My Son's Ex-Wife:

The Aftermath

My Son's Ex-Wife:

The Aftermath

Shelia E. Lipsey

www.urbanchristianonline.net

Urban Books, LLC
78 East Industry Court
Deer Park, NY 11729

ISBN 13: 978-1-60162-854-1
ISBN 10: 1-60162-854-4

First Printing September 2010
Printed in the United States of America

10 9 8 7 6 5 4 3 2 1

*This is a work of fiction. Any references or similarities to actual
events, real people, living, or dead, or to real locales are intended
to give the novel a sense of reality. Any similarity in other names,
characters, places, and incidents is entirely coincidental.*

Distributed by Kensington Corp.
Submit Wholesale Orders to:
Kensington Publishing Corp.
C/O Penguin Group (USA) Inc.
Attention: Order Processing
405 Murray Hill Parkway
East Rutherford, NJ 07073-2316
Phone: 1-800-526-0275
Fax: 1-800-227-9604

My Son's Ex-Wife:

The Aftermath

What Readers Say About Shelia E. Lipsey's Books

Shelia E. Lipsey is one of the few authors who sets my heart to blaze with her writing. Her writing is intense, complex, unforgettable, and most of all, needed in the world today. Shelia's novels have everything Christian fiction novels need: brilliant plots, timely conversations, and faith building passages! Keep your eyes on Shelia E. Lipsey . . . she is definitely a legend in the making." — Ella Curry, president of EDC Creations. Publisher of Black Pearls Magazine. Based on novels *Beautiful Ugly* and *My Son's Wife*.

Wow, Shelia E. Lipsey takes it there with *My Son's Wife*. She masterfully wraps the subject content of religion around that of molestation, homosexuality, and skepticism. The quotes at the beginning of each chapter set the mood for what will occur. Often times I found myself nodding in full agreement with what they represented . . . This book was a great read and one I recommend to everyone. Reviewed by Chantay, APOOO BookClub

I loved Shelia E. Lipsey's *My Son's Wife*. Five stars are simply not enough. In addition to the drama, it was an eye opener about Christianity. If there's one lesson to be learned, it's that people shouldn't be so judgmental. I didn't like how it ended, and I am hoping it's because there will be a sequel. *My Son's Wife* is good reading, and I recommend it. Reviewed by: Marcella

Sheila E. Lipsey should be applauded for the work she created for *My Son's Wife*. She has brought up a subject that some do not like to speak about and just want to sweep under the rug. She doesn't miss a beat with the way she ties in the Christian community in this novel. The detail and the characterization she gives each person in *My Son's Wife* are commendable. She touched on some subjects that some authors like to stay away from. You understand what Francesca, Rena, and Stiles are feeling when they realize the dissent the first lady has caused. *My Son's Wife* is a great read. Reviewed by Jackie for Urban Reviews

Shelia E. Lipsey is without a doubt a great writer. The story she tells is one you can relate to. It's not too over the top with preaching, and not the typical urban Christian novel. Her detail for writing is of expertise. She has the passion in *My Son's Wife*. I highly recommend *My Son's Wife*. Not only does Lipsey teach the Word of God in this urban tale, she allows us to walk in her characters' shoes. You will know more about yourself when you are done reading this story. Tamika Newhouse AAMBC Reviewer

Shelia E. Lipsey has done a masterful job of showing how imperfection is part of the daily walk of religious life. Envy Wilson, Layla Hobbs, and Kacie Mayweather are friends in their 30s who look to each other for support yet still are unable to find what they need most. Sex, men, lies, attempted murder, and redemption await the reader in this story of understanding how imperfect people can do great things when they understand that GOD's grace is sufficient and HIS mercy is forever.***** (5) stars out of 5. Tanya R. Bates Reviewer for C&B Book Distributor, Amazon, Barnes & Noble, International Grant Writer

Novels by Shelia E. Lipsey

Into Each Life
2007 Shades of Romance Readers' Choice Award for
Best Multicultural Christian Romance Author of the Year
Best Multicultural New Christian Romance Author of the Year
Best Multi-cultural Christian Fiction Book of the Year
Best Multi-cultural Christian Fiction Author of the Year
Sinsatiable
2008 Conversations Book Club Author of the Year
My Son's Wife
2009 Shades of Romance Readers' Choice Awards for
Author of the Year
Best Book Cover Award
Best Christian Fiction Book of the Year
Best Christian Romance Book of the Year
Best Fiction Book of the Year
Urban-Reviews Top Shelf
Beautiful Ugly
2009 Black Pearls Magazine Top Books

Dedication

To those that need to be forgiven and to those who
need to do the forgiving.
At once, Moses fell to the ground and worshiped,
saying, "Please, O Master, if you see anything good in
me, please Master, travel with us . . . Forgive our iniquity and sin. Own us, possess us. Exodus 34:9 (The
Message Bible)

Acknowledgments

To God be all of the glory, all of the honor, and all of the majesty forever!

Thank you, Lord, for endowing me with the gift of placing your words on paper. Thank you, God, for showing me that despite my physical challenges, you are still able to use me as you see fit. I pray that I will always make myself available to you, Lord.

Thank you, God, for every reader of my work, every naysayer, every doubter, every person of faith, every prayer warrior, every interceder, every believer, every non-believer, everyone and anyone who picks up a book written by Shelia E. Lipsey. These people are the ones who keep your message of non-condemnation and redemption spreading worldwide.

May those who read my works see that you are a good God, a merciful, kind, and loving God whose mercies are new each and every morning. You are the bright and morning star, the lily of the valley, the alpha and the omega, the beginning and the end.

You are the God that promises me that if I obey your commandments, that I will be the head and not the tail, that I will be above and not beneath, that I will be blessed going in and blessed going out; you said that the fruit of my womb would be blessed, so in obedience to you, Father, I write.

I write because you've blessed me to write. And so I write because you've given me stories to tell about imperfect people

Acknowledgments

who are in need of your perfect love and your never ending forgiveness. And so I write, so that someone somewhere might be touched, changed, saved, forgiven, and reminded that you do love them. Yes, I write because one day you chose me. Before I was even in my mother's womb, you chose me, Lord, and predestined my final destination on life's journey.

I love you, Father.

Chapter One

"What most people need to learn in life is how to love people and use things instead of using people and loving things."
  Unknown

Audrey and several ladies from Holy Rock Women's Ministry gathered in one of the church meeting rooms for their quarterly meeting. Toward the end of the meeting, the ladies sat around and talked, rather they gossiped.

"First Lady, may I ask you something?" one of the ladies spoke up.

"Certainly," Audrey replied.

"What really happened to your son's wife? It's like she disappeared off the face of the earth."

Audrey threw up one hand and waved it carelessly. "Honey, she left town after he divorced her. I tell you, it was the best thing she could have done. It was enough that she pretended to love my son, only to leave him heartbroken."

"I know she put him through a lot," another woman commented.

"Yes, I tell you, my son's wife was not all she pretended to be. All of the years I thought I knew that child, and she turned out to be a deceitful little phony. And to think, we've known Rena and her family since they first moved to Memphis. Well, she sure had the family fooled. Who would have thought that she was only using Stiles? That's why you have to be careful these days."

A fair skinned, older woman agreed with Audrey. "Yes, you sure have to be careful, First Lady."

This fueled Audrey's flame, and she kept on talking. "You think you know somebody, and find out you don't know them at all."

"Lord, these women today are scandalous. I tell you, our men of God have to stay in prayer," a short, dark complexioned woman added.

"You sure are right," another commented. "We have to stay prayed up on their behalf."

"Is Pastor Stiles all right, First Lady, since the divorce is final?"

"Yes, he'll be fine. Of course, the pain of divorce is something that takes time to heal; even more so, for a man of God like my Stiles. He tried, but there was no way to mend their marriage. The girl was promiscuous, and she wasn't about to change. I tell you, I cried almost every night for months for my son. Thank God for Pastor; he keeps Stiles encouraged. And since he appointed Stiles as the full time pastor of Holy Rock, Stiles doesn't have a lot of time to mope around and feel sorry for himself."

The fair skinned older woman was named Sister Jean. She readily agreed with Audrey. "Don't worry," she said and waved her hand. "He'll find another woman. That's for sure. A smart, intelligent, handsome man of God like him won't have a problem at all. This time, she'll be the kind of woman that will be worthy of being his wife and the first lady of Holy Rock. We're going to keep praying that next time he'll meet a fine Christian girl with true morals and respect. But we all know that whoever it is won't be half the first lady you are, Sister Audrey."

Audrey blushed. "Thank you, Sister Jean."

"The truth is the truth," Sister Jean remarked, and so did

several of the other women that were gathered in the lunch room.

Audrey's face brightened like the morning sun. She was astonished at the sense of fulfillment she felt as she spoke. "I know one thing, whoever she is, she will have to be more than special. She's going to have to definitely prove that she's worthy if she ever plans on becoming, *my son's wife.*"

On her way home, Audrey was flying high on praises. Rena had been revealed for the two-faced, double-life leading, unworthy woman that she was. "What the devil meant for bad, God meant it for good," Audrey said followed by her laughter over the way things had turned out. The gall of Rena trying to ruin Stiles's name with her vulgar, nasty, abominable lifestyle with Francesca. It was bad enough that her child was a practicing lesbian, convict, and a drug user. Audrey turned up her nose at the thought of the vile life Francesca led. She couldn't begin to imagine how Francesca turned out to be the kind of terrible, shameful daughter that she was. She was a disgrace to the Graham name and especially to Holy Rock Church.

Audrey hummed along to a song on the 95.7 gospel station to help replace the terrible thoughts of Rena and Francesca with positive ones. She was thankful that Pastor was on the mend from his stroke. God was really healing him in a 'nothing but God can do' kind of way. His speech was markedly improving daily, and his gait was becoming stronger with each round of physical therapy.

Audrey thought about Stiles. She was sad that he'd been hurt so badly by Rena. If only she could have seen warning signs of Rena's devilish ways, then she would have been able to save her only son from Rena's evil intentions. Audrey believed that Rena's purpose had been to latch on to Stiles in an effort to cover up the affair she was having with Francesca. But God has a way of bringing things to light.

Audrey continued to hum and think about the fact that Francesca and Rena had a lot of reaping to do. As for Stiles, Audrey had her eye on a few young ladies at Holy Rock who would make a good wife for him. There were also a few more she planned on checking out from two or three of the other churches that Holy Rock interacted with on a frequent basis. This time around she would make sure she checked into the background of the young lady, her parents, finances, and any other thing she could find out. No more surprises like the one with Rena.

"And to think, that, that, oh, Lord, you know I can't call her what I want to call her," Audrey said out loud as the song on the radio ended and she was left with her own thoughts bursting forth like mighty waters through her mind. "But Lord, she has to pay for how she hurt my baby. It's been close to five months since their divorce, Lord, and my baby is still beside himself with embarrassment, a broken heart, and mistrust about receiving another woman into his life. Lord, fix it. Fix it for my child," pleaded Audrey with the tiniest trace of forced tears trickling down her made up face. "You know he doesn't need to be preaching Sunday after Sunday without a first lady in his life. You said, 'he who findeth a wife findeth a good thing and findeth favor with you,' so fix this mess that Rena caused in his life."

Audrey swiftly went to the next thing on her mind, like she had a mental to-do-list. She called Pastor to see if he wanted her to order takeout from one of the local restaurants. Since she'd eaten at the quarterly meeting, she didn't want to think about standing over a stove cooking anything for dinner. When he answered, she told him her suggestion, and without hesitation, like most of the time, Pastor agreed to eat takeout. She stopped at one of the neighborhood soul food restaurants and ordered two dinner plates of turnip greens, hot water cornbread, fried corn, baked pork chops and peach cobbler.

While Audrey waited on the food to be prepared, she went into mental overdrive. This time she thought about Francesca. Where in the world could that wayward child be? She hadn't seen or heard from her in weeks, and it worried her a little. She was used to Francesca running off and getting locked up or going on one of her drug binges, but this time around Audrey felt somewhat different about Francesca's no show. Maybe she was with Rena and the two of them were making an ungodly life for themselves. That certainly was something to be considered.

For Audrey, the good thing that came out of the mess that Rena and Francesca created was Pastor and Stiles could see the women for who they really were. Rena and Francesca needed to fall before the Lord and beg for His forgiveness. But Audrey couldn't imagine Francesca ever going before the Lord to ask Him anything.

Chapter Two

Ring. Ring.

Stiles listened, hoping to hear the tender voice he once adored, answer the phone. Instead, he listened to the automated voice of what used to be Rena's cell phone number.

"At the subscriber's request this phone does not accept incoming calls, message SEL9324," the robotic sounding voice informed him.

He closed his cell phone and lay back on the bed, with his head resting in the palms of his hands. It had been months since he'd seen his ex-wife. He opened the phone again and scrolled through his contacts until he saw the listing, The Jacksons; Rena's parents.

Should he call? His mind and heart were confused. Part of him missed her. He thought about her laugh, her smell, and her touch. "But why did she have to turn out to be so deceitful? "God, I don't understand why all of this happened? I can't get over it. I can't get past it." Stiles dropped the cell phone and bolted upright in the bed like he'd been electrocuted. He stood and paced the floor in front of the bed.

Looking upward, he stopped. "God, I preach to hundreds of people two to three times a week. I tell them about your love, your forgiveness, your grace and mercy. Rena was my love, the woman I dreamed of having babies with, Father. She was the perfect wife in every way. So why?" He rubbed his hands over his head. "Why did she have to be... I don't know what to call her."

Stiles's body jerked. He looked around the room as if he expected to see someone. *A sinner?* He heard within his spirit. *Why did she have to be a sinner like you, and all of my children?*

Tears streamed from Stiles's eyes. "Who am I to judge anyone?" He sat back on the bed and clasped his hands together. "I am a sinner; a sinner saved by your grace, Lord. You forgave me, and you love me unconditionally. But I don't have the strength, or the kind of heart that can allow her back in my life. Part of me yearns and aches for her because I still love her, but it's time for me to make a fresh start. It wouldn't be fair to Rena to have a man who couldn't love and accept her for who she is. I'd probably never be able to trust her again. I repent for any wrong I've done toward her and Francesca. Father, forgive me. I know now that this is your will. You want me to close the door to my past, to my hurt, and my heartache." Stiles felt his heavy heart lighten. It was time to let go of the past and look forward to what God had planned for his future. He would always love Rena, but he finally realized that although he didn't understand the ways of God, God was the one in control of everything. It was time to trust Him totally and completely.

"Whatever tomorrow brings, I'm ready, Lord." Stiles looked at the cell phone, and then opened it and scrolled through it again until he came across Rena's old number. He deleted it. He scrolled again until he found The Jacksons. He paused again, and then he deleted it too. Closing the phone, he threw it on the other side of the empty bed before going into the kitchen and pulling out a frozen dinner.

While Stiles sat and waited on the man-sized dinner to get

ready, he thought of everything that had transpired over the last year of his life. The timer went off and yanked him away from his thoughts. He gulped down the fish nuggets and steak fries hurriedly.

After he finished his supper, he stood up, threw the empty container in the trash, wiped his mouth with his paper towel, and headed to the den to study his mid-week sermon notes. He couldn't concentrate.

Stiles missed Rena, but he didn't really understand how he could still miss, and yes still be in love, with a woman who betrayed and deceived him. He had placed his trust in Rena, given her his whole heart, and she crushed him by sleeping with his sister. Stiles rubbed the top of his head back and forth. His tears were fresh and heavy. His heart ached, and he didn't know what he was going to do. Probably almost everyone at church was whispering and coming up with their conclusions about the reasons for the divorce. Stories continually surfaced in the most unlikely places. Stiles no longer felt the anointing of God over his life. He felt more like a wounded man, vulnerable, fit to be tied and disbarred from the ministry he once believed God had called him to serve.

He went to his bedroom and sat on the edge of the unmade bed. For a few minutes he sat, and then lay back on the propped up pillow. He needed to find Francesca. He wanted to hear her side of the story, plus he wanted to see if she was all right. He had gone to a private physician to get tested for STDs and God had been favorable; all of his tests were negative. The doctor recommended that he return every three months over the next year, plus Stiles was supposed to make an appointment if he felt or saw any changes in his body. He thought of what Francesca might be experiencing. She actually had an STD and she was HIV positive. Stiles understood that his sister had to bear the consequences of her actions and sinful decisions, but somehow he felt that God had been too harsh.

He was just as confused when it came to Rena. "Why? Why couldn't she just tell me the truth in the beginning? Why did she have to build our relationship on lies and deceit?" Stiles said out loud, and then sat upright in the bed and crossed his legs Indian style. He used his fist to pound the bed over and over again. "Rena, why couldn't you have just told me the truth? You could have told me you were in love with my sister. You could have saved me from all of this grief. But, noooo," he screamed out loud. "You let me love you, knowing that you loved her. Both of you are sick, sick, sick," he kept yelling.

"And Mother, how could you keep a secret from Pastor and your sister about what Fonda did to Francesca? What kind of woman of God are you supposed to be? You're partly to blame for all of this too." Stiles looked upward at the bedroom ceiling as if answers would pour from the sky any minute. Only silence answered.

Stiles disrobed and took a shower. Thought after thought. Hurt upon hurt. Love that he wanted to deny but couldn't, kept flooding his mind and thrashing at his heart until he screamed under the pounding sprays of water. "God, why? What am I supposed to learn from this? What do you want me to do? I can't forgive her like I know that I should. I want to, Lord. Help me. Help my unbelief." Stiles fell to his knees and on to the marble tiled shower floor. Water washed away the tears that wouldn't stop flowing. "Rena," he cried out. "God, I still love her. God, I can't do this. I just can't do this." His cries went on until he felt the water turning cool. He slowly stood to his feet and rinsed his body.

Before getting into bed, he fell to his knees again. This time, Stiles prayed for God to renew a right spirit within him. He prayed for Rena, Francesca, his parents, and for his congregation. He ended his prayer with a request for God to help him become a man who could trust love and loving again. Then he got up, climbed in bed, and reached over on his nightstand to retrieve his Bible.

Chapter Three

"The hottest love has the coldest end."
~ Socrates ~

Rena found her pain more bearable after she confided in her mother. Initially she'd told her father only about her and Stiles. She didn't have the nerve to tell him everything. She believed he would be so disappointed in her and the choices she'd made in her life when she was in Memphis. Rena's mother became Rena's confidante, her godly counsel. Two weeks after she arrived home, her mother had convinced her to tell her father everything from beginning to end.

Rena sat next to her mother while she told him all about Francesca, the STD, their relationship, and her deceit. He listened attentively. At times he frowned, and at other times his face remained stoic, almost unlife like, but Rena continued until she got everything out in the open. When she was finished, she waited on the verbal onslaught from her father. But it never came.

Mr. Jackson was extremely upset when he heard the truth about everything, but one thing that he was not was condemning. Rena watched his eyes glisten. She saw hurt sketched all over his almost wrinkle free, burnt by the sun skin. But what Rena didn't see was disgust. Her father sat in his recliner, quiet for several seconds.

Rena's mother took hold of her hand. Suddenly, Rena's father opened his arms and outstretched them toward his child. Stunned, Rena paused momentarily, then stood up and rushed into the waiting arms of her father.

"Oh, Daddy, I'm so sorry. I'm so sorry that I messed up. I'm so sorry that I hurt so many people." She cried all over his shirt while he held her and patted her on the back like he used to do when she was a little girl.

"You've done nothing that God won't forgive you for, honey. You just have to yield yourself to Him. I am not the one to judge or condemn anyone." He pulled her away from him slightly while she remained on his lap. He looked her directly in the eyes, and rubbed her hair gently. "We all make mistakes, sweetheart. No one is perfect. No one walks the straight and narrow. Yes, you've done some things that are not pleasing to God. But confess those things, something I'm sure you've already done."

Rena answered with a nod of her head.

"Then you have been forgiven. God is the only judge. You have to move on with your life. Forgive yourself. I know Stiles is hurt. He probably feels like he was purposely deceived, and maybe he was. You do owe him an apology, along with all of those whose lives you've hurt along the way. Seek their forgiveness and get this heavy burden off of you. If they don't accept your forgiveness, then that's on them. They'll have to answer to God for that. Rena, it's the only way you're going to be set free."

His words were spoken so gently. Rena leaned back against his broad shoulders and tear-soaked shirt. He held her for a very long time. This was where she needed to be; at home with family who loved her no matter what.

Rena settled rather quickly in Andover. She found and leased a two bedroom, cottage-style house in the suburbs, several miles from her parents. She thought of Stiles, Frankie, and the entire Graham family often, but each time, tried to push thoughts of her past behind. There would be a time she would have to own up to the mistakes of her past by seeking forgiveness from the Grahams. Her father was right about that, but she couldn't do it right now. Her hurt was too fresh.

Rena was offered a position as lead librarian at Andover Mass Preparatory, one of the prominent private schools, which proved to be quite rewarding. She found it enjoyable and challenging working with middle school-aged children on a daily basis. It was definitely a far cry from what she'd been accustomed to doing at the public libraries in Memphis and Arkansas. This position was hers, and hers alone, to operate as she saw best. She decided on most of the reading materials that would go on the library shelves; and she set out to make sure that the children had plenty of books that would provide them with the gift of knowledge often overlooked because of the lack of reading.

Rena learned the names of most of the 275 plus children who attended the school because they came to the library on their assigned Class Library Day. Many of the students also spent their free time in the library doing homework, working on special projects, meeting up with friends, or reading.

Overall, Rena was doing quite well in her new life as a divorced woman of God. There was no denying that she regretted the damage she'd caused in Memphis, but thank God her small, intimate church family openly welcomed her. She returned to feeling secure in her life, which allowed her to slowly forgive herself.

Thoughts of Frankie's well-being and whereabouts often drifted through her mind. Where was she? How was she doing? Was she suffering from the results of having HIV? Was she incarcerated again? Had her HIV turned into full blown AIDS? And what about Stiles? she thought as she placed computerized library stamps on a fresh load of books that had been delivered.

Talks with Mr. Bolden, her former supervisor in Memphis, were sporadic. There was nothing he could tell her anyway about Stiles, Frankie or any of the Grahams for that matter. But he was a great resource of information that helped with her present position.

Rena resigned herself to making good things happen in Andover. Thus far, she'd had a pretty good start in the form of Dr. Robert Becton. He was one of the physical science teachers and assistant basketball coaches at Andover Mass Preparatory. When she first started the job, Robert was one of the first teachers to bring his class to the library to gather information for an upcoming science project.

He was more than easy on the eyes, and a confident air about himself drew Rena toward him like a magnet. He must have felt some attraction to her as well, because after releasing his students to seek their required reading materials, he seemed to focus his attention on Rena.

"So you're the one who ran Mr. Holloway off, huh?" His baritone voice caused Rena to feel somewhat anxious when he approached her.

"Excuse me?" replied Rena. She wasn't sure if he were serious or not. He certainly wasn't flashing a smile.

"Hey, don't look so serious," said Robert. This time he flashed a wide smile, and immediately, Rena exhaled lightly. He extended his hand out toward her. "I'm Dr. Robert Becton, Physical Science, Class Two, grade eight. And you have to be Mrs. Rena Graham, right?"

"Yes, that's me. Present and accounted for." Rena smiled.

"Mr. Holloway was the school's previous librarian, but he retired at the end of the past school term after thirty-eight years; but you probably already know that."

Robert didn't give her much time to respond. Rena nodded her head in agreement. He had a hint of what Rena surmised was a New Yorkian accent. Like most New Yorkers, Robert came off, though pleasantly, as being direct, opinionated, and confident. And he certainly seemed to enjoy talking.

"I missed meeting you at the AMP Staff Welcome Reception. I was attending a science convention in Boston," explained Robert, like he owed her a viable explanation for his absence.

Rena had done some research of her own. She learned from the booklet given to her at the Welcome Reception, the names and titles of the staff at Andover Mass. Dr. Becton's picture in the booklet did not do him justice. "It's nice to meet you, Dr. Becton. I believe there are two or three more staffers I've yet had the pleasure of meeting," she told him. "I hope they're all as engaging as you."

Rena's nervousness vanished as Robert effortlessly engaged her in conversation about Andover Mass and the layout of the accelerated science programs the school offered. With what could only be described as confidence, Robert sat in the chair parked next to Rena's desk.

"Why don't you tell me something I don't know about you?"

"I'm sure that would take quite some time, Dr. Becton."

Robert smiled, glanced at the watch on his wrist, and then replied. "I have exactly thirty-seven and a half minutes. Fill me in."

Rena flashed a smile again. "Well, let's see. Where do I start?" Rena decided to tell him what he more than likely already knew about her from the staff booklet. "I'm a native of Massachusetts."

"Uh-huh; know that. Staff Members Booklet," he said

quickly. "But keep going." He gestured toward her with his right hand, like he was shooing a fly away.

"Okay. Ummm." Rena pretended like she was in deep thought. "I've lived in Memphis and Marion, Arkansas since I was fourteen years old. I worked as a librarian in both cities before I made the decision to return home."

"Okay, I think we're getting warmer. But let me help you out," Robert urged in a non-pushy manner. "The staff booklet doesn't say anything about there being a Mr. Graham. Can I be so lucky as to assume there isn't one?" He flirted openly but tastefully.

Rena blushed. "My, you are something else. You get right to the nitty gritty, don't you?"

Robert paused and checked the time again. "I only have twenty-nine minutes before I gather my future scientist protégés and prepare for my next class. So I'd like to learn as much about you as I can."

"I'm sure there'll be plenty of time for that, Dr. Becton."

"Oh is that so? And please, call me Robert."

Rena decided to flip the script. "Okay, Robert. Why don't you tell me something about *you* that I don't know?"

"That's easy. The moment I saw your picture in the staff booklet, I know you might think it's corny, but I felt like you were going to become an important part of my life." This time Robert wasn't smiling. He sounded so serious that Rena's heart picked up its pace. Without effort, she laid her left hand on her chest.

She pursed her lips before she responded. "Look, Dr. Becton, I don't play games. That's something you definitely don't know about me, so it's best to let you know that from the get go. If you did, you wouldn't be sitting here trying to play one with me. Save that for your wife and kids. And be careful what you say because that was in your bio in the staff book."

"No, I don't think so." Robert looked directly into her eyes. Rena quickly shifted hers to a copy of *The Native Son* lying on her desk. "What it did say was that I have two children. It said nothing about there being a Mrs. Becton. And your bio, by the way, did not mention there being a hubby."

"Since you insist on going there, and why it would matter to you anyway, I don't know. I will tell you this much, I recently returned to Andover after a traumatic divorce. Now," Rena patted the book and sighed, "is there anything else you insist on knowing about me, Robert?" Rena tried to smirk, but her lips turned upward in a smile once again.

"Now, that wasn't so hard was it?" asked Robert. "But there's one more thing." He raised one finger up at the same time he spoke.

"And what is that? Rena asked. "Do you want to know my height, age, weight, and social security number too?" She tried to sound sarcastic, but it didn't appear to faze Robert at all.

"Like I said, and I'm serious, Rena." Rena liked the way he called her name. "I couldn't wait for the chance to meet you in person. There was something about your picture that captivated me, other than you being beautiful. It was like God speaking to me. And when God speaks, I listen."

Rena didn't know what to think, and there was nothing she could say but, "We all should listen when God speaks."

"See, we already have something in common; the most important thing too; and that's God. You know, there are so many scientists today who do all of this research." Robert waved his hand upward flippantly. "And yet they choose to give scientific reasons for how the earth came to be, how man came into existence. It perturbs me to no end," he said.

Rena realized she could probably listen to Robert tirelessly. He didn't present himself as annoying or conceited. He gave information about himself freely, especially his belief in God.

He had a vivacious personality, wide smile, and before he ushered his class back to the classroom, Rena had agreed to join him for lunch in the school's food court.

Rena laughed at Robert's humorous anecdotes between taking tiny bites of her chicken sandwich. It was refreshing to talk to someone of the opposite sex, something she hadn't engaged in since she left Memphis and Stiles. At least she hadn't on a personal level.

"So, Dr. Becton," she said teasingly, "tell me about your family."

"Okay, let's see." Robert took a swig of his lemon water; he bit his bottom lip like he was choosing what he should say. "I'm new to the divorce scene myself. I'm a single dad raising my four-year-old daughter, Isabelle, and my ten-month-old son, Robbie."

"I don't have children of my own, but you don't have to tell me that it's a pretty big job. Raising children these days can't be easy. I don't envy you," remarked Rena

Robert smiled slightly. "I love my kids. Yet I can't deny that there are times when I ask God, why they have to grow up without the love of their mother?"

Rena nodded, sipped from her glass of tea, and lowered her eyes, afraid she might see the hurt that she heard in Robert's voice.

"My wife, Karen, ex-wife," Robert corrected himself, "was diagnosed with manic-depressive disorder. It worsened over the six and a half years of our relationship. I prayed and believed for her healing and thought that things were changing when she became pregnant with our first child, Isabelle." Robert smiled. "I remember Karen being happy back then. She was the amazing, beautiful, funny woman I first fell in love with. Then within a month of giving birth to Isabelle, her battle against mental illness returned with a vengeance.

She began to withdraw from me, from her family, and more from Isabelle. I mean, there were days, or moments when she was what I guess we equate as normal, but those days became more sporadic."

The more Rena listened to Robert, she understood that his reasons for divorce were far different and much sadder.

"Did you seek professional help for her?" Rena looked at Robert with an aching in her eyes.

"Of course. She was even hospitalized a couple of times during the course of our marriage. And she was on a long list of medications, which also had an even longer list of side effects. But the thing about Karen was that she wanted to love me; she wanted to love our daughter. No one is going to make me think differently. But she couldn't. I'd come home from work sometimes and Karen would be gone. I wouldn't hear from her for days at a time. Made me believe she was strung out on crack or something, but I wasn't far off course. I found out that was not entirely the case. I did discover through some people we both knew that she dabbled in some other drugs like cocaine and methamphetamine.

"Did she take your little girl with her when she went on these disappearing trips?" asked Rena, her concern showed on her browed face.

"Thank God, she had the mindset to leave me a note~ well most of the time~ that told me where she'd left our daughter. Sometimes it was with one of the neighbors; other times it was with my mother, my sister, or Karen's half sister. At first, I'll admit I tried everything I could to help her, to work things out between us, but it was hard. Soon it became downright impossible. Karen stopped taking care of Isabelle and totally ignored me. There was nothing but mounting turmoil in our marriage, which wasn't good for our daughter, and it was unhealthy for us and it was scary. We agreed, both Karen and me, that divorce would be better for us.

"Didn't you try to get some counseling? Did you all do anything to try to salvage your marriage?" Rena asked. She thought of her and Stiles. Could their marriage have been saved? No, was her immediate answer. Not if Audrey Graham had any say about it. And like it or not, Audrey always had something to say.

"I suggested counseling, but Karen refused. It takes two people to make a relationship work. So we divorced when Isabelle was three years old. Shortly after the divorce is when we found out that she was pregnant with our second child."

Rena's eyebrows arched upward. "What's up with that if you all were so at odds with each other?"

"Well, what's up with that is I kept pursuing Karen. I thought if I could somehow convince her to see a psychiatrist, that we still had a shot at reconciliation. There were times when Karen was as sweet as a Georgia peach, and other times she was mean as the devil's wife. Needless to say, it was during one of her sweet moments that she got pregnant with Robbie. Believe me, it was a surprise to both of us." Robert stopped and inhaled.

"You don't have to talk about it. Believe me, I understand how difficult it can be when you have to see your loved one, especially your mate, disintegrate from sickness," said Rena, with thoughts of Frankie racing through her mind.

Robert either didn't hear her, or he needed to talk, to get some of the hurt out rather than hold it all inside. "Our intimate moments were extremely rare, but nevertheless, she got pregnant at a time that turned out to be the end of the end of any hope of reconciling. During the pregnancy, she lived with her half sister, although I tried several times to convince her to come home. Whenever she did let me see her, she was irritable, depressed, and suicidal. She never asked about Isabelle, and she didn't want to see her. I was still foolish enough to hope that it would all pass over, and that if I gave her the space she said she needed, then once she had the baby, things would be better. She could get back on most of her prescribed medications that she'd been accustomed to receiving."

Rena spoke up. "I guess she had to stop taking a lot of the meds because of her pregnancy, huh?" she asked in a concerned voice, because she was.

Robert nodded his head and kept talking. "Anyway," Robert said, sighing and balling up his napkin and pushing his plate away, "I didn't hear from her or see her again until she gave birth to our son. She called me from the hospital and told me she was in labor. Two days later she and Robbie were discharged from the hospital. We were divorced, but she agreed to go home with me. I thought things were going to go just as I'd predicted. But her battle with post partum depression, along with her lifelong struggle with mental illness pushed her over the edge. Three days after I brought her and Robbie home, Karen disappeared, leaving me with Isabelle and Robbie. The only time I hear about her is through her half sister and her parents who live in Maryland. They love their grandkids, and they've visited a couple of times. They told me the last time they heard from Karen she said she was fine and that she was free at last to live her life the way she wanted. That's been almost nine months ago." Robert spoke softly but recovered his happy demeanor immediately. "Look, now you know all about me. So let's say we shift the subject?" asked Robert.

"Sure."

"Good. Now tell me, Ms. Graham, what can a guy do to get a pretty lady like you to go out on a real date, or am I going to be forced to meet you here every day?" Robert's eyes roved around the food court. "In this public place with probing eyes and wondering young minds all around us." He grinned.

"I'll have to think about it," replied Rena and giggled.

Rena and Robert finished lunch and exchanged friendly chitchat before he returned to his class and Rena, to the library.

Rena daydreamed on her way to the library. Her subconscious compared Stiles to Robert. She smiled at the thought of having another man interested in her. But on the other hand, she couldn't understand why it couldn't have worked for her and Stiles. She arrived at the library and slowly pushed the door to the library while at the same time pushing thoughts of Stiles out of her mind. If only she could push him out of her heart.

Chapter Four

"Blues are the songs of despair, but gospel songs are the songs of hope."
~*Mahalia Jackson*~

Audrey hummed to one of her favorite gospel tunes as she drove off the church parking lot, after attending the Golden Friends luncheon for seniors. She felt such relief to have been given a chance to have a new beginning that included her two favorite men in all of the world—Pastor and Stiles. As for Francesca, another two weeks had come and gone and still no word from her. Audrey prayed that Francesca would one day accept Christ as her Savior and stop living the lesbian lifestyle to which she was so enamored.

When it came to her ex-daughter-in-law, Audrey had a few choice thoughts as well for Rena, but God would take care of that little lying woman. Audrey's cell phone rang just as the end of the song played.

"Hello, Clara. I missed you at Golden Friends today." Audrey listened to Clara's explanation of why she wasn't there.

"I'm sorry that you're not feeling well. I'll be praying for you. I hope you feel better, and please let me know what I can do to help. Buh-bye, Clara, and God bless you." Audrey pushed the END button.

When she eyeballed Baskin-Robbins, she pulled in and bought two berry smoothies, one for her and one for Pastor.

Pastor loved berry smoothies no matter what time of the year. She made a second stop at the sub shop and bought Pastor a chicken Philly salad before she set off in the direction of Emerald Estates.

She sighed with relief when she turned on to her street. She pushed the remote that was clipped on her visor, pulled into the garage, grabbed her things, and walked inside the kitchen. She placed the salad on the counter and the smoothies inside of the freezer.

"Pastor, I'm home. The meeting was one of those where ladies love to gossip," she said out loud as she removed her cream colored, waist length jacket.

"Pastor," she called out again. "You here?" She knew that he had to be since his car was in the garage. He rarely got behind the wheel since the stroke. Audrey surmised that Stiles had probably come by and picked him up. Stiles would do that sometimes, taking Pastor to the church with him or to run errands just to get him out of the house.

It was fall and it was quite cool inside of the house. Audrey checked the thermostat and set it to seventy. Why did Stiles have to take Pastor out in all of this cool, unpredictable Memphis weather, especially knowing that Pastor still had not completely recovered?

Audrey huffed at the thought. She suddenly felt agitated. A hot bath might do her good, she decided. She went into their master bedroom and stepped out of her skirt, folded it in the walk-in closet, and as neat as she was, she stepped out of her high heels and placed them directly in the hole that the shoes went in.

Audrey still grew enraged every time she thought how Francesca and Rena almost sent her dear beloved Pastor to an early grave with their nasty, sick affair. And Rena, her ex-daughter-in-law from hell, was nothing more than a wolf dressed in sheep's clothing that had destroyed Stiles's life. "Thank God Stiles had sense enough to kick Rena to the curb and divorce her. Lord, I tell you, children can be the death of you. Always lying, trying to play one parent against another. Got Pastor all mad at me," she continued to rant. Without missing a beat, Audrey began humming, "Amazing Grace," as she completely undressed and walked into the oversized master bathroom.

Indescribable screams emanated from the depths of her belly, up and out into the empty house at the sight of what lay before her when she stepped inside the bathroom. The thin, frail body and the pool of blood petrified her.

Audrey hollered in a voice so loud it could have shaken the earth. "Ohh, nooo, Pastor." She knelt beside him. Her screams of panic grew louder if that were possible. Pastor's body lay on the marble tiled bathroom floor like a block of ice and stiff as a wooden board.

Audrey shook her head and bolted upright as the bad dream awakened her. She looked confused, especially when she saw that she was still in the bathtub. The water in the tub had turned cool so she must have been in there for some time. She was frightened upon the realization that she had fallen asleep in the bathtub—again. It was something Audrey found herself doing more of lately, falling asleep while taking a bath, watching television, or reading. There were other times she seemed to forget the simplest of things that had once been routine for her. For instance, she always prepared sandwiches and something to drink for her and Pastor to watch their favorite TV shows, starting with *Judge Mathis*. Lately, she not only forgot to prepare the sandwiches, but she darn right forgot about the *Judge Mathis* show completely.

Audrey blamed it on being overly consumed with everything that had happened the past few months with Pastor's stroke, the shameful scene involving Rena and Francesca, followed by Stiles's divorce. It had all been too hard on her. Everything happened so fast. During the months that followed, her blood pressure meds were increased by her primary care doctor.

Audrey reached on the edge of her Jacuzzi style tub for her face cloth. She wet it, wrung it out with both hands, and used it to dab her forehead. She felt flush and somewhat confused. It took a few seconds for her to determine whether what just passed before her was a dream or reality. When she realized she had been dreaming, Audrey whispered, "Thank you, Lord. I couldn't take it if I lost Pastor." She completed her bath in the almost frigid water and stepped out of the bathroom and into an empty bedroom. She reached for her terry cloth robe hanging on the hook on the bathroom door. Audrey remained confused and thought it would be better for her to sit down until she could collect her thoughts. She walked over to the bathroom chair and sat there until she heard familiar footsteps.

It was Pastor. "Audrey, honey," he called.

"I'm in the bedroom," she answered in as normal of a voice as she could. She stood up just as he stepped into the bedroom.

"Oh, you just got out of the tub, huh?" he remarked. He walked over to his wife and kissed her on the lips.

"Where were you? With Stiles?" she asked.

"No, I was next door talking to Thomas. We hadn't talked in awhile, so I thought since I was moping around, that I would go over there and see how he was getting along."

"That was thoughtful. He's a good neighbor," commented Audrey.

"And you, my love, have always been the perfect wife." He kissed her again.

Audrey returned his kiss with deep passion. The dream

had frightened her to the point that she was terrified. She didn't want to be by herself like Thomas was since his wife's recent death.

Pastor and Audrey embraced. He loosened Audrey's robe and smiled at the sight before him.

Audrey knew what he wanted and she wanted the same. She never denied Pastor. She unbuttoned his shirt. Her anxious feelings had passed. All that was on her mind was pleasing her husband.

Chapter Five

"Family quarrels are bitter things. They don't go according to any rules. They're not like aches or wounds; they're more like splits in the skin that won't heal because there's not enough material."
~Anonymous~

Stiles became troubled again in the middle of reading a book by one of his favorite Pastors, Joel Osteen. He set his chocolate brown leather briefcase to the side. As if on auto pilot, he rushed to the kitchen, grabbed his car keys, and within minutes, he was on I-240 driving in the direction of Emerald Estates. He felt an urge in his spirit like he hadn't experienced in a long time. It was time for him to do what he'd put off long enough—confront his mother and tell his father everything about what led to the break-up of his marriage and caused the rift in the Graham family. Part of it had come out when Pastor had his stroke, but Audrey had managed to smooth things over by taking advantage of Pastor's weak mind and short-term memory loss he endured after his stroke.

Stiles loosened his striped tie and moved his neck from side to side. He steered the coral blue Infiniti with his free hand. He spoke out loud while he headed to Emerald Estates. "Should I call and let them know I'm coming? Should I tell Mother what I'm planning to do? Lord, I need you to guide me." He gritted his teeth and tucked his bottom lip. "The truth must be told. I can't allow Francesca to go on living a life of self-condemnation. Not when I know the truth. I don't want to hurt Audrey either, but she was wrong for not telling anyone about Francesca's molestation. Why didn't she tell Pastor? Mother, what were you thinking?" He hit the steering wheel with an open palm.

Stiles didn't want to be the one to remind his father of the truth, the whole truth at that, but Rena was gone, plus there was no telling where Frankie was, and it was time for the truth to be told. *No more hiding,* his spirit pressed him.

Stiles thought about the conversation he'd had with Pastor after Rena left town and Frankie disappeared to only God knows where.

"I'm going to make you a promise right here and right now, Pastor," he had said. "I'm going to do what I can to find out what happened to Frankie. I don't know what the outcome will be, but whatever I find out might tear this family even further apart. And if what Fonda said about mother turns out to be true, we both have a lot to think about."

Unfortunately, Stiles's suspicions had been right. When he went to Chattanooga and confronted Fonda about Francesca's allegations, Fonda reluctantly broke down and confessed to her horrible acts. She admitted that Audrey knew about it, just like Francesca said that she did.

Stiles's thoughts about his family, particularly Francesca, flooded his mind like a tidal wave. "God," he said. "How could Audrey have turned her back on her little girl; her own flesh and blood? And then for Francesca to be raped by Pastor Travis a couple of years later, what was it all for, God? Why didn't I see that something was wrong? Was I that busy with my own life that I missed what was happening to my sister? God, please forgive me. Why couldn't I have talked to her more, or spent more time with her? Maybe then, she would have known she had someone to talk to. But I was too busy doing my own thing. I didn't want to be bothered with her. I was wrapped up in being the popular guy around school and church. But my baby sister wasn't safe at home or at church. It doesn't make sense." He cried out to God bitterly. Salty tears rested on Stiles's upper lips as he shook his head in anguish over what laid ahead.

Stiles continued to drive in the direction of Emerald Estates. Once he finished confronting Audrey and Pastor with the truth, he had plans to find his sister to let her know that she was free to move on with living the life God designed for her to live. He pushed the button on the steering wheel and audibly said to the car, "Parents." The phone automatically dialed the number.

"Hello, sweetheart," the voice on the other end said politely.

"Hi, Mother. How are you this afternoon?"

"I'm fine, darling. Where are you?"

"I was calling to make sure you and Pastor were at home. I wanted to stop by and talk to the two of you about something."

"Why, of course, honey. You know our doors are always open to you."

"Yes, I know, Mom. Look, I'll be there in about ten minutes or so. Do you need me to bring anything? Something to eat? Ice cream and cookies? Anything?" offered Stiles.

"No, we're fine. You just bring yourself on over here. Pastor is going to be glad to see you. It's been almost two weeks since you came to visit. Seems like we only get the chance to see you at Sunday worship services or mid-week Bible class."

Stiles apologized. "I'm sorry about that, Mother. It's a hectic life. Being pastor of a growing church like Holy Rock keeps me busy. There aren't enough hours in the day for me to accomplish all of the tasks that need to be taken care of."

"Is that so?" Audrey sounded somewhat perturbed. "So that's what Pastor and I amount to now, one of your tasks?"

"Mother, please. You know I didn't mean it like that. I was just saying that I'm still in transition mode. Pastor left large shoes to fill. He made it all seem too easy, but really and truly it is a tough, demanding responsibility. Being the leader of a church, responsible for teaching, preaching, and leading others to Christ, plus managing the day to day operations of a church . . ." Stiles paused and wiggled in his seat. He was uncomfortable with Audrey's way of grilling him.

"Enough said," Audrey stopped him, sounding like she was satisfied with the response Stiles had given her. "We'll see you in a minute. Bye, baby."

"Bye, Mother." Stiles hit the button to disconnect the phone. "Father, guide my tongue. This is not an easy thing for me to do, but I know you want me to bring it out of the closet, Lord. I can't do it without you. I pray that Pastor and Mother will listen with open ears and a non-condemning spirit. I pray that my mother will open up her heart and admit her wrongs. Help me, Father. Help your servant. In your name I pray. Amen."

Stiles turned in his parents' driveway, turned off the ignition, and sat for a few seconds before he eased out of the car and walked to the front door. Before his balled up hand met the oak door, Pastor opened it.

"Hello, son," he said. His speech was near perfect now. The evidence of a stroke was present only in his slow gait.

"Hello, Pastor," Stiles answered. He stepped inside the door. His affection and adoration for his father was evident when he leaned over and hugged Pastor tightly. "How're you doing, Dad?"

"Blessed, son. Everyday God allows me to be on this earth is a blessing. I won't complain about a thing," Pastor remarked, and then turned around with his left foot dragging and went toward the family room.

"Where's Mother?"

"She's back there getting dressed." Pastor tilted his head. "You'd think she was getting ready to go somewhere, but all she's doing is dressing up for her son. You know your mother." Pastor laughed.

"That I do," replied Stiles, and he chuckled too.

"How are things going with the church and the ministry? It's been awhile since you've called and asked for any advice. Must mean that things are going well, huh?"

"There's no such thing as enough advice from you, Pastor. You've led Holy Rock since I was a young boy. I've taken in all of your teachings; and your guidance along the way can never be replaced. I guess what I'm saying is I'm flying now. I'm out of the nest, and God is guiding me along step by step."

"Praise the Lord. That's what I want to hear."

"I'll be out in a minute," yelled Audrey from the back of the house.

Stiles answered her with a yell of his own. "Okay, Mother. I'm not going anywhere."

Pastor chuckled again. "That wife of mine. I tell you, she's one of a kind." Stiles watched Pastor as he spoke of Audrey. The look that was etched on his face was one of happiness and contentment. His father almost glowed when he spoke of his beloved wife of thirty years. Why couldn't he and Rena have had that same, priceless kind of love toward one another? Stiles sat for a few seconds while lightning flash thoughts of Rena saturated his mind.

"I'm glad to know you're leaning and depending on the Lord, son. That's the only one who can sustain you. God is the only one whose steps you should follow. Don't be swayed by anything outside of God's will."

"I'm praying every day that I will be receptive to God's will and way."

"Good, good. Have you heard from Francesca?" The look on Pastor's face changed from one of happiness to a face that appeared to be full of wrinkles and deep lines of worry over his daughter.

Stiles hated to break the news to his father. "No. I'm afraid I haven't, and that's part of why I'm here. Or should I say, it's the reason I'm here."

"What's going on, sweetheart?" Audrey asked Stiles as she made her grand entrance into the family room. She was dressed stylishly in an African style three-piece, silk tangerine and soft cocoa pantsuit. Audrey accented the outfit with a pair of wide-heeled sandals.

Stiles stood when his mother waltzed into the room. He walked over to where she stood like she was posing for a photo shoot. "Mother, you look stunning," complimented Stiles and kissed her on her cheek. "Ummm, and you smell like a sweet slice of heaven," he continued lavishing her with compliments. Audrey seemed to soak all of it in like a sponge.

"Stiles, Pastor, would you like some lemon tea and a sandwich?" Audrey offered.

Stiles waved his hand, "No, but thanks, Mother. I ate well and the kitchen ministry keeps me well fed." Stiles patted his belly.

"I'll take a glass of tea," Pastor said.

"On second thought, I'll have a glass of tea too," said Stiles.

Without hesitating, Audrey darted in the kitchen and returned with two cold, tall glasses of Pastor's favorite beverage. She gave each of them a glass. She took a seat next to Pastor on the sofa that faced Stiles.

Pastor was the first one to speak after he took a nice, long swallow of tea. "Son, you said that you wanted to talk to us about Francesca? Did you find where she is?" His look was one of anxiousness and hope. "Is she all right?"

Stiles moved around in the oversized camel chair, displaying his nervousness. He took his time and inhaled before he spoke. "No, I haven't located Francesca yet. But that's only a matter of time. I am confident that God will open the doors for me, so I can find my sister."

Pastor nodded in agreement while Audrey sat still as a statue, quiet as a mouse.

Stiles clasped his hands together. Within, he prayed, *Lord, help me.* "I don't know where to start."

"Just let it out, son. We're listening. We want to know whatever it is you have to say. Isn't that right, honey?" asked Pastor and nudged his wife lovingly.

Audrey remained quiet, like she wasn't so sure. She barely moved her head in agreement.

"Okay. Here goes. A few weeks ago, well, a month ago I should say, I took a road trip."

"To where? Andover to see that ex-wife of yours?" Audrey said harshly.

"No, although I sometimes wish I had gone to see Rena. I think about her all the time. I wonder if there was anything I could have done to make things better for the two of us. Maybe I should have tried harder to forgive her for her betrayal. Maybe, being a pastor and man of God, I should have gone before God and laid it all before Him, but I couldn't do that." Stiles dropped his head. "I acted from my own emotions. I acted out of my own selfishness and my anger."

Pastor intervened. "Stiles, son. It's not too late to seek forgiveness. If God is convicting you for a wrong you've done, then there's still time to make things right. As long as the blood is running warm in your veins, you've got a chance to make your wrongs right." Audrey exhaled loudly and Pastor continued to speak. "Don't be one of those pastors that preach one thing and practice another. Don't stand in the pulpit Sunday after Sunday with unconfessed sins in your life. The Bible teaches us that we are not to regard iniquity in our hearts. No one is perfect, son. And I'm not saying that you and Rena will get back together. What I am saying is that whatever you need to do to make sure your part in what happened is cleared with your wife, then that's what needs to be done."

"Ex," announced Audrey rather boldly.

Pastor and Stiles acted like they didn't hear Audrey. "Son, you are God's man. You move, act, and speak according to what God instructs."

"Yes, sir. You're right, which is why I have to speak the truth now, even though it might hurt. Like I was saying, I took a road trip. I visited my cousin, Fonda in Chattanooga." Stiles saw Audrey's eyes loom large and her body appeared to stiffen like a piece of wood. "I had to find out the truth for Francesca's sake." Stiles spoke slowly, weighing his words carefully. "I asked Fonda about the accusations Francesca made about her."

"About Fonda molesting her when she was a child?" Pastor said in a somber voice.

Audrey sat frozen.

"Yes, Pastor."

"And what did Fonda have to say?" asked Pastor.

"She. She. She admitted that everything Francesca said was true. She said she didn't know why she did what she did to Francesca. She also said she was jealous of our family; especially Francesca because it seemed like Francesca had a better life than she had. She pleaded for me to forgive her. But I'm not the one she needs to ask for forgiveness. I told her she has to answer to God, and she needs to make things right in her own life by first asking Francesca for forgiveness and letting Francesca know that none of the things Fonda did was my sister's fault."

"Oh my Lord." Tears trickled down Pastor's face. "Not my Francesca. Why? How could I have been so blind to what was going on?" Pastor trembled. Audrey remained staunch.

"And I'm afraid that isn't all," said Stiles. His voice was shaky and his hands trembled. He glanced at his mother who watched him with eyes that glinted like steel. It was the first time his mother actually evoked fear in him. He turned his eyes away immediately. He wouldn't let the devil win this one. It was time that his sister be vindicated.

"What else is it, son?" asked Pastor. He used the back of his hand to wipe the tears away.

"Fonda confirmed what Francesca said." Stiles paused, and then glared at his mother. "Fonda said that you, Mother, you knew all along what was going on." Anger began to mount in Stiles. "Not only did you know about it; you saw what happened. You chose to, and I said chose to do nothing. You let Fonda continue to molest my sister again and again. Then a few years later, Pastor Travis stole her precious, sacred virginity by raping her!" Stiles jumped from the chair. He was so full of anger.

"Well, I never heard lies like the ones being told," screamed Audrey. "And you dare to come in this house with this, this evil, contemptible mess? How dare you?" scolded Audrey.

Pastor jerked away from his wife, who he had been holding around the waist. He moved back and looked at her. Hurt like Stiles had never seen, filled his father's watering eyes. Stiles hated to tell his father and mother what he'd learned, but he had to do it. There was no time for any more lies and secrets.

Pastor turned and faced Audrey. "How could you, Audrey?

All of the years we've been together, I've trusted you, believed in you. When I heard Francesca and Rena talking the day I had my stroke, even when Francesca said that you knew about Fonda, I refused to believe her. I thought I was confused and that I had to be wrong about what I heard. I blamed it on her being angry and the fact that she may have felt shame about being a lesbian. But to be molested and raped, first at the hands of our own flesh and blood, then by a man I trusted to help lead young people to Christ! Oh, Lord, what happened to my spiritual discernment? My poor baby. My poor, poor darling Francesca." Pastor started crying like a baby. His sobs moved Stiles until Stiles's tears pushed forward and out. Pastor continued to sob loudly. "How could I forget something like this?" He continued crying.

Stiles moved next to his father, not paying any attention to what Audrey was doing. The two men hugged each other. Their tears meshed.

Audrey continued to sit down quietly, almost stoically. What now? What did the future hold for the Graham family? And where and how was Francesca?

Audrey dashed up from the sofa again and forced Stiles and Pastor to part. "Listen to me. Okay, if you want me to say that I saw what happened all those years ago, then I'll say it. I did. I didn't know what to do back then. I couldn't believe what I was seeing. I mean, my baby, my dear little, Francesca was doing disgusting, nasty things. I was furious, hurt, and confused. All at one time. I couldn't process what happened. I couldn't believe that Fonda, my sister's child, would be part of something so evil."

"But you could believe that your own daughter could?" Pastor lashed out at Audrey.

Audrey screamed and cried. Her arms flailed, spittle spewed from her mouth. She begged Pastor and Stiles. "Please, Pastor.

Please forgive me. I didn't know what to do. I know what I did was wrong. I turned my back on my own daughter. I blamed her for what happened. Who else was I to blame when the same thing happened to me when I was a child! My uncle did far worse than Fonda ever did to Francesca. He was the most evil person I've ever known. When I heard about Minister Travis, I blocked that out too."

Audrey shook her head from side to side. Pastor and Stiles stood in silence, stunned at the confession pouring like a flood from Audrey's mouth. "Pastor," Audrey grabbed hold of her husband's hand. "Please, forgive me. I didn't mean to hurt our daughter. I didn't mean to do it. It was like living all over again, the terrible violation I suffered. I'm sorry. God," Audrey looked up toward the ceiling before she placed her hands over her face. "Oh, God, please, please, please! I'm so sorry. I'm so sorry, Francesca, wherever you are. I'm so sorry," she cried.

Probably relying on Pastor's forgiving and nurturing spirit, Audrey continued to cry. Pastor, however, reacted totally the opposite. Stiles's eyes bulged when he heard the thunderous voice of Pastor roaring at Audrey. The only time he'd heard Pastor's voice this strong was when he was in the pulpit.

Pastor jerked his hand away from Audrey. He stood upright and yelled. "All of these years, I wanted to believe you. All of these years, I did believe you and whatever you said," he corrected himself. "What am I to believe now, Audrey? That you hid all of these secrets from me about our only daughter, about my darling Francesca because of your past?" Pastor looked at Stiles with eyes blazing like fire.

"And you," he pointed an angry finger at Stiles, "how long have you known this? There's no wonder Francesca turned out the way she has. In and out of jail, turning against God and her family, involved in homosexuality." Pastor's hands flew up in the air as he continued his tirade. "And my wife, my help meet of thirty years, turns out to be part of all of this sin sick madness."

Audrey interrupted hastily. "But Pastor, it's not like you make it out to be. I was afraid. I didn't want to face the same things I had to face when I was a child. My mother told me that it was my fault when my Uncle Larry molested me. She told me how bad I was and that I should be ashamed of myself." Audrey's tears flowed heavily down her face. She tried to use the back of her hand to wipe them away, but the more she wiped, the more she cried. She stood next to Pastor, while Stiles surveyed the shocking scene playing before his very eyes.

"Audrey, I don't know whether to believe a word you're saying. All the years we've been married, and you've never said a mumbling word about this so called molestation. Now, when it's convenient, you want to tell me and your son about this." Pastor raised his hands in a tirade. "Again, it's all about you. It always has been. I've tried to be there for you, Audrey. I've tried to be the man, the spouse that God desires of me. I've loved you and I still love you, but what you've done to Francesca is something I have to go into prayer about. I have to seek God. I've been so blind, so blind." Pastor's own tears fell down his face and on to his honey gold polo shirt. "I can't take all of this right now. I need time for this to soak in."

Audrey's pleading tone disappeared as fast as a cheetah chasing after its prey. "You can't sit here and try to blame everything on me. If you weren't so busy at church all of the time, maybe you would have noticed something too," she yelled.

Stiles didn't know if he should intervene or allow his parents to keep going at each other's throats. He chose the latter. Maybe all of this needed to come out now. It had been far too long and too many lives had been destroyed because of everything that happened. He sat on the edge of the sofa and listened.

"I've been nothing but supportive of you, Pastor. And you want to make this all my fault. How dare you? How dare any of you?" she said in a voice of anger. She watched Stiles as if waiting on his reaction. He had nothing to say. She then looked back at Pastor and continued lashing out at him. "All the time you paraded around like you were the top dog or something. Holy Rock is all you've ever cared about. But what about me--your wife? What about your children? Everything concerning Holy Rock came first in your life. Don't pretend you didn't see the change in Francesca, just like I did. Don't act like you're Mr. Innocent. You're just as much to blame as me. You're the one who purposely had such a great relationship with your daughter. If that were so true, why didn't she feel free to turn to you for help? And you heard everything before now anyway." Audrey pointed at him. "Or don't you recall that the reason you had a stroke was because of the conversation you overheard. Answer that?"

Pastor could barely contain his fury. Audrey was right. He had failed his daughter too. He had failed his family as well. He looked away every time Francesca came up with a different attitude, or an outlandish wardrobe, or when she changed her room drastically. He'd closed his eyes to everything that happened around him. But to be molested and sexually assaulted is something he never would have allowed to happen. He made himself available twenty-four seven to his congregation, but he was blinded by the happenings in his own family.

"So think about what I said. I won't be in this alone. You," Audrey continued to point an accusatory finger at Pastor and yell. "You have a lot of explaining to do before God yourself. And Stiles," Audrey whirled around and looked at him again, still with bitterness, "find your sister. I want to get this out in the open and over and done with as soon as possible." With that being said, Audrey abruptly left without saying another word.

Pastor's arm lovingly enveloped his son and pulled him into the safety of his arms. Stiles held on.

"Son, I'm sorry. I have a lot of repenting to do. I have to talk to God about all that's happened. I need some time away from Emerald Estates." Pastor's eyes appeared dark and marked with sadness as Stiles pulled away and looked at him. "Maybe healing can begin, but only if Francesca can be found."

Stiles eased himself away from his father. "We're going to make it through this. With God's help, we'll make it. Where are you going to go? Are you saying that you're leaving mother?"

"Yes and no. I'm not leaving her because of what she's done or not done. I'm leaving because I need to spend some quiet time talking to God. I think I'll drive up to the cabin in Gatlinburg for a few days."

"Drive? Pastor, are you up to that? Gatlinburg is about a six-hour drive or more. I don't know if that would be good for you."

"God will take care of me. That's for sure." Pastor patted Stiles on his shoulder. "Your mother has done some wild and crazy things in the past, but I never saw this coming–never. Where did I go wrong? I thought my relationship with God and with Audrey was better than this." Pastor shook his head and cried.

"Pastor, look; come over to my house. You can sleep in the guestroom." You can stay there as long as you want. Plus, it's on the other side of the house, so I won't be a bother to you. You can have all of the time alone that you need. There's plenty of food in the fridge too. I mean, Dad, the devil is a lie, and believe me when I tell you that with God's help and direction, I am going to find Francesca. It's the only way healing can manifest. As for Mother, she has to own up to her mistakes. She has to be the one to go to God for forgiveness, and then she has to ask Francesca for forgiveness and maybe even Rena. But that's between her and God."

Through tears, Pastor raised up his bowed down head. "Yes, I know she does. I feel like a ton of weight has been placed on my back. I'm just so sorry. So sorry all of this happened . . . and right before my very eyes. Stiles, please find Francesca. Bring her home; bring my little girl back home where she belongs. And," he sighed, "I think I'll take you up on the offer to stay at your place for a day or two. I'll be there later." Pastor turned and walked away.

"Good, let me go to the car and get my extra garage remote." Stiles returned and gave the remote to Pastor. "I'll get the bed turned back for you too." Stiles left and Pastor stood still for a moment. The tears in his eyes had dried and crusted.

Later that same evening, Pastor came to spend the night. Like Stiles promised, he allowed his father his privacy. He showed him to the guestroom, told him where everything was, and then disappeared to his bedroom.

Audrey felt the emptiness of having Pastor gone. It did calm her down somewhat to know that he was spending the night at Stiles's house — that much he had told her. She hoped he would be home tomorrow. She and Pastor had been together too long for their marriage to be in trouble. He had always been her provider, her nourisher, her lover, and her best friend. He loved Stiles like he was his biological son; and to prove it, he had adopted Stiles when they first got married. Audrey looked in the bathroom medicine cabinet and took her nightly blood pressure and arthritis medications. She climbed in the king-sized bed and looked over at the empty side. She caressed the place where Pastor always laid. Her hand remained there.

The following morning, Stiles woke up early. He listened

to the whippoorwills singing praises to God; their morning tunes. It was five forty-five. The automatic coffee machine had done its job. Stiles lay in his bed for awhile and read his daily morning scripture. He said a prayer to God, then went to the bathroom to groom himself.

When he finished in the bathroom, Stiles sat at the kitchen counter and began to think about last night's visit. He assumed that Pastor must have been still asleep because Stiles didn't hear him shuffling around, nor had the extra coffee cup been touched that Stiles had sat out the night before for Pastor. He pressed the garage remote, and Pastor's car was gone.

When Stiles left his parents' home the night before, he'd left them in a terrible state; especially Audrey. It had been tough to expose his own mother, but he had to be true to the man God had called him to be. Audrey was wrong, so wrong for turning away from the hurt and pain experienced by her own child. But the past was the past, and now the only way for positive change was through finding Francesca and bringing her home to the family that loved her.

Stiles thought a time or two about his life. The reflection he saw standing in the bathroom mirror earlier was not one that he was proud of either. Part of him felt like Audrey. He was no better than his mother. How could he talk about forgiveness and repentance when he had allowed Rena to leave town without so much as telling her good-bye. He let her walk away, knowing that she was sorry for the wrong she'd done. He had condemned and judged her. But he was the man of God, the one who based his teachings on God's forgiveness and the fact that there is no self-condemnation with God. How could he let his wife walk away? The man in the mirror had quite a bit of soul searching of his own to do.

He finished his coffee, and then got dressed. He peeped in

the guestroom to check on Pastor. Stiles half smiled when he saw the bed was already made and empty, as if Pastor hadn't slept in it at all. Stiles shrugged and then turned and walked to the kitchen. He didn't act too surprised when he saw that Pastor's car was gone too.

Stiles faced a long day, complete with staff meetings, answering church e-mail, and studying his sermon for the week. The day turned out just as Stiles had predicted. There were numerous church issues to discuss, people to counsel and visit, and a host of other pastoral duties. By the time he made it home, it was close to seven o'clock. One of the first items on his agenda was to start a real search for his sister. He went online and searched for the next two hours without finding a clue that could possibly lead him to Francesca. Tired, exhausted, and no closer to finding Francesca, Stiles decided that a piping hot shower might help ease some of the tension.

The shower did its intended job. He felt a little more relaxed when he stepped out of the shower into the steam filled bathroom. He draped a bath towel around his defined waist and walked into the bedroom. He dried off, and then shuffled through one of the dresser drawers until he pulled out a pair of deep blue pajama pants to put on.

Stiles strolled slowly down the hallway and into the kitchen. He prepared himself a plate of left over spaghetti and meatballs he had in the fridge, warmed two pieces of garlic toast and made a nice size garden salad. While he ate, he went over his notes for Sunday's sermon until his eyelids became heavy as lead. He stood, stretched, went to the sink, and washed his plate and fork.

Outside, heavy drops of rain started to pour, released from the black clouds looming over the city of Memphis. Thunder roared mightily. Stiles smiled and said, "The angels are bowling," something the Grahams often told him and Francesca when it thundered. Lightning flaunted its power with round after round. Stiles peeped out of the kitchen window over the sink. Trees, hundreds of years old, swayed against the rushing winds that only God could make cease. The fall of the year was his favorite season. Tonight it seemed like the earth itself was in a rage all of its own. With each bolt of lightning and thunderous clap, Stiles jerked. The power of God was beyond his comprehension. The handiworks of God could only be felt through his finite mind. Stiles watched the storm longer than he intended, then turned and walked up the hall to his bedroom. He would put off his online search for Francesca until the thunderstorm ceased.

Stiles knelt down on the side of his bed and praised God for all He had done. He prayed for his search of Francesca, for healing of his family, and most of all, forgiveness for the wrong he'd committed.

Stiles went boldly before the congregation the following Sunday morning and explained that he was searching for Francesca and asked for the prayers of his congregation. Audrey and Pastor were not there, but Stiles couldn't allow their absence to interfere with what God had called him to do. He didn't feel it was necessary to go into all of the details, but he did believe that it was God who directed him not to shield his congregation from what was going on in his own life. Most of them had probably come up with their own conclusions anyway. Maybe in all of this, people would see that he truly was an ordinary man, called to do extraordinary things for God. He emphasized how much he needed them to intercede on behalf of himself and his family.

Daily, Stiles searched and held weekly update meetings with his search team. On his days off from church, mostly one day a week, Stiles spent his time trying to locate people who knew Francesca. He especially wanted to find Francesca's sidekick, Kansas. It seemed likely to him that if Kansas could be located, then the puzzle pieces to Francesca's disappearance might begin to fit together.

It took several weeks, but Stiles did find out information about Kansas. She had died from AIDS about two weeks prior. Stiles had been told by one of Kansas's street friends that she was buried at the Pauper's Cemetery. He went there and there were no headstones, only small markers with names inscribed on them. It took awhile, but he managed to find the spot where Kansas lay. He placed a bouquet of flowers on her grave and prayed over her soul.

Chapter Six

"I'm starting with the man in the mirror . . ."
~Michael Jackson~

Francesca had adjusted well to her new life in Newbern, Tennessee. She loved her cozy apartment and the many new friends she made both in the complex and at church. Since giving her life totally to Christ and being baptized for a second time, Francesca believed there was nothing that God couldn't do. She had not had a herpes outbreak since before leaving Memphis, which had been months ago. She found a great doctor in nearby Dyersburg whom she liked. The doctor happened to attend the same church as Francesca too. Continued testing, eating healthy, living healthy, and having a positive attitude aided in Francesca's well being. There was no reason to believe that she would ever get full blown AIDS. Her faith refused to allow her to believe such. As for the old Frankie, she was gone and had been transformed into Francesca Graham. No more getting high, no more cigarettes, no more same sex relationships, no more ill will toward her life and the mistakes she'd made over the years. She still wrestled with the molestation and rape, but God was dealing with her in that area of her life too. And as for the feelings she had about her parents, she was still seeking God in that area as well.

Francesca was definitely on her way to full recovery in more ways than one. Her spiritual journey had certainly begun. During one of her regular counseling sessions at her church, she learned that true forgiveness was evident when those who believe in God can truthfully and sincerely pray for those who wronged them. Francesca had a difficult time with this part of her journey. Every time she kneeled down to give God praise and honor and to pray for others, somehow she always managed to bypass Fonda, Minister Travis, and Audrey. She prayed easily for Rena, Stiles, Pastor, and Kansas too; not knowing of Kansas's death. God had brought her a long, long way.

Francesca sat on the floor of her living room. Her eyes were focused on the documentary about planet Earth, but her mind was fully not on the images before her. She thought back to how she'd come to this awesome point in life.

"What can wipe away your sins?" she remembered the preacher asked and answered himself. "Nothing but the blood of Jesus. Someone in here needs the stench of sin wiped away from their life. Someone in here needs to know that God is a forgiving God." His voice escalated. "I tell you, someone in this very place needs to know that God is a habit breaker; that he is a healer and a deliverer. Someone, I tell you, needs to know that God is the God of second chances, third chances, and unlimited chances. Someone needs to know that God is a God of suddenly. He can suddenly turn your darkness into light. The God I serve can suddenly right your wrongs. He can suddenly save your sin sick soul, and he can make a broken life whole. Oh yes, God can."

The preacher stretched out his arms toward the gathering of people. "Come to Jesus. All who are burdened and heavy laden. He will give you rest. Surrender your all to Him. He will work it out."

From the back pew that day, Frankie listened to the

preacher. At that moment, she felt like there was no one else around. He was speaking directly to her. She saw him. The spirit within that she had closed the door on so many years ago, began to speak to her heart. She needed what she now had come to understand that only God could give her – deliverance. Easing from her seat, she excused herself and moved past each person until she stood in the aisle. Walking slowly, limping and wounded in more than her physical body, she moved toward the front of the church and yielded her broken life and spirit to God.

On that Sunday, when Francesca walked to the front of the apartment church and was ushered inside, she returned to her own apartment renewed and restored. She quickly became known by the ever growing congregation. The main church was located several miles from Francesca's apartment, but she didn't let a lack of transportation hold her back. When the church discontinued the services at the apartment due to its phenomenal growth, Francesca made arrangements for the church's van to pick her up every Sunday and for mid-week service.

Once wounded and with a life that had spiraled out of control, Francesca began to see herself the way that God saw her. She was blessed, saved, much loved and adored by God–she belonged to Him, and for the first time in her life, Francesca believed that God loved her.

Chapter Seven

"In real love you want the other person's good. In romantic love you want the other person."
  ~ *Margaret Anderson* ~

The next few weeks went by quickly. Rena and Robert spent more time together. It didn't take long for them to discover they were alike in many ways. Both were lonely. Both of them were dealing with the agonizing blows caused by broken hearts. Rena didn't share as much depth about the break-up of her marriage, but she did let Robert know as much as she could without divulging the ugliness of her past, which haunted her more times than not.

Being in a semi-relationship, with a man like Robert, was awkward at times for Rena. First of all, dating a man with children, small children at that, was new, but Rena found it refreshing as well. She loved children, but often believed her hopes had been dashed of ever having children of her own because of the horrid mistakes of her past that she lived with everyday. She had not had many outbreaks since moving to Andover, probably because she was under less stress. Her mother had been the catalyst to helping her accept God's forgiveness and talking to her about forgiving herself. She'd had another HIV test since returning to Andover too, and it had turned out negative. But knowing that she had herpes, an incurable STD, forced her to do all she could to keep her emotions in check with Robert, whom she was growing to like more each time they spent time together, whether it was an evening at home watching movies with his kids, or sharing private, alone time with each other over an intimate dinner, or a walk in the park. Robert was invigorating. He wasn't pushy at all; probably because he was still wounded from the piercing shot to the heart left by the absence of his wife.

On one of their evenings spent together, Robert, Rena, and his kids had an explosive time at Rena's house. The evening had gone perfectly. It was on a Friday night, and Robert, Rena, and the kids had a fun evening watching a family comedy, eating pizza, and drinking fresh homemade smoothies that Rena made. After a long evening, the children had both fallen sound asleep. Robert and Rena carried them into her guest bedroom, and she and Robert cuddled on the sofa, her head nestling on his shoulder. It was times like these when thoughts of Stiles popped in her head. Tonight she pushed them aside and instead tried concentrating on what Robert was saying. Tunes from the seventies were playing at a low volume on the music channel.

Robert's hands twirled the curls in her hair. "You know, I love times like this," he said softly. "You're such an amazing woman to accept me and my kids. They're crazy about you, you know."

"I feel the same way about them," answered Rena and cuddled closer to Robert when he started caressing her shoulder. She could feel his breath blowing slightly against her forehead. He kissed her lightly on the cheek.

"Rena, I like you. I really do. You're the first woman I've even thought of seeing since Karen walked out on us. I want you to know that I would never take you for granted or hurt you in any way," he whispered in her ear. "You mean too much to me," he said and lifted her chin so her eyes met his intense gaze. Before she could respond to his words, he kissed her with fervor and unbridled passion. He used the back of his hand to caress her face lightly.

Rena returned the intensity of his kiss and held on to him like she was afraid if she released him, he would flee. With each kiss, their desire reached a higher pitch. His hands explored and her body responded. When Robert's words turned to groans of want, Rena hesitated before she pulled away from his embrace.

"What is it, sweetheart?" he asked her in a panting voice. "Did I do something wrong?"

Rena looked away. *Oh God. What do I say? How do I get through this?* "Robert, I want us to take things slowly. We've both been hurt. We've both gone through a traumatic divorce. We still have a lot of baggage and a lot of soul searching to do before either of us can think about a relationship. You're a great man, a wonderful father, and a man who fears God." She continued to talk, not sure if she were making any sense. "I just think we need to slow down and let our friendship grow at its own pace before anything. And I don't want to have sex outside of marriage. I know it might sound old fashioned to you, but it's what God has placed in me, and I can't disobey Him." She exhaled, and then dared to look at the expression on his face.

She was surprised to see a smile form on his lips. "You know, that's what makes you so special." He kissed her again, this time it was a peck on her lips. "I totally understand, and I agree with everything you've said. I want you; that I won't lie about. But I don't want to compromise our relationship. I don't want to jump into anything too fast myself, especially because of the kids. I have to be cautious who I allow in their lives. You're great with them, but like you said, we need to grow into this thing. We need to see where it's going. And

I do, more than anything, want to please God, Rena." After having said that, he stood up from the sofa and jiggled his right leg before he turned and grabbed hold of her hand. He helped her get up from the sofa.

Rena looked somewhat puzzled. "What are you doing?"

"I'm going to go and get my kids, bundle them up, and we're going home. I've had a great time with you, Rena, like I always do. But you and I both know if I stay here one minute longer, I won't be liable for what I desperately want to do – make love to you." Robert sighed.

Stuttering slightly, Rena agreed with him. Though reluctant, she knew there was no way she would make love with Robert. She couldn't think of the possibility until she saw exactly what the future held for them, if it held anything. Then and only then, as much as she liked him, would she even consider telling him about her STD, and the real reason for the dissolution of her marriage.

Rena and Robert headed for the bedroom and put coats on the sleeping children. After she and Robert put on their coats too, she helped him carry the children to the car. They placed them in their car seats without either of them waking up. With her arms clasped inside each other, she danced around in the midnight cold while Robert kissed her again before getting inside his car.

"Go back inside before you turn into an icicle," he teased.

"Okay, call me when you make it home," she said and blew him a kiss before dashing up the walkway and back inside of the house. She closed the door when she saw him pull out of the driveway. Leaning against it, she thought of Robert before thoughts of Stiles invaded her mind.

No matter how much she liked Robert, she couldn't keep Stiles out of her thoughts. Part of her despised him for the way he treated her. The other part of her loved him like she'd never loved anyone before. She thought of all the fun times they had together. Rena sat on the couch and curled her feet underneath her. With her head leaned back against the soft head cushion, she reached for the throw at the other end of the couch and placed it over her to warm her. She imagined how it would have been if things had turned out differently with her and Stiles. Maybe she would be pregnant by now, preparing for the birth of their first child. She would be walking proud and happy. But she wasn't married to Stiles anymore. The tawdry past had made certain of that.

As for Francesca, Rena hoped she was doing well too. They had their major differences about a lot of things, but Rena still looked at Francesca as her best friend. There was a time that nothing could come between their friendship. When they crossed the line and experimented with each other, Rena felt guilty, but she would do anything for Francesca. Francesca was the one who reached out to her when Rena's family first moved to Memphis. It was Francesca who Rena formed a solid alliance with. There was nothing she couldn't or wouldn't tell Francesca. Her loyalty toward Francesca is what made her offer her body for Francesca to experiment with. Rena never meant for it to be the beginning of a lesbian relationship that spanned for years. She found herself locked in, caught up with Francesca. Why couldn't Francesca have been as trusting of Rena as Rena had been toward her? If she had confided in Rena about Fonda and Pastor Travis, they could have worked things out differently.

The best and worst events in her life came from one family — the Grahams. She had to find a way to let the past be the past. Robert may be the answer, but she would have to tell him everything about her past before they could ever think of moving forward in a committed relationship. She had learned harshly from her relationship with Stiles, how much it could destroy people when the truth was hidden.

Rena got up, walked to her bedroom, and lay across her bed. She had no more tears to cry. Momentary sadness and loneliness for the man she really loved enveloped her. Stiles Graham was gone out of her life forever, and she had to come to terms with it some way. But how, Rena didn't quite understand. Only God could heal her wounded spirit and her broken heart.

Rena stood up and slid out of her pants and top. She crawled under the quilt and curled in a knot. She prayed for God to open the doors to a new beginning.

Chapter Eight

"*Anyone who has a continuous smile on his face conceals a
toughness that is almost frightening.*"
~*Greta Garbo*~

Pastor sat on the edge of the bed in Stiles's guestroom. He
couldn't deal with the span of emotions that he had experienced earlier. He felt betrayed by the person whom he loved
the most. Spending the night away from home because of a
disagreement was something Pastor and Audrey had never
done. He heard the scripture play in his mind, *don't let the sun
go down upon your wrath.* He understood what he had to do; go
back home where he belonged.

At Emerald Estates, Audrey tossed and turned; she couldn't
sleep. She slowly got up out of the bed and moved around the
perimeter of their bedroom. She saw Pastor's charcoal pajama
pants and shirt neatly folded over his recliner. She walked
toward the chair and picked up the pants and began kneading them gingerly between her hands and laying them on her
face.

The sound of footsteps startled her and she dropped the
pajamas where she stood. "Pastor, is that you?" she asked out
loud. She grabbed hold of her pineapple satin robe, put it on
and cautiously walked out of the bedroom and into the hall,
but no farther.

Pastor appeared just as Audrey took another bold step. She

threw both hands up to her face and started laughing with joy.

"I knew you'd come back," she said and reached out toward him only to have him slightly but firmly pull back.

"I'm a man of God, Audrey. You know that. I couldn't stay at our son's house when I know God doesn't want me to leave a bad situation. But I can tell you that we," Pastor pointed to himself and to Audrey, "have done a grave injustice to this family, especially to Francesca. You were right." He spoke with sadness ringing from his voice. "I'm no better than you. I was so caught up in working for the Lord, so to speak, that I neglected the needs of my own family. I've prayed for many a person since I answered God's calling on my life at the age of eighteen." Frowns formed deeper than the wrinkles on his aging face. "But for every person I've prayed for and ministered to, I missed the most important thing, my own family. I'm sorry for that, and I've asked for God's forgiveness." Tears pushed forth from Pastor's hazel brown eyes. His body shook like a person sobbing over the loss of a loved one.

Audrey shed fresh tears of her own. She moved close to him again and held him by the shoulders. This time as they stood in the hallway, Pastor didn't flinch. "You're right about some of what you said, but you're also wrong too. You can't take the blame for what's happened in our family."

Pastor lifted his head up and his slumped shoulders perked.

"Chauncey Graham, you have never neglected this family," she said firmly. "You've always shown us nothing but unconditional love, and you've been the best husband a woman could ever hope or pray for. You've been the type of father some children wish they had. They know you love them and that you've always been there for them. But our children are full grown now. I'm certain that along the way, we did make mistakes when it came to raising them. But I will not take full responsibility or let you take full responsibility for their actions. Francesca was not driven to homosexuality, she chose that lifestyle. She chose to become entangled in situations that landed her in jail. She is the one that turned her back on her family and God. As for Stiles, I know he isn't your blood, but you embraced him and adopted him as your son. And look at him. He turned out just fine. So you see, sweetheart, the pendulum could have swung either way. Francesca had an outlet. She could have talked to someone. And yes, I'll be the first to take some of the blame for what happened back then, but on the other hand, I can do nothing to change the past. I have to press forward and so do you." Audrey sniffed, and then stepped into Pastor's arms fully.

While he spoke, Pastor slowly welcomed her and hugged her tightly. "The Word says we are to confess our faults one to another. God alone judges. He has the first, middle, and last word in all things. I have gone before Him and repented." He released Audrey from his embrace and they faced each other.

"I love you, Chauncey," Audrey said in tears. I love you more than life itself. Maybe you are right. I need to go before the Lord and confess too, and so does Francesca, Rena, and everyone who played a part in nearly destroying this family." Audrey spoke with more boldness and fewer tears fell.

Looking stunned, Pastor responded and started to walk up the hallway. "You still don't get it, do you? Why can't you own up to your mistakes? Where is your heart, woman? Who have I been married to all of these years? It's like I don't even know you anymore. You sound so callous. You talk about our daughter like she's a nobody. You need to go before God for yourself. Listen to Him and plead for your compassion to be restored because you act like you have a hardened heart." Pastor brushed past her and went to the bedroom.

Audrey didn't try to pursue him. Instead, she walked toward the kitchen. Once there, she made hot, spiced raspberry tea for the two of them. She was glad Pastor had returned home. All she needed to do was to give him a little space and time; and he'd come around to being the pastor she knew and loved--he always did.

She brought the tea to Pastor. He was sitting in his chair next to the bedroom window, staring outside at the blackness of night. He looked up and accepted the steaming cup from Audrey. The hot brew warmed his chilled insides. Audrey returned to the kitchen and drank her cup alone. When she returned to the bedroom, Pastor had finished his tea, and had changed into his pajamas. Audrey followed by removing her robe, and then she got in bed. A thick wall of silence separated them.

Pastor climbed in bed next to Audrey. She made it known in no uncertain terms, by her prissiness, that she wanted him to make love to her. Pastor, still in the throes of hurt and disappointment in his wife, ignored her seductive tactics and turned so that his back faced her.

Audrey wasn't perturbed in the least. She knew Pastor inside and out, everything about him, and she wasn't going to lose him to anything as silly and contrite as what Stiles had said.

As for Stiles, he was another mission Audrey had to accomplish. There was no way he should have come to Emerald Estates and confront her and Pastor in the manner in which he had. She'd have to remind him that he was her son, and he owed it to her to tell him when he learned something that could cause problems in the family. No one was going to mess up the relationship that she had developed with Pastor; no one, including Stiles.

Audrey finished putting on the last dabs of make-up. She went toward the study where she knew Pastor would be finishing his daily morning devotion with God. "Good morning, sweetheart," she said as she opened the door slightly. "I hope you slept well in your own bed and at your own home." She saw him sitting back in his chair, and laying his Bible on the desk.

"I slept okay. I see you're up rather early," he told her as he got up and walked toward her. He could smell her enticing aroma from across the room. He opened the door completely and hugged her. He never could resist Audrey. She had all of him outside of his love of God, and Pastor loved her dearly. She could do some things that would set him off, make him angry, like what she had pulled all of these years by keeping what happened to Francesca away from him. For that, he was more than angry; he was hurt. Plus, he felt that he should have noticed more of what was going on in his family. Audrey had been right when she said he'd spent so much time dealing with church matters that he didn't see what was going on at home. The short time he spent at Stiles's house gave him a chance to do a lot of thinking. Pastor believed Stiles was a lonely man. He'd lost his wife, his sister, and he'd lost his zest for loving again. Pastor didn't want to lose Audrey. No matter what she'd done, she could be forgiven. God said to forgive seventy times seven, and Audrey was no saint, but then again, no one was. Pastor pushed his hurt and anger aside and prayed to God for restoration of his family.

Audrey not only smelled good but she looked gorgeous as she stood in the doorway dressed stylishly in a cream brulee' pantsuit that flattered her figure.

"I thought I'd go to the mall to the one-day sale at Macy's. I need to invest in some new outfits. I know that officially I'm no longer the first lady at Holy Rock, but I still need to keep up my appearances you know. Until Stiles finds a woman worthy of being his wife, I want to make sure I," she posed and pointed at herself, "look the part of a first lady, so that the blessed woman he chooses will know how to maintain herself for her husband before the church."

"I'm sure Stiles would appreciate that, sweetheart. But you know you'll always be my first lady." He kissed her on the lips and lightly tapped her butt. "And about last night, I shouldn't have left. I should never have left our home in anger. That's why I had to come back. I couldn't stay away. God convicted me."

"I understand. I really do. And a lot of it was my fault."

"I'm sorry, Audrey. But hearing all that Stiles said yesterday, really got to me. I should have known that our family was in peril, Audrey. I should have known."

Audrey placed two polished fingers against his lips. "It's all over, Pastor. That's all in the past. We've sought God's forgiveness, and now it's up to Rena, Fonda, Minister Travis, and Francesca to do the same, if they haven't already. They're adults, and they can't live off the mistakes of the past, honey." Audrey took hold of his right hand. You're the one I have to worry about. You're my life, my man, and I love you. I'm so sorry I hurt you, but believe me, everything I did or didn't do was because of you. I never wanted to hurt you, and I sure didn't want anyone else to hurt you. I see now that I went about it the wrong way, and I'm sorry. I'm so sorry." Audrey rubbed the side of Pastor's face tenderly. "I need you to tell me that you forgive me, Pastor. Because if you don't forgive me, I don't know how I'll go on living. God brought you into my life, and I will never let you go. I love you just that much," she told him.

"And I love you, my darling. No matter what, I love you," he repeated, and then kissed her deeply.

"I never doubted that." Audrey turned and resumed being Audrey, with her quick movements and commanding performance like she was playing in a starring role. "Coffee's brewing, and I made you some grits and sausage that's on the stove. I want to be at the mall when the doors open so I can get back home before the storm sets in. The weather-man said we're supposed to get severe thunderstorms, so I need to make it to Macy's. I'll bring us something back for lunch." This time Audrey pecked him on his lips, then wiped the smudge of coco-raisin lipstick from his lips. "I'll be back as soon as I can," she told him.

"Okay, I'll be waiting," he said in a flirtatious voice and with raised eyebrows.

Audrey set off for the mall, which wasn't more than a twenty minute drive from Emerald Estates. She was glad Pastor had come to his senses, like she knew that he would. He had to have realized that the garbage Stiles had been fed was just that-garbage. She would have to find a way to make this entire mess blow over. The devil was not going to get her man nor wreak any more havoc in her household.

When she arrived at Macy's, she was just in time because the salesclerk was unlocking the door for several waiting customers. She went inside and browsed around the store. She found two not too casual outfits that Pastor was sure to love. To get things back on track, she invested in a gorgeous flowing and flattering ivory, ankle-length nightgown and another one that was a luscious fireworks color chemise with pearl accents, crafted lace, sweet ruffles, and edgy detailing, both sure to whet Pastor's insatiable appetite for her. When she stepped outside of Macy's, armed with several new pieces for church and for play, it was shortly after noon. Audrey decided to stop at Chick-fil-A and pick up a chicken strips tray. She would fix a Caesar salad and lemonade to go with it. *Pastor will love this*, she thought. There was one thing Audrey was sure of, and that was Pastor couldn't stay angry at her long. His coming back home so quickly had proven that.

Audrey placed the order at Chick-fil-A, and then drove in the direction of home. Like usual, she had her radio tuned to the gospel station. With each song that played, Audrey sang right along with it.

She fumbled in the bag of food, searching for a chicken strip to ward off a sudden bout of nausea that overcame her. The car that crossed in front of her seemed miles away. Was the traffic light green? Red? Yellow?

Audrey closed the bag of food without taking a bite. She felt nervous, and extremely thirsty. The end of the hit gospel tune played in her mind over and over again like a scratched CD.

Chapter Nine

"A person who has never made a mistake has never tried anything new."
  ~ Albert Einstein ~

After less than a month long search, Stiles, with the help of the church volunteers, had researched until they found a contact number for Francesca. Stiles hadn't told Pastor or Audrey yet. Sitting behind the desk in his church office, he looked at the blue sticky note with her number on it. For some reason, he was shaky, almost jittery at the thought of not having talked to Francesca for what must have been close to eight months. He said a silent prayer and asked God for intervention and direction as he made the call. As much as he wanted it to be a celebratory reunion, the news he needed to convey to her was all but joyful. But he had to do it. He succumbed to his inner voice and dialed the number. Sure enough, Francesca answered the phone. He could recognize her voice anywhere, and this time was no different.

Hearing Stiles's voice over the phone appeared to cause unsettling thoughts to rush through Francesca's mind all at once. She paced the floor back and forth with her hand over her head, and tried to force herself to listen to what he had to say. She could hardly digest anything that he said. It sounded like Charlie Brown's parents, "Wah, wah, wah."

"How did you find me?" she asked.

"It wasn't easy. One of your friends from the past told me that she heard you had gotten mixed up with some support group connected to one of the churches here in Memphis. It was an uphill battle, but after several calls and visits, I finally located the church. They didn't know you, but they did tell me about a mission church in Newbern. They gave me the contact number after I told them who I was and why it was so important to find you. And I'm sorry about your friend," Stiles said with sincerity.

"What or should I ask who are you talking about? I don't have any friends, at least not in Memphis. That's part of my past, part of letting go," she said strongly. "So I'm telling you now, I'll never forgive you if you tell anyone, and I do mean anyone, where I am."

"I hear you." Stiles responded without making any promises. "I was talking about Kansas. She was one of the people I went searching for. I'm sorry to hear about her death," he said.

"Kansas is dead? Oh my God." Francesca cried into the phone. "When, how did it happen?" she asked him.

"I'm sorry. I thought you knew. She died from complications of AIDS a few weeks ago, from what I heard."

Stiles listened as Francesca cried over the phone.

"I'm sorry to be the bearer of such bad news, Francesca. Will you let me come to see you? Tell me where you are," Stiles pleaded.

Francesca didn't answer.

"Francesca, are you all right?" he asked.

"Sure. I just didn't know; I can't believe Kansas is dead. Here, I am doing well. I've made a great start by joining a church; I attend services every Sunday, joined the choir, and I attend a recovery support group at the church twice a week. I haven't tried to reach out to my friends like Kansas; I haven't heard from any of my old sidekicks since I moved away, so I didn't know about her."

"How are you doing, really, sis?" Stiles asked.

"Well, as for my HIV, I learned through the recovery group that it's another one of those things I'll have to accept and learn to live with; and that it hasn't turned to AIDS. The most important thing I've come to understand is that none of the molestation and rape that happened to me when she was a child was my fault. I've learned that God has somehow made me stronger even though my life was a total wreck at one time." She sniffled into the phone. "God breathed a new breath into my physically ill body. He's shown me how to be a help to others who are in similar situations and endured similar circumstances. Through the church ministry, I'm embraced, loved, and shown the forgiveness of God. I speak at schools and other churches in the area and always leave feeling invigorated and cleansed. For the first time in my life, Stiles, I know what it means to be accepted, loved, and most of all, forgiven.

"Thank God for His tremendous favor over your life," Stiles told her, but Francesca said nothing. Only silence penetrated the phone lines. "Francesca? Francesca, are you still there?" Stiles asked her after silence passed back and forth between the sister and brother.

"Yes, I'm here. It's just that I can't say what I'm feeling right now. It's so much to take in. I mean you calling out of the blue. Then Kansas; man, Kansas is dead. That's wild. What's that all about? I mean I've been trying to live my life. Tryin' to be me. Then you pop up and want to get all up in my business and stuff. I don't need it from you, man. I don't need it from Pastor, Audrey, nobody." Francesca yelled into the phone receiver.

"Just let me come to see you, Francesca. I promise I won't

stay any longer than you want me to. But I really do need to talk to you, and I don't want to do it on the phone."

Silence.

Francesca finally spoke and told Stiles he could come to Newbern. She gave him the address and told him to Map-Quest the directions.

Stiles agreed, and the two of them hung up. Stiles thought about the news he had to share with Francesca, as if telling her about Kansas wasn't bad enough. Audrey had been in-volved in a wreck two days before while leaving from the mall. She fell asleep at the wheel, which was not like Audrey at all. Tests were still being done to determine what happened, if anything, to cause her to fall asleep at the wheel when Pastor said she had just gotten up out of the bed cheery and ener-gized. It wasn't the type of news Stiles wanted to share over the phone. He wanted to be face to face with his sister, to comfort her and to hold her and reassure her that everything would be all right.

The next afternoon, around mid-day, Stiles visited Franc-esca. It was raining harder than ever. Thunder clapped and lightning danced across the darkened sky. It was a spectacle of beauty. For Stiles, it symbolized one of God's many ways of showing mankind that He is the one who rules the heavens and the earth.

Stiles took I-40 West to I-55 North until he came to I-55 East. He made record time to the city of Newbern, arriving in less than two hours despite the heavy downpour. He lis-tened as his GPS navigated him directly to Pattie Lane Apart-ment Community, which turned out to be a small, beautifully landscaped property. He was stopped by the steel gate and asked to enter his card or to call the person he was visiting. He called Francesca, and she answered right before he was about to hang up.

"Hey, it's me. Can you let your brother in," he teased as his shirt sleeve got soaked with rain water. The signal buzzed and the gate slowly opened. Stiles drove directly to her apartment, which was right behind the manager's office. He parked and grabbed his umbrella and dashed inside. Francesca was waiting at the door.

"My, aren't you soaked. Why didn't you just wait until some other time to come? It's not like this was so urgent you needed to tell me face to face. You could have easily told me whatever it is on the phone."

Stiles eyed his sister. "You look good, sis," he complimented.

"So do you, except that you're drenched. Strip down and I'll get you one of those whatchamacallits they advertise on TV all the time. You know the ones you slip your arms into and you can still do whatever it is you want to do?"

"Yep, I think I know what you're talking about. That will be just fine. I had no idea the weather was going to get so nasty. And in a hurry too," remarked Stiles.

"It doesn't take God long to make up his mind when it's something He wants to do," commented Francesca as she threw him a pink whatchamacallit.

"Oh, thanks a lot." Stiles giggled.

"It's that or get butt naked. Your choice."

"I think I'll use the whatchamacallit," he said and laughed again. "Well, thanks a lot, but I'm here now. I've got to get out of this soaked shirt and these shoes and socks if you don't mind."

"Knock yourself out. The dryer is behind that door next to the kitchen," she said and used her finger to point in the direction. "You want something to drink? Tea, decaf coffee, or water?"

"No, I'm fine right now. I just want to get dry first." A

boisterous round of thunder caused both of them to jump. Afterward, Francesca laughed. "Remember what Mom and Dad used to tell us when it was thundering and lightning?" she asked with a wide grin on her adorable face.

"Shush, God is talking," answered Stiles.

They both laughed, and at the same time embraced each other. It was good to see his sister. She looked rather healthy. Her face was radiant and her skin was smooth. Her body was thin, and she appeared to have lost some of the color of her skin, so much so that it was a mixture of what Stiles would describe as apricot and milky. Her face was a little pale, but she still was Francesca, standing proud. Her hair was no longer cut close to her scalp; it was thick dark hair that shined like glass. The potholes and brown stained teeth were no more. This was the Francesca he remembered. This was the Francesca he had missed.

"Girl, you look good," Stiles told her again. "I like the hair."

"Thanks," was all Francesca said.

"I'm glad you finally gave me your address. I've wanted to see you for a long time, sis." Stiles held both of Francesca's hands and spread the gap between them so he could have a good look at his sister. She still walked with a limp, but she was more beautiful than ever. Her hair was to her shoulders, and the outfit she had on was feminine. A casual pair of jeans, a pale yellow pullover, with yellow and white dangling heart earrings. "I'd say you clean up nicely," he teased.

Francesca smiled. Her teeth glistened, Look, I'm glad you came. I told you it wasn't necessary but since you insisted, you may enter my palace, sir," she said with a slight bow and an extended hand pointing further into her apartment. The apartment was quite cozy. Stiles was somewhat taken aback when he saw the huge gray-striped cat stroll across the room with no fear or hesitation. It only stopped long enough to stare at Stiles, obviously to let him know that he was the ruler of this palace.

"Wow, he's big. I never knew you were into cats?"

"There's a lot you never knew about me, or maybe you just didn't care to remember. There's a lot none of you knew about me. Umm, I wonder why that is?"

"Oh, I don't know," Stiles responded sarcastically in kind with Francesca's tone. "Let's see, maybe it's because half the time we had no idea where you were; or maybe it's because you were in and out of jail so much that we couldn't tell if the only habits you had were smoking weed and snorting coke. Didn't know you had it in you, to care for anyone or anything, when you didn't give a darn about yourself."

The color drained from Francesca's face for only a moment. Long enough for her to shoot an arrow of words back at Stiles. "Well, there's more to me than that. That was how I used to be. I did the streets in order to avoid the nightmares that I faced at Emerald Estates."

Stiles shifted his eyes downward and didn't respond to her statement. "What's the cat's name?"

Francesca answered, "Jabez."

"That's deep. Taken from 1 Chronicles, 4:10"

"You want a ribbon for knowing that verse or something?"

"No, I don't want anything. I came here to see you and to tell you about our mother."

Francesca ignored his response. "He's a Maine coon cat. Come here, Jabez. Come to Momma." The cat meowed heavily, then began to purr as he strolled over to Francesca's waiting arms. She picked him up and rubbed him tenderly and gently underneath his chin. "Oh, wait a second, did I offer you anything to drink or eat?"

"Yes, you offered."

"Sure you wouldn't like a slice of bread and a lukewarm glass of water? I've grown accustomed to that since I spent so much time in and out of jail, you know." She laughed hysterically while Stiles looked at her with contempt shining in his eyes.

"You know what?"

"No, but I'm sure you're going to tell me," was her curt response.

"You're still self-consumed, full of anger, rage, and unforgiveness. Maybe we didn't have a home life straight out of the movies. Maybe bad things happened, but they were not your fault, Francesca."

Francesca moved suddenly, and Jabez jumped off of her lap. She placed both hands over her ears and screamed, "I'm not listening. I'm not listening." She said it over and over again until she opened her eyes and saw Stiles standing up with his hands searching for a pocket that wasn't there in his semi dry boxers, one of his nervous habits.

"Well, you need to listen to this," said Stiles rather angrily. "Audrey was involved in a terrible car accident. I don't know what she was thinking, but she was driving on the wrong side of the highway and hit a car with two kids and their parents. One kid and its mother died, the other two are in critical condition. As for Mom, she severed her spine. She's permanently paralyzed from the waist down. She's in bad shape. Right now they have her on a breathing tube and heavily medicated. She's going to need full time around-the-clock care. The doctors say that she can understand everything, so you already know she's devastated. She speaks low and real slow, but in time, the physician said, she should regain use of her voice and her upper body will become stronger too." Stiles told her in a voice filled with agony.

Francesca basically ignored Stiles. She had loved Audrey so much when she was a little girl, but in the end, she somehow believed Audrey let her down by turning her back on the hurt she had been subjected to. There was no sense in feeling one way or the other toward her mother now.

All she could say in response to Stiles was, "I'm sorry to hear about Audrey." Pause. "Listen, I have an appointment in a few hours. No need for you to hang around if that's all you came to tell me. This storm doesn't seem like it's going to let up, so really you might need to let me make you a sandwich or something, and then leave.

Stiles reluctantly agreed, and Francesca fixed him a fried smoked sausage sandwich, a handful of potato chips and a soda.

While Stiles ate, he and Francesca continued to talk. "Like I said, I'm sorry about Audrey, but there's nothing I can do about it. I can put her name on the prayer list at church, and I am glad you came and I got the chance to see you, but seriously, I don't see a reason for us to keep in touch.

"What are you talking about? I'm your brother; you're my sister; our mother is in a hospital paralyzed from the waist down and faces two counts of vehicular homicide, and you tell me you don't see a reason for us to keep in touch!" Stiles couldn't believe what had just transpired.

Francesca didn't display one ounce of emotion.

"What do you want from me? You expect me to drop everything here and come to Memphis and act like I'm so sorry and that I'll be there to take care of her, or something? Well, sorry to burst your bubble, big brother, it's not like that. I don't feel a connection to Audrey. I don't feel anything for her. I have my own life now. I've forgiven everyone that wronged me, but that doesn't mean I have to insert myself back into her life or anyone's life from my past."

"No, but I did expect you to have some compassion, some concern for our mother, for Christ's sake! How can you say you're healed and you've forgiven everybody," said Stiles as he threw up his hands.

"I'm not you, Stiles. I can't and won't go back to the same old thing. I won't be involved in the discord in our family any longer. I am trying to live a life that's acceptable to God. I am HIV positive, Stiles. Do you hear me? Do you understand me?" Francesca limped toward the laundry door and opened it. She checked to see if Stiles's clothes were dry. They were. She threw them at him, and he hurriedly put the warm clothes on.

"But all I can tell you is, thanks for coming here and thank you for letting me know about Kansas and Audrey."

Rain continued to pour down and the thunder clapped outside.

"I understand what you're saying, Francesca. You won't let anybody love you. You won't give your family a chance to redeem themselves. Yes, I admit, our family screwed up," Stiles said as he dressed. "But we need each other. You say that you've forgiven everybody, but have you really? I went so far as to tell Pastor everything about what happened. I searched for the truth and I found it."

Francesca snapped her head around and closed the laundry door behind her.

"Yes, you heard me correctly," Stiles said boldly. "I visited Fonda and she admitted what she'd done to you all of those years ago. I told Pastor and Mother about Minister Travis. I told them that Mother knew about you and Fonda all along and did nothing."

Tears poured down Francesca's reddened face. She braced herself on a nearby chair. Her body heaved and tears broke loose like a bursting dam.

Stiles fastened the last button on his shirt, and then walked over to Francesca. He grabbed her in his arms and held on to her. She cried like she'd had tears stored up for years and they were finally able to release.

"That's right; cry, baby sis, cry." Stiles rubbed and kissed her hair. "I'm so sorry, Francesca. I'm so sorry for everything you've had to endure." He held on to his sister and she held on to him. "Please, think about coming to Memphis to see Mother and Pastor. Pray on it, sis.

Francesca lifted her head and looked at her brother. "I can't, Stiles. I just can't see that woman ever again. I'm sorry."

"Still, think about it. Okay?"

"Okay," she muttered.

Stiles didn't believe that she would relent. He asked himself, *Why should she?*

Chapter Ten

*"Be sure that it is not you that is mortal, but only your body.
For that man whom your outward form reveals is not yourself;
the spirit is the true self, not that physical figure which can be
pointed out by your finger."*
~ *Cicero* ~

Several weeks of being in a rehabilitation facility didn't improve Audrey's mobility. It was like she'd given up her will to go on, to move forward, and to fight for life. Stiles and Pastor visited her every day, but she refused to accept visitors from members of Holy Rock or from her neighborhood. She told Pastor and Stiles that she couldn't bare them seeing her sitting up in a special chair like she was a vegetable. Even in her illness, pride was strong enough inside of Audrey to rear its ugly head.

As for Francesca, Stiles confided in his father that he had spoken to her. He kept his promise to Francesca and did not tell Pastor that he had actually seen his sister. He told him about Francesca's request not to call or bother her anymore. This upset Pastor as much as seeing his beloved wife lying in a hospital bed day after day, with no desire to get better. The only thing Audrey was insistent about was the nursing staff keeping her cleaned and bathed. She fussed when they didn't keep her room clean enough for her likes, or if they didn't check on her colostomy bag often enough. She was one demanding patient. From the looks on most of the nurses and certified nursing assistants, it appeared they did not like being assigned to care for her.

Life in the Graham home had truly changed. The family was ripped apart in so many ways that Pastor began to question God. He prayed out in the prayer closet in his bedroom. He asked God questions about Francesca and about Audrey and even about himself. "Why, Lord? What has your servant done to displease you so much? Tell me, Father, and I will repent and do it no more. Lord, I'm praying for restoration for my family. Healing for my wife, forgiveness from my daughter, and your precious will to be done in our lives."

Audrey was what one would call a tough patient. She was hard to please, more than ever after she was allowed to come home. Her depression and dark days were frequent. She refused to see anyone, and that often included turning her own son away. She couldn't comprehend why God would allow something so horrific to happen to her. She was still facing possible vehicular homicide charges for killing innocent people. She didn't remember how it happened and didn't want to know. All she knew was that Pastor told her that she was driving on the wrong side of the highway when the oncoming car swerved to try to avoid her. But it was too late. Audrey had to be cut out of the car with the Jaws of Life, and two people in the other car were pronounced dead on the scene.

It had been on all the news stations in the mid-south, and had been documented in the newspapers as well. Pastor did what he could to shield any news about the accident from his wife. He didn't want to get her upset more than she already was. The lawyer he hired told him that Audrey would have her driver's license permanently revoked, and since this was her first major accident or accident of any kind, and no drugs or alcohol were involved, then she might get off with a few years of probation.

When the lawyer visited Audrey at home, he explained much the same thing to her. She burst in tears while she slowly maneuvered her hand toward the box of tissue sitting next to her on the nightstand. "I can't believe this. I can't believe any of this happened. Two people are dead because of me. What was I thinking?" she cried to Pastor, like she was searching for him to give her the answers.

"Please, honey. Don't get yourself upset. All you should be doing now is concentrating on getting better. Let the lawyer handle everything. Prayer for your healing and for the members of the family that were killed has been going up before God each and every day. Stiles has been holding nightly prayer vigils. He even went to see the family of the people who were killed. As much as it hurts them to lose their loved ones, they were grateful for Stiles coming to see them to express how sorry we are. Everyone, as you can tell from all of the cards, balloons, and gifts in here, and there are more in the family room, have been thinking of you and praying for you.

"For real?" she said in a sort of vain tone, and quickly cleared her throat.

"Yes, for real. There isn't a day that goes by when the phone isn't ringing and the person on the other end is inquiring about your health. People want to come to see you, Audrey."

"No, no, I can't let anyone see me like this. Wait until I'm up and walking again," she said.

Pastor found it impossible to tell her again what the doctors said, that she would never walk again. Her lower spine was completely severed as the result of the accident. He allowed her to talk. "Yes, honey, faith changes things, and there's nothing impossible for God," he told her. "But I sure wish you would let some of the ladies from the auxiliary visit. They've been calling so much that it's driving me up the wall." Pastor chuckled. "All I'm saying is there are people who love you, Audrey. Think about allowing some of them to stop by to see you and to do for you like you've done for so many of them. The ladies auxiliary wants to prepare a nice lunch for you and spend the day chatting like you all do every second Saturday of the month."

Audrey repositioned her head on the pillow. "I'll think about it," she said.

"Good, that's all I ask. Now why don't you get some rest? You had quite a workout with the therapist today."

Pastor stood up from the chair next to Audrey's hospital bed that was placed in one of the guest rooms of the house. He leaned down and kissed her on her lips. Audrey smiled, turned her head to the side and drifted off.

Just as soon as Pastor closed Audrey's door and headed for his study, the doorbell rang. He went to answer it and Stiles stood on the other side with a bouquet of mixed flowers in one hand and a large plastic bag in the other.

"Come on in, son. Let me help you with that load."

"No need. I can handle it, Pastor." Stiles shuffled into the kitchen and set the plastic bag on the counter top and the flowers on the table. "Is Mom awake?" he asked.

"No, she just went back to sleep. She had a pretty intense workout. You know how she dreads having therapy every day, but it's a must if she's going to gain any strength in her upper body. She somehow still thinks she's going to walk again, son, and that worries me a lot," he confessed.

"Pastor, what's that saying?"

Father and son spoke together, "If you're going to worry, then don't pray. If you're going to pray, then don't worry." The two of them laughed. Stiles stepped closer to his father and gave him a bear hug.

"Let's see what you've got here," Pastor asked while at the same time peeping into the plastic bag. "Ummm, Piccadil-ly's."

"I stopped by there so you wouldn't have to worry about conjuring up something for you and Mother this evening."

"That was nice of you. I'm glad you did it too, because me and cooking just don't seem to get along." Pastor chuckled again.

"It's no problem. I'll make sure you two always have a home cooked meal, but just remember, I won't be the one doing the cooking." This time Stiles laughed, and then pulled out a chair from the kitchen table and sat down. Pastor placed both dinners in the refrigerator for later.

"I'll warm these up later on. You know what, son?" Pastor sat down in the other chair.

"What is it, Pastor?

"This makes me think about Rena. You remember when I had my stroke you and her would stop by Piccadilly's every Sunday afternoon and bring me and your mother a hot dinner plate?" Pastor smiled.

Stiles smiled slightly too. "Yep, I remember."

"Have you heard from her? Do you know what she's up to these days?"

"Not really. The last I heard she was back in Massachusetts. I tried calling her a couple of times when she first left, but her phone was disconnected." Stiles said sullenly.

"You know she should be easy to find, that is, if you really want to find her." Pastor's eyebrows quipped.

"I know, but I don't know what I'd say to her. Pastor, I've been praying so hard for God to help me forgive her for lying and deceiving me. If I can pray for Francesca, and I have forgiven her too, then why can't I forgive Rena? I don't understand."

"God says for you to trust in Him with all of your heart. Don't lean to your own understanding, just trust Him and He shall direct your path. The Word also says that if you regard iniquity in your heart, the Lord will not hear you. Son, you've got to bring some resolution to all this madness that's been going on in this family. Now I'm not saying you have to get back together with Rena, unless you truly still love her and want her, but what I am saying is that you can't be an effective leader, minister, preacher, teacher, or anything connected to God if you don't obey His commandments."

All the time Pastor was speaking, Stiles shook his head in agreement. He would love to hear Rena's voice again and her contagious laughter. He missed holding her and smelling the sweetness of her body. He missed his wife. But how could he ever think of going back to someone or reaching out to the one he loved when all she had done during their relationship was lie to him? She had deceived him, and it still hurt. His heart was still an open wound.

"Pastor, if only she had told me," Stiles said as he rubbed his head back and forth with his hand. "Why didn't she just tell me the truth?"

"And would you still have married her? Can you imagine what she went through? She was involved in an unnatural act with your sister, and from that she contracted an STD. Are you telling me that you still would have married her had she told you that?" Pastor waited on the reply he knew was coming.

"No, I wouldn't have."

"Do you believe she loved you, son?"

"Yes, but then again, I don't know. It's all so confusing. How can you love someone and betray them at the same time? How is that love?"

"Son, look at your mother. You think that this is the only time she lied to me, when I found out she saw and knew about Francesca's abuse? Do you think I've always been one hundred percent truthful to her?"

"What do you mean?" Stiles leaned forward and placed one hand under his chin.

"I mean I've done things in my past that I lied to your mother about, or should I say stretched the truth. I've said and done things that I'm not proud of. Some of those things your mother knows about, and yet she forgave me and kept on loving me. But the fact of the matter is that you have to give the other person that chance to make the decision. You didn't give Rena that chance. You didn't give Francesca that chance."

"I know it, but it's too late. I'm sure Rena's gone on with her life. I mean, she's beautiful, smart, intelligent, witty, ambitious, and she loves the Lord," said Stiles.

"Yet, you cannot find it in your heart to forgive her? Which brings up another subject–Francesca. Have you had any luck in finding her? I know you said you talked to her on the phone, but has she told you where she is?" Pastor looked hopeful and waited on Stiles to respond.

"Dad, so much has gone on these past couple of months that I feel like my head is spinning around and around like a Ferris wheel and I can't get off. But to answer your question, I did locate her. I meant to tell you and Mom, then the accident happened and it never seemed like the right time. After Mother had the car accident and I found out that Francesca's friend, Kansas, had died, I convinced her to tell me where she was living. She agreed to see me."

"Kansas died? Oh, I know Francesca was disturbed about that. But it's still great news that you know where Francecsa is. Is she okay?"

"Yes, she's fine."

"Your mother will be happy to hear that."

Stiles pushed his hands up. "Hold up, it's not all that easy. Francesca is doing well. She's involved in a great church, a recovery program, and she has a place of her own. She even has this giant cat that looks like a dog. She calls him Jabez." Stiles laughed at the thought.

"She always loved cats. Remember Charlie?"

"Oh yeah, I completely forgot about Charlie. Anyway, she doesn't want to be bothered, Dad. When I told her about Mother, she practically brushed me off. She's still holding on to the hurts of the past. Somehow, she can't let go of yesterday."

"Somewhere, my Francesca lurks inside of the young lady who is full of rage and hurt. She's inside of there, and I'm going to pray until the devil releases his stronghold over her life. She may not know it yet, but we need her as much as she needs us. We're family. Families are meant to hold one another up, to love one another no matter what, to treat each other with the utmost respect, and most of all, to forgive one another no matter what mistakes the other has made. Keep reaching out to her, son. Promise me that. And when God directs me, then I am going to see my daughter and so is your mother. It's time for restoration. And with God's help, it's going to happen." Pastor reached across the table and grabbed hold of his son's hand. "Where two or more are gathered in my name—"

"There am I in the midst also," finished Stiles.

Chapter Eleven

"We cannot change our past. We cannot change the fact that people will act in a certain way. We cannot change the inevitable."
~*Unknown*~

Audrey was tormented again with bad dreams about the accident. Since the accident, she had been sued and stood to lose all that she and Pastor had worked hard for over the years. Insurance didn't begin to cover all the damages she had caused and the lives of those who were snuffed out because of her. The court permanently revoked her license, and she was sentenced to ten years in prison, which a good attorney managed to have converted to probation.

The reason for her accident was determined to come from Audrey lapsing into a diabetic coma. The times she couldn't remember, the night flashes, her mood swings, all of it was contributed partially to Audrey being a diabetic. It was a shock, but a relief as well, to learn the cause of her irrational actions the night of the accident. Her high blood sugar level sent her into a diabetic coma, where she lost consciousness at the wheel. It had forever changed Audrey's life and the lives of those involved in the accident.

Audrey withdrew more deeply into a state of depression. She was a paraplegic, unable to feel anything from her waist down. Each time she looked at the colostomy bag hanging on the side of the bed, she became more distraught. She would never be able to make love to Pastor again. She would never again know the feel of his touch, a slight rub of his hand on her thigh. Audrey lay in her hospital bed and cried.

"God, is this payback? Have I been so wrong, done so badly that you've brought this upon me?" Audrey wept. "Lord, I'm so sorry. I'm sorry for the lives I've destroyed. I'm sorry for the family whose loved ones are gone because of me. I'm sorry, God, for everything I've done. But please don't let me be like this for the rest of my life. Heal me, God. Don't be cruel to me." Audrey's tears deepened and left track marks down her face.

Pastor walked in and saw Audrey crying and praying. He went to her bed and tenderly held on to her hand. He leaned over and kissed her on her lips. "Everything is going to be fine. Don't you worry, darling. Don't you worry about a thing."

"How can I not worry?" Audrey allowed Pastor to wipe her tears away with a tissue. "Chauncey, I'm paralyzed. I can't feel a thing. I can't walk. I can't even go to the bathroom and pee. I can't take a bath. I can't do anything. Oh, Pastor, does God hate me this much that He would let me suffer like this?"

"No no no. You know God doesn't work like that. It was an accident that caused this, Audrey. God is still with you. He loves you and you know that." Pastor spoke to her gingerly.

"If He loves me so much, then why this?" Audrey managed to look down at her lower body. "If He loves me so much, why did He allow me to kill an innocent mother and child? If He loves me so much why do I have diabetes and have to be stuck with a needle three times a day? Why!" Audrey wailed.

"Audrey." Pastor wiped the hair from her forehead. "Don't get yourself worked up. You have to allow God to heal you from the inside, baby." Pastor's voice was so tender and loving. He stroked her hair gently while he talked soothingly to her. "You aren't strong enough to carry this burden of guilt and self-condemnation. You had no idea you were a diabetic. None of us did. God knows your heart. God knows you didn't mean to kill anyone. Please, honey. Don't keep beating up on yourself. As for being paralyzed, yes, you are paralyzed, and no, I don't know if you'll ever regain the use of your lower body, but even if you don't, God hasn't forsaken you, Audrey; neither have I. I'm not going anywhere. You're still my Audrey Poo," Pastor said with a deep smile that caused crevices to appear on his face.

"I'm nothing but a burden to you now, Pastor. I want to die. I wish it had been me who died in that wreck. I wish it had been me." She started weeping again.

"But it wasn't you, Audrey. This means God still has work for you to do. You may have to find other ways to do things, but nevertheless, God still has a purpose for your life. Maybe you'll minister to others who've experienced such an accident, or who have lost the use of their limbs. We don't know yet how God is going to work everything out. But this I know for sure, that everything that the enemy means for bad, God can and will work it out for our good. I don't know what that good is right now, but in time, it will be revealed to you, Audrey. Just be strong, my darling." Pastor sat in the chair next to Audrey's bed and held on to her hand. He kneaded it softly. "Is there anything I can get you?" he asked.

Barely speaking above a whisper, Audrey said, "No, no one can do anything for me." She turned her face away from Pastor.

Pastor held on to her hand until he heard her breathing becoming labored. She had fallen asleep. He wiped tears from his eyes when he stood up and looked down on his sleeping wife. Pastor pulled the cover up to her chest, kissed her again and walked out of the room.

Pastor went into his study and sat down. His hands were trembling, and he fought back a strong desire to cry. He sat back in his office chair, intertwined his hands, and cuffed them underneath his chin. He remained in the chair for sometime without uttering a word. It wasn't until the ringing of the phone, that he was yanked from his inner thoughts.

"Hello," Pastor said into the receiver. He didn't hear a response. "Hello," he said again.

"Pastor...it's Francesca," the child like voice said.

Tears pushed forth from Pastor's eyes. "My Francesca. Oh, God, my sweet, sweet, baby. How are you? I'm so glad to hear your voice." He could barely contain his joy.

"How are you, Daddy?" asked Francesca.

"Oh, baby. I'm fine. Now that I hear your voice, I'm even better," he told her. "Honey, are you all right?"

"Yes. I'm doing well. I just wanted to hear your voice too." Francesca paused. "And I wanted to see how Audrey was doing since her accident. I know it's been awhile, and you're probably wondering why I haven't..."

"Stop it. I'm not wondering anything. I'm too glad to hear from you. You sound so good. I miss you, baby. And as for your mother, she's doing okay. She's resting right now. She's having a hard time dealing with never walking again and being a diabetic. You know how much your mother loves to go and to do things. So right now, she's finding it hard to cope." Pastor tried to explain in simple terms.

"Oh, I see. And you? Are you taking care of yourself?"

"Of course. I'm fit as a fiddle."

"That's good." Francesca's voice sounded nervous and apprehensive. "I just wanted to call and say hello. And of course, check on Audrey."

"Good, very good. What have you been doing?"

"I guess Stiles already told you that I'm back in church.

I'm working a lot with youth and at risk people. I've started a group recently for people who aren't sure about their sexual orientation. We don't meet at the church. I have a private meeting at my apartment so everyone at the church won't be eyeballing this person or that person if they find out they're part of the group. You know, church folk are still judgmental."

"Francesca, I'm proud of you. You know, God always gives me a pick up when I'm down. You've been my pick up for today and many days to come. Sometimes we have to go through the valley of darkness and over the mountaintops of abuse and hurt in order to fulfill our calling and purpose in this life. I know you've certainly experienced your share of some of life's challenges, but you've managed to come out on the other side stronger and wiser. I thank God for that."

"Yeah. I'm glad I've gone through what I have too, Pastor. It's made me more compassionate and more in tune with people who are hurting, bruised, and whose lives are messed up."

Pastor hesitated like he was wondering if he should ask what he was about to ask. "How is your health?"

"You mean my HIV and herpes? You can say it, Daddy. It's what I have, but it's not who I am. I'm taking it one day at a time. God is keeping me strong. I'm on a lot of meds and there are some days I don't feel too well, but it's mostly because of my bad leg. It gives me the blues some days. But I'm learning to not complain. I just lean and rely on God."

"Good, honey. Hearing you talking about the Lord and His goodness, is an answered prayer. I feel like shouting," he said in a raised voice.

"I'm just speaking the truth," replied Francesca. "Look, Pastor. I just wanted to check in with you. I have some other things I need to get done. But I'll call again."

"Promise?" asked Pastor.

"Sure. Bye for now," said Francesca and ended the call.

"Bye," responded Pastor to the dial tone in his ear.

No sooner than hanging up the phone, did it ring again. This time it was Stiles.

"Hi, Pastor. How are you two doing over there today?" he asked.

"Oh, so so. Your mother, well, she's in a bad way right now; questioning why God allowed her to have the accident and diabetes. She's really been coming down on herself. The nurse should be here soon to get her up and in her chair. I know she's going to fight tooth and nail against that. She wants to give up, son."

"We can't let her do that, Pastor."

"Yes, I know. Hey, your sister just called. I was so glad to hear from her."

"Amazing. God is working, isn't He? I haven't heard from her since I went to see her."

"She sounded good on the phone," said Pastor. "She didn't give me her number, and the ID said private number, so I didn't push her about it. I know she'll call again."

"Did she ask about Mother?"

"Yes, she did. We had a nice conversation. She really does sound like my Francesca. I miss her so much." Pastor's voice weakened.

"Just don't give up, Pastor. God is always in control. Right?"

"Right," Pastor readily agreed.

"I'll stop by later on this afternoon and bring you all something to eat."

"Piccadilly special?" remarked Pastor.

"Nope, not this time. It's straight from Holy Rock's café," said Stiles. "Prepared by none other than Sister Detria. You remember her, don't you?"

"Umm, I can't say that I do."

"She's Brother Mackey's middle daughter. She was away at college for awhile, then settled in Arizona for five years. She's a certified nutritionist."

"Oh yeah; Detria Mackey. I remember her. I used to call her Lil Dee Dee. I don't recall you telling me that she was back in Memphis. Has she reunited with Holy Rock? Is she here for good or what?"

"Yes. She's here for at least a few years. She moved back to be closer to Brother and Sister Mackey since Sister Mackey's been in poor health. She leads the volunteers in the kitchen ministry. She said the church should provide good meals, but nutritious meals as well."

"Is that so?" quipped Pastor. "Sounds like there's a little something going on that I might not be aware of," replied Pastor. "Is she married?"

"No, she's not married, and there's nothing going on. She knows you and Mother aren't in a position to prepare meals for yourselves, especially the kind of meals you need, so she volunteered to come up with some delicious meals that both you and Mother can eat without worrying about if it's good for you or not. I thought it was nice of her to offer her time."

"Sure. Whatever you say, son." Pastor giggled.

"Anyway, I'll see you guys later this afternoon. Hang in there, Pastor. I love you."

"I love you too, Stiles. Bye now." They ended their call, and Pastor whirled slowly around in his chair. A huge smile came over his face.

The nurse arrived soon after Audrey awoke from her nap. Against her patient's wishes, she insisted that Audrey get in her wheelchair and practice maneuvering through the house. Audrey hated to see the nurse coming, and was often mean toward her. There was no reason for her to practice being in a wheelchair when it was only temporary. She would soon be up and walking around running her own household again.

Audrey sat in the chair while the nurse cleaned her room, bed, and then proceeded to groom Audrey. She brushed Audrey's hair while she squealed like a little girl, accusing the nurse of pulling too hard on her head, or insisting that she style it in a certain way.

Pastor heard her complaining all while the nurse was in the house. She stopped long enough to push the joystick hand control on the electric wheelchair and sail into the front of the house. The nurse followed closely behind her.

"Pastor, I don't see the need for all of this," she told him. "I don't think I'm going to be in this chair too much longer, so why do I have to learn how to use it? I can't get out of the bed anyway by myself to get in it, and God knows you aren't strong enough to help me."

Pastor eyed the nurse and smiled. "Audrey, do it for me, please." He kissed her cheek.

"Pastor Graham, call me if you need me. I'm going to go back to Mrs. Graham's room and finish cleaning. I'll be back and give you your insulin injection," the nurse said to Audrey.

"Oomph, I don't need you to do that. My husband can give it to me," she said smugly.

"That's fine, Mrs. Graham," the nurse responded. "Would you like to give it to her, Pastor Graham?" the nurse asked, seeking his final approval.

"Of course. I'll give it to her. Don't you worry about a thing. Come on, Audrey. It's almost time for *Judge Mathis*. I'll go fix our sandwiches and you park in a good spot in the family room in front of the television. Then I'll give you your shot. How does that sound?"

"Okay. But if you need any help, just call me," Audrey told him.

Pastor turned around and headed toward the kitchen. He chuckled along the way.

Chapter Twelve

"Remember, we all stumble, every one of us. That's why it's
a comfort to go hand in hand."
~Emily Kimbrough~

"I can't thank you enough for your time," Stiles told Detria. "I know you're working a full time job, and then to come
here during your lunch and volunteer at the church as much
as you do is a great blessing."

Detria swished around slightly, like she was showing off
her well proportioned body. She smiled at Stiles, and then
lowered her head like she was shy.

"It's no problem at all," replied Detria when she looked up
at Stiles. "Good nutrition is one of the main factors of being
healthy."

Stiles smiled in return. Since his divorce, he had received
his share of women at Holy Rock and other churches, vying for his time and attention. But no one could replace the
thoughts of Rena. There was not a day that passed when he
wasn't bombarded with thoughts of how much he handled everything wrong in his marriage and break-up. He could have
tried harder, been more considerate and more level headed.
But he was too embarrassed to feel anything for a woman who
had slept around with not another man, but with another
woman, and of all the women out there, it had to be his sister.
The devil really stuck it to him. He tried Stiles's manhood
and the devil won.

Detria, whether he wanted her to or not, had a way of lifting Stile's spirit. Her genuineness made him comfortable around her. It was the first time that he felt safe about letting his guards down, even if it were only a little. She was easy to talk to. Whenever he was around her, she had an uncanny way of making him smile.

Detria didn't come off like some of the other women who Stiles had come to believe from experience were only after the title of First Lady. He didn't understand it at first. But there were women in the church who were ready to go to battle about being the next first lady.

Stiles was determined to tread carefully. If there was a woman for him, if God wanted to give him another chance at being a husband, and possibly a father, then Stiles wanted to have clear, divine direction from God. No more love on the run.

"Pastor Stiles," Detria pulled him from his day dreaming. "I enjoyed noon Bible Study today." Detria nervously wiped her hands on her spotted white kitchen apron. "I'm glad you chose to hold it here in the banquet hall. That way people can come from work during lunch, enjoy a free, nutritious meal, and listen to the Word of God, all within an hour. It was a great decision on your part to start doing this," she gracefully complimented him.

"Thank you, Sister Detria. The numbers are growing every Wednesday too. I've received several e-mails, letters, and phone calls about the noon Bible Study. It's not only enticing some of our working church members, but it's proving to be a good time for our senior citizens. You know, because of crime in this city, many of our seniors don't like to venture out after dark, so the noon session fits them perfectly. The church van picks them up and some of them drive themselves when they wouldn't drive at night. God is truly good," Stiles said and reached for a glass of orange juice Detria held out toward him.

"Thank you, sister," said Stiles.

"No matter how many times I've heard the Word of God, there is always something new I take away from it," Detria said and took a small swallow from a glass she poured for herself. She sat down at one of the round tables and Stiles followed suit.

"Like today's Bible teaching," Detria said with an interesting look on her smooth, coal black skin. She was slender, with fiery eyes that seemed to glow.

"What about today's teaching?"

"First of all, I'm ashamed to say this." She shifted her eyes away from his.

"You never have to be ashamed to talk about the Word of God, Detria. Tell me, what's on your mind."

"It might sound silly, but I'll say it anyway." She smiled and showcased her dazzling white, even teeth. "When you were talking about Deborah; I wasn't surprised to learn that she was a prophet, but I had no idea she was...that she was something like what we would call an attorney. I mean, people actually came to her and asked her to solve their legal cases?"

"Yes, they did. That's something preachers and those who study the Bible sometimes fail to mention. Deborah was a great woman of God. A wife, prophet, a leader, and as you say, an attorney of sorts. People took great confidence in what she said and followed her advice," Stiles told her.

Detria beamed and added. "Deborah would sit under Deborah's Palm Tree. Wow, that's amazing to know, Pastor Stiles. Since I've returned to Memphis and to Holy Rock, I feel myself growing in the Word of God tremendously. Don't get me wrong, your father, Pastor Graham, Senior was an excellent teacher, but you; well, I have to say, Pastor Stiles, that you bring a whole new level of enjoyment to learning about the Word of God."

"Now that's a compliment. I have big shoes to fill since my father had to step down from being the pastor of Holy Rock. I've gone through some dark days, and I don't always feel like I should be standing in the role I'm standing in."

Detria toyed with her glass of juice. She looked like she was in deep thought.

"What are you thinking?" asked Stiles.

"I don't want to come off as brazen, so forgive me if I do. But do you feel unworthy to be in the pulpit because of your divorce?"

Stiles was somewhat startled, but he was relieved, too, that Detria spoke her mind, and she did it in such a loving way.

"You don't have to answer the question if you don't want to," she told him.

"No, it's not that. You're right, Sister Detria." Stiles looked around the empty banquet hall before he continued speaking. "I do feel unworthy sometimes. How can I lead others to the path of God when I'm such a failure myself? How can I be effective when I couldn't even keep my own marriage together? There, I've said it." Stiles threw up his arms in the air and exhaled like he released a giant helium balloon of air. "I know God has forgiven me. It's me who hasn't forgiven me." He patted his chest. "Maybe I should have or could have handled things differently. I believe that marriage is for a lifetime. Especially when we're yoked with whom God has joined together." His words were slow and he raised his eyes and stared at Detria.

Detria reached across the table and took hold to Stiles's trembling hands. "You, of all people, know that God is loving. You know that there is no mistake, no mess-up, nothing that we can come to Him with that He won't forgive, if we are sincere and repentant about it. Just because you're a pastor doesn't mean that you won't make mistakes. You're still human."

Detria's voice quickly calmed down Stiles's warring spirit. Her words were not condemning; they were like salve being lightly rubbed across his broken heart. "One thing I notice about you, Pastor Stiles," she said in a happier tone.

"And that is?"

"That you are a strong man. You remind me so much of Pastor Graham. You're transparent. You don't try to pretend like you're a man of God who walks around perfect and with all of the answers. That's one of the things I believe that draws people to Holy Rock. It's your realness, Pastor Stiles. It's your ability to be who you are and not some man standing in the pulpit like he's trying to win a badge for getting the most people to join the church just to add to the church roll. When you preach; when you teach; you do it with conviction and with love." She removed her hands from holding his. "Don't allow the enemy to make you feel like you shouldn't be doing what God Himself has called you to do."

Stiles looked at Detria for what seemed like hours, but in actuality was mere seconds. Tears dimmed the corners of his eyes. "Thank you, Sister Detria. You don't know how God has used you today. And I can't believe that I released this heaviness I've been walking around with these past months. I don't know where all of this is going to lead me. I do know that I need to make some kind of contact with my ex-wife."

Detria listened intently. By the look on her face, she appeared to be glad that Pastor Stiles had confided in her.

"If that's what you know you're supposed to do, then do it. You won't be satisfied until you do what God tells you to do."

"Sounds like you're the counselor here. People come to me for advice and here I am, sitting across the table pouring my problems out to my Deborah today." Stiles raised one hand up. "I didn't mean to sound condescending. It's just that there is so much expected of pastors. We're often looked at as these perfect people of God who can't fall, who shouldn't fail, and it's impossible to be what people want us to be. It's a hard job. A difficult duty and responsibility." Stiles rubbed the top of his head.

"I wouldn't want to be in your shoes, I know that," remarked Detria. "You are responsible for people's souls, and that has to be a massive responsibility, to know that people cling to your every word and watch to see if you're going to fail. But I know better. I didn't grow up as a preacher's kid, but I'm sure you know that my daddy is about the next closest thing to being a preacher." Detria and Stiles giggled.

Stiles glanced at his watch. "I'm sorry I have to end this, but I've still got several more things to complete on my schedule." He stood up from the table and grabbed his juice. He took the last giant swallow of it. "The lunch was splendid today, Detria."

"Thank you, Pastor Stiles. Hold on just a minute. I need to give you the plates of food that I put aside for Pastor and Mother Graham." Stiles watched Detria as she turned and went into the kitchen. She returned with two plastic bags of take out containers.

"Here you go," she said with her infectious smile.

"Detria, thank you. Thank you for the food for my parents, and thank you for being my Deborah today. God bless you," he said and embraced her.

"Anytime," remarked Detria. "Anytime."

Stiles completed the remainder of his busy day by teaching his University of Memphis religion class, reading church reports, and checking in on the sick and shut in before he stopped by his parents' to deliver the food Detria had prepared.

Stiles's BlackBerry chimed. He read the message for his to do list. He slapped his forehead as he drove toward Emerald Estates. "That's right, I have to do the *Loretta McNary®* television show at twelve-thirty tomorrow afternoon." He said to himself. "Thank God for this little reminder," he said and looked at his red BlackBerry. The *Loretta McNary®* talk show came on weekly and featured various guests from various places and walks of life, concentrating on more of the mid-south. With the growth spurt happening at Holy Rock, popular television and radio host, *Loretta McNary®'s* staff had contacted Stiles about being on her show to talk about what the church is doing for communities throughout the city of Memphis. Stiles gladly accepted the invitation. It would be a great way to reach out to the unchurched and to let them know about Holy Rock and the forty-five different ministries they offered. Being on such a huge, successful television show was another great blessing and avenue to spread God's Word. He dialed the telephone number and reached Ms. McNary's assistant. She confirmed the time that he was supposed to arrive at the studio and reminded him to be on time because it was a live taping. Stiles assured the assistant that he would be there and that he looked forward to meeting Ms. McNary in person.

On his way to Emerald Estates, he started thinking about Rena again. Why couldn't he get her out of his mind? He had to make amends some kind of way. He guessed that he loved her and probably had never stopped loving her. But the thing that bothered him most was did she still love him? Would she even talk to him? It was time to stop wondering what she would or would not say; it was time for him to step out and just make it happen.

He passed the intersection where his mother had her accident, and Rena left his mind. He tried to fight the feeling of guilt about his mother's condition, another one of the nagging feelings he dealt with on a day to day basis. When he confronted his parents with the family's hidden secrets, it wasn't long after that when Audrey was involved in the car accident. If Audrey had been preoccupied with worry about the family's skeletons pouring out of the closet, she may not have been concentrating fully on driving. Stiles tried time and time again not to take on an unnecessary worry, because it was diabetes that was the major cause of Audrey's accident.

Guilt was definitely a mighty tool that the devil used to get at his intended targets. It didn't matter that he was a man of God; Stiles still felt the blame for a lot of things. He picked up his BlackBerry, and without thinking, he scrolled through his contacts list. There was nothing there for Rena's parents. He remembered that he'd deleted Rena's old number and her parents' numbers. He hit speed dial.

Pastor answered the phone promptly. "Pastor, will you do me a favor?" asked Stiles.

"What is it, son?"

"I don't know how to ask you."

"That's simple." Pastor chuckled. "All you have to do is form the words, and ask me whatever it is you want to ask."

"Could you get the number for Rena's parents? Rena's old cell phone number is no longer in service, and I deleted her parents' phone number."

Pastor paused before answering. "I'll be glad to get it for you. I'll have to call you back later this evening. It's in my study with all of my other one hundred thousand things." Pastor laughed. "Me and your mother are watching one of our shows right now, so I'll call you tonight or tomorrow. Is that okay?"

"Oh, yeah. No hurry. I'm glad to hear that Mother is up. How is she feeling today?"

"Who is that?" Stiles could hear Audrey in the background.

"It's Stiles, honey."

"I want to talk to him," Audrey insisted.

"Hold on, son. Your mother wants to talk to you. And I'll get that church information for you," Pastor told him so Audrey wouldn't bug him with question after question about why he wanted to get in touch with Rena.

"Stiles," Audrey said. Her voice was strong, but it still didn't match up to the bold, commanding voice that she used to have before the accident.

"Hi, Mother. It's so good to hear your voice. I'm glad you're up today. Dad says the two of you are watching television."

"Yes, we are. You know your father. He has his favorite shows, and he won't miss them for the world," she said without admitting it was really her that Pastor was pacifying.

"I'm going to stop by briefly and drop off dinner for the two of you. You remember Detria Mackey, Brother and Sister Mackey's middle daughter, don't you?"

"Yes, I sure do. Is she back in Memphis?" Audrey asked and raised her eyebrows in curiosity.

"Yes. She's a nutritionist. She's the one who's been preparing meals the past several weeks for you and Pastor."

"Oh my, that is so nice of her. She was always a nice girl. So the two of you are friends, huh?" Audrey asked in a curious voice.

"Mother, it's not like that. Don't start making something out of nothing. She volunteers in the kitchen ministry, and she knows the two of you aren't the best at fixing meals," Stiles said with a chuckle.

"Well, it's nice of her. And she was always a sweet, mannerable, Christian girl. It's time you start looking for a wife anyway. Don't close your eyes to what God brings before you. You hear me, Stiles?"

"Yes, I hear you, Mother. I'll be there shortly, but like I

said, I can't stay long. It's been a long day for me, and I'm exhausted. I still have to get home, study my sermon, and catch up on some house cleaning."

"I don't know why you won't hire a housekeeper. You make enough money, Stiles."

Stiles tried not to allow his voice to reflect his agitation. "Mother, I'm fine. I'll be there in two shakes and a tail feather. Bye now," he said.

"I love you, baby," Audrey told him. "See you soon."

"Love you too. Bye, Mother." Stiles hung up the phone. He'd done it. He'd asked Pastor to help him get in contact with Rena's parents. It would be the first step he made toward whatever it was God intended for him to do. He didn't know the words he would say if he got the chance to speak to Rena. He prayed that she would, first of all, take his call, or that her parents would tell him how he could reach her. He would have to play it by ear. He'd come too far to turn around.

Stiles drove in the direction of Emerald Estates to take his parents the food Detria had prepared. Detria was another great lady. Stiles felt comfortable with her, and talking to her came easy as slicing pudding pie. He liked her; he liked her a lot, but until he could come to a closure with Rena, there was no way he was going to try to establish a relationship with another woman. He never wanted to experience the hurt he had when he went through the divorce with Rena, and he didn't want to hurt anyone the way he was hurt.

Still, thoughts of Detria brought a smile to Stiles's face. In some ways, she did remind him of all that he had lost when he and Rena split. Rena had an uncanny way of making him laugh. She could bring out the best of him. She complemented him. Rena was a true helpmeet, or so he thought. "Why did everything have to fall apart, God?" He slammed his fist on the leather passenger's seat of his car.

Stiles approached his parents' house and relieved his mind of all thoughts of Detria and Rena. He hated to think it, but the truth of the matter was that he wanted to take the food in to his parents, spend a few minutes with them, and then skedaddle. He had college essays to grade, assignments to post online, and if Pastor had retrieved Rena's parents' phone number, he had plans to call before the hour grew too late and before his resolve weakened.

"Hi, Pastor," he said as Pastor opened the door to allow his son's entrance. Pastor patted Stiles on the back and smiled. "Here's the food. Do you want me to warm it up for the two of you?" asked Stiles.

"No, that won't be necessary. I can handle it. You go on back there and speak to your mother. You know she's waiting on you," Pastor said.

"Where is she? In her room?"

"Yes, the nurse helped her get back in bed right after you called, so she's in for the night. She balks every time her nurse puts her back in that bed, but you know I can't lift her. I barely can maneuver around this place myself," said Pastor. "I wish I could be of more help to her than I am, but that's what age and a stroke does to you, son."

"Pastor, I know Momma can be more than a hand full at times. She's a pretty tough cookie," Stiles said.

"You got that right. Stiles, I know your mother has made a lot of mistakes, but I hope you won't hold any of them against her," commented Pastor.

"Where did that come from?" asked Stiles and twitched his eyebrows.

"I don't know. I guess it's because this family has seen some tough times. Francesca, you, your divorce, my stroke, and now your mother is permanently paralyzed. Sometimes if we aren't careful, we can find ourselves blaming God for all that has gone wrong in our family. I just want to make sure you remember that every good and perfect gift comes from God. God is our source and our strength. He knows our ways, and He knows that we are not perfect by a long shot. As for the relationship between you and Rena, that's not my call. I can't tell you what to do or what not to do." Pastor passed a sticky note to Stiles. It had the phone number of Rena's parents scrawled almost illegibly on it. "All I'm going to say to you, son, is to let God lead you and guide you. Don't make matters worse because of what your flesh wants to dictate." Pastor patted Stiles on the back again and ambled off to the family room.

Pastor's tone of voice reminded Stiles of the fearless preacher that his father was before he had his stroke. Pastor loved the Lord, and no matter what downs he experienced, not once had Stiles ever heard him blame it on God. Unlike his father, Stiles couldn't say that he did the same. He was too ashamed to admit it, but there were times he did feel like God had forsaken him. There were times Stiles wanted to ball up his fist at God. When he looked out at the congregation Sunday after Sunday, Stiles felt like he wasn't fit to be standing in a place as holy as the pulpit of Holy Rock. He could never fit into the shoes his father left. Shoes that bore the weight of a man like Pastor, who was upright, decent, loving, and forgiving.

Stiles knocked on the slightly ajar door to his mother's room. "Mother, you asleep?"

"No, I was waiting on you, sweetheart. Come on in," she said in an angelic like whisper.

Stiles walked over to her bed and leaned over and kissed her. "Hi, Mother. How do you feel this evening?"

"I'm tired of this bed, Stiles. I want to get up and walk again. I feel helpless. I don't know how much longer I can stand this," Audrey said. Without undue warning, Audrey began to sob like a baby.

Stiles took hold of his mother's upper body and hugged her close to his chest. He rubbed her hair and shed tears with her. There was no reason for Audrey to suffer like this. No matter what she'd done in life, Stiles didn't want to see his mother in the condition that she was in. Being a paraplegic was robbing her of her dignity day by day. The number of friends visiting from church and in the neighborhood had decreased tremendously, mostly due to Audrey's refusal to see them. She barely received phone calls anymore for the same reason. The most Audrey could count on was seeing her name on the sick and shut in list printed every week in the church's Sunday bulletin, along with the first Sunday sacrament the deacons brought her.

Life for Audrey had taken a drastic turn, so much so that Stiles had no words of comfort to deliver to his mother. He held her in his arms until he felt her tears subside and her breathing become labored. Like a little child, she had cried herself to sleep. Stiles sat next to her in what was Pastor's favorite recliner. It was the same recliner Pastor sat in and from the bedroom window, watched the birds fly by when he had his stroke. The same bedside chair that Audrey sat in when Pastor was recovering. Now Pastor had moved the recliner in the room with his wife, so he could sit by her and be close to her. An installed baby monitor sat on a nearby table so if anything went awry, Pastor, the nurse or whoever was in the house could hear Audrey. *A sad existence, God, for such a proud woman*, thought Stiles.

Assured that his mother was asleep, Stiles crept slowly out of her room. He went into the family room and said his good-byes to Pastor.

"Take care, son. Remember what I told you," remarked Pastor as he trailed behind Stiles to the front door.

"I will and I do," said Stiles. He hugged Pastor before he turned to leave.

Stiles opened the door to his car at almost the same time that his cell phone rang.

"Hello, Pastor Stiles?" the caller stated.

"Yes, this is Pastor Stiles."

"I hope I'm not interrupting you," the sparkly voice said on the phone.

"Sister Detria," answered Stiles when he recognized her voice. "Of course, it's no bother. I wouldn't have given you my cell phone number if I thought you would abuse it." He laughed.

"Good. Because I was thinking about something, and I wanted to hear your thoughts about it."

"Okay, what is it?" he asked with a smile stretched on his face. He got in, shut his car door, and started it up. He listened to her as he backed out of the driveway and drove toward the direction of the expressway.

"I wanted to offer my services to your family. I've been praying and seeking God about this for more than a week or so. Today when I gave you the plates of food, it was as if God gave me confirmation about what I should do."

"What is it, Sister Detria?" Stiles's curiosity was definitely piqued.

"I'd like to extend my services to your parents. What I mean by that is I want to be their personal nutritionist. I'll monitor the food they eat, help Pastor learn how to prepare simple, nutritious, and healthy meals, and I'll prepare as many meals myself as I can that will at least provide one meal a day for each of them for a week."

"My goodness, that sounds perfect! But I don't want you giving up your free time for my parents. I'll be glad to compensate you," countered Stiles as he steered onto the acceleration lane leading to the interstate and his home.

"If I accepted payment, then I wouldn't be doing what God

instructed me to do. This isn't about money, Pastor. It's about using the gifts that God has blessed me with to further His kingdom, and according to His direction, not yours," she said bluntly.

"Excuse me, Sister Detria. I don't want to be the one to come between you and God," replied Stiles. He was still smiling while he talked.

"Do you think your parents will accept my services?" she asked.

"I don't see why my father wouldn't. My mother, well, you'll find out for yourself that Mother can be a bit feisty and stubborn." Stiles's laughter vibrated through the cell phone. In return he heard the sweet laughter of Detria's voice. "I'll talk to my father tomorrow, and then get back to you. How does that sound?" he asked.

"It sounds like we have ourselves a possible deal in the making here," she said happily.

"Is this the number I should call?" he asked her, referring to the number that showed up on his cell phone screen.

"Yes, it is. I'll wait to hear from you tomorrow."

"Sure thing, Sister Detria."

"Good-bye and goodnight, Pastor."

"Wait, Sister Detria," he said hurriedly before she hung up the phone.

"Yes, what is it, Pastor?"

"Thank you for following the guidance of the Holy Spirit. Thank you for all that you've already done for me, for my family, and for the church. Your kindness will not go unnoticed," Stiles said seriously.

"You're welcome." Stiles heard the click of the phone. He continued his drive home with a flurry of emotions rushing through his head like hurricane forced winds. Sister Detria was the kind of woman that a man would be proud to have by his side. He hadn't noticed her in church with anyone in particular, other than her family. And when she came to volunteer during midday Bible studies, she was always alone, unless some of the staff from her job came to Bible Study, which was quite often.

Stiles placed his BlackBerry on the console. He reached inside his suit coat and pulled out the sticky note Pastor had given him. "Rena, where oh where are you? And will you talk to me when I find you?" The remainder of his drive home was made in silence as thoughts infiltrated his mind, bobbing from Sister Detria to Rena, like playing ping pong.

When he arrived home, Stiles walked into a house that felt emptier than ever. No one to greet him, not even a dog or a cat. No one but loneliness and the harried thoughts of his past. He removed his clothes, took a shower, and then sat at his office desk. He went over the syllabus, and then placed it online for his students before he remembered that he needed to save Detria's number into his cell contacts. He did that and then went into the kitchen to make himself a hot cup of decaf coffee. He passed by his jacket and remembered the phone number Pastor had given him. He reached inside and pulled it out again. Looking at the number, Stiles considered what to do. He went back to his office and sat down, grabbed his BlackBerry, and dialed the number. He was about to disconnect the call when he heard Mrs. Jackson's familiar voice. It was now or never. Time to find out if the damage he'd caused was irreparable or not.

"Hello," Mrs. Jackson said.

"Uhh, hello, Mrs. Jackson," Stiles stammered. "This is Stiles. How are you this evening?" he asked, while he imagined sounding like a total klutz.

"What is it you want?" she replied in what, to Stiles, sounded like an offensive tone, and rightfully so.

"I don't mean to bother you, but I was wondering if you could tell me how I can get in touch with Rena, ma'am?" Stiles felt sweat beads forming on his head.

"Why do you want to talk to Rena? You have no reason to be dredging up anything with my daughter, Stiles. I don't care whether you're supposed to be a man of God or not; you are not going to call here and start up mess," she said in an adamant tone that caused Stiles's heart to pound hard against his chest.

"No, that's not why I'm calling, Mrs. Jackson. Honest, it's not. I've been doing a lot of thinking lately, and Rena keeps popping up in my head. I know I treated her badly, but we were both to blame for what happened in our marriage. I don't want to hurt her anymore. I just want to talk to her, to talk things out like I should have done in the first place," Stiles said in an almost pleading type of voice.

"I don't think Rena wants to talk to you, or see you, or your family ever again. And you shouldn't blame her for that. My goodness, what kind of family are you? Your twisted sister, your evil mother, and then you. You're just like Audrey. Selfish and always concerned with your feelings and disregarding everyone else's. You're going to pay for what you did to my Rena," shouted Mrs. Jackson into the receiver. "You're going to pay dearly."

"Please, Mrs. Jackson. I don't want to get you all upset. That's the last thing I called to do. All I ask is that you give Rena my phone number, and ask her to call me, or she can call me at the church office. I promise not to call or bother you again. Please, Mrs. Jackson, please just give her the message. Or you can call her on three-way now. That way I still won't have her number, I just want to talk to her," Stiles repeated.

Stiles held on to the phone and listened to the silence that penetrated the lines.

"Mrs. Jackson, please will you at least give her my phone number?"

Mrs. Jackson didn't know what to do. After a few seconds of silence she relented and wrote Stiles's phone number down on the message pad that was close by the phone.

"Thank you, Mrs. Jackson." Stiles felt somewhat uplifted that she'd agreed to take his number.

"I'm taking your number, but I will not call her on three-way, and I don't know how you could ask me to do that to my daughter anyway without her knowing about it. As for giving her your message and phone number, I'll have to think about it. Good-bye," she said and hung up the phone.

Stiles hit the button to end the call as well. He had done what needed to be done. It was hard, and he felt lower than scum when he heard the hurt that was still present in Mrs. Jackson's voice. Stiles finished putting the syllabus online, and then followed by reading his nightly scripture. When he hit the bed, he fell asleep from pure exhaustion, and to think, it was only Monday.

Chapter Thirteen

"Someone to tell it to is one of the fundamental needs of human beings."
~ *Miles Franklin* ~

Rena slowly opened up a space in her heart and reserved it for Robert. Their relationship had taken a rather positive turn. He didn't pressure her anymore for premarital sex, nor did he try to convince her to define their relationship, other than the two of them being good friends. Rena filled spots of loneliness in Robert's heart, and he did the same for her. It was refreshing not to be plagued with thoughts of her past. The past seven months had been blissful for Rena. There continued to be times when she thought about Stiles and what was going on in his life, but she reminded herself that it was a part of her past. It was something that could no longer be rekindled, and with each day she spent with Robert, she came to the realization even more. As for Francesca, Rena prayed for her safety and well being constantly. Francesca would always be in her heart and stamped in her memory. Not because of their relationship, but it was because Francesca had been her friend; her best friend at that.

The church Rena attended played a positive role in her life. It offered her a fresh start in Andover. It had been almost a year since the nasty breakup, and it was time for her to leave the past where it was; in the past. At first she attempted to reintegrate herself at the church where her parents raised her, but she had outgrown its traditionalism and needed somewhere that she could fit in. Grace Baptist turned out to be the right place. Robert had invited her to attend the medium sized church family and she had agreed. She was glad that she did because everything about Grace Baptist spoke revitalization, restoration, and redemption. The pastor was close to her and Robert's age, and his message was befitting for today's times.

Almost every Sunday, Rena met Robert at church after he'd dropped off his children in the children's church area. After church, they often went to lunch before going their separate ways. Rena formed a close bond with Robert's children, and finally, life in Andover seemed to be going well for her. She became involved in the greeters' ministry, sports events at Andover Mass, and spending time with Robert and her parents. Life appeared good.

Rena relaxed at home after attending a football game at school. She sat in her Boston recliner, pulled a throw over her legs, and watched one of her favorite weekly sitcoms she had recorded on TiVo. Her eyes drooped as the call to sleep began to overtake her. The sound of her house phone startled her and stopped her head nod bobbing. She looked at the time; it was almost 10:30 at night. When she saw her parents' phone number flash on the caller ID, Rena hurriedly picked up the phone, afraid that something terrible had happened. "Hello, Mom, Dad, what's wrong?" she asked before the caller had time to say one word.

"Calm down, honey. Nothing has happened. I'm sorry to cause you alarm, but settle down. I had to call you tonight. I didn't think you'd want me to wait until morning," her mother said in an edgy voice.

"What? Tell me what's going on," responded Rena, still somewhat panicky.

"You won't believe who just called here asking about you."
A nervous knot formed immediately in the pit of Rena's belly.
The first thought that came to mind was Francesca. Francesca could be the only person bold or desperate enough to
track her down. If she was in jail, it would be too bad because
Rena was determined not to go down that road ever again.
She wanted Francesca out of her mind, her heart, her everything - forever.

"Mother, if Francesca calls again, please do not tell her
where I am. I don't even want you to tell her that I'm back
in Andover. If she comes here, I'll move. I can't have her in
my life ever again," Rena started blurting out hysterically. In a
flash, she could see the hurt on Robert's face and the embarrassment Francesca could cause on her job and in her life,
period.

"Hold on, hold on; stop it, will you?" her mother insisted.
"It wasn't Francesca."

Rena released a heavy sigh of relief. "Then who was it?"

"Stiles, honey. It was Stiles who called."

Rena held her hand against her chest and gasped. "Stiles?"
She couldn't identify her feelings at the time. Hearing Stiles's
name being called, other than in her head, proved to be electrifying. "Mother, did I hear you correctly?" asked Rena.

Yes, dear. You heard me just fine. I'm just as shocked as
you. When I heard his voice, I didn't know if I felt angry,
mad, hurt, or what. He's caused you so much pain, that I
wanted to reach through the phone and give him a swift kick
in the you know what," Rena's mother said.

"What did he want?" Rena ignored everything her mother
said except the name, Stiles. Her heart raced. Her mouth became dry. She stroked the arm of the chair in a nervous manner.

"He said he wanted to talk to you. Asked me if I would give
him your contact information. "

"What did you tell him?"

"What do you mean, what did I tell him. You know that I told him, no. Just think about it. The unmitigated gall of that man. After putting you through all that he did, and now he wants to all of a sudden call here and ask about your whereabouts. I'm glad your father didn't answer the phone. That's all I can say," her mother said. "You and I both know he would have given Stiles more than an earful." Anger ripped over the phone from her mother's voice so strong that it transferred to Rena.

"I don't know what he wants, and I really don't care to hear what he wants. The divorce is over and done with." Rena paused before she spoke again. This time her voice resonated fear instead of anger. "Mom, what if...what if he has... you know." Rena stopped. She didn't want to think the unthinkable. She silently prayed that Stiles wasn't calling to tell her he had an STD. It could very well be. Sometimes it takes months, even years before a person knows that they have an STD. "Mother, I'm scared."

"Honey, I don't think that's why he was calling. He was far too calm for that. He sounded almost pitiful, like a little lost boy. He was polite to me and apologetic for the hurt he caused our family. But I just couldn't receive it, honey. I mean, I know we're supposed to forgive, and I took him before the Lord a long time ago. It's not that I have any iniquity or a grudge against him, but I just don't want him back into your life again to bring up the past. Let sleeping dogs lie is what I say."

Rena teared up. She curled her freshly shaved legs underneath her bottom and pulled the throw around her neck. "Momma," whispered Rena, "did he say why he wanted to get in touch with me?"

"No, he just sounded sad." Her mother's angered voice had

subsided and changed into the calm after the storm. "Do you know he wanted me to call you on three-way, but I refused. I couldn't do you like that. If you decide you want to talk to him, that's on you. I'm not one to interfere in your life, Rena, or try to tell you what to do. I never have, and I never will."

"I know that, Momma. And you don't know how much I thank you for that. You've never judged me or even given me a reason to feel bad about myself or the decisions I've made in life. I'm so grateful for you. But this time, I need you. I need you to tell me, to help me. I don't know what to think."

"He left a contact number. He asked me to call you and give it to you. He wants to talk to you. He did say that he wasn't calling to make trouble. I hope he means what he says. God knows enough trouble has surfaced dealing with that family to span a lifetime," said Rena's mother. "Do you want the phone number that he left?"

"I don't know." Rena twirled her fingers through her hair. After seconds in thought, she said, "Yes, I'll take it. But I don't know if I'll call him," she quickly added.

"All I can tell you is to pray about it before you do anything, honey. Prayer never fails. Talk to God and seek clear direction. I'll be praying too. If you want to talk more about it tomorrow or whenever, then you know I'm here for you."

"Thank you, Momma. I love you so much." Rena twisted her body slightly and reached for the pen and paper sitting on the end table next to the chair. "I'm ready. Give me the number." She wrote it down, and after chatting for a few minutes, Rena ended the call.

Rena twirled the piece of paper with Stiles's number on it over and over in her hands like she was kneading dough. She stopped, looked at the number, and then looked at the phone. She looked at the time on her table-sized grandfather clock. Memphis was an hour behind Andover. Stiles, if he hadn't changed his routine, was probably still awake and watching the news. She could call him and use the code that would block out her number. Rena picked up the phone and dialed the first few numbers on the paper. Before she finished dialing, she hung up.

"God, help me. What do I need to do? What is your will? Should I call him or not?" Rena almost dropped the phone when it started ringing. "He..Hello."

"You asleep?" the soothing voice asked on the other end.

"No, I just got off the phone with my mother," replied Rena. "I thought you would be asleep by now," she told Robert. "Are the kids down for the count?"

"Yep, and I'm about to hit the sack myself. You were on my mind, and I thought I'd call to tell you to have a good night. That's all," Robert said in his gentle tone.

"I hope I do. Robert," she called his name affectionately.

"What's wrong?" he asked, obviously detecting some change in her voice.

"Stiles called my momma tonight. He wants to talk to me. I don't know why he wants to talk to me now, and I really don't know what to do," she said in a tearing voice.

"Hold up, don't get yourself all worked up for nothing. Maybe he misses you, Rena. You are a good woman. Any man in his right mind can see that," he said.

"Thank you, Robert. You're such a good friend to me. I don't know what I would do without you and my parents. I'm just nervous and uncertain, is all."

"And I understand that. I would be too if I were you. If one day my kids' mother called or showed up on my doorstep, I would freak. The only advice I can give you is to follow your heart, Rena. Pray before you act because what you fight you ignite."

"Robert!"

"Stop, Rena. There's no need to say another word. Get off the phone and try to get some sleep. You've had a long day, and you can't process everything that's happened all at one time. God will direct your path if you let Him, trust in that. We'll talk more about this tomorrow at work, okay?"

"Okay. Robert?"

"Yes?"

"Thanks again for being such a good friend. G'night," said Rena and hung up the phone.

She followed Robert's and her mother's suggestion and went to bed. Before she slept she bowed down before God and praised and petitioned Him on behalf of others as well as herself. She didn't want to act too hasty when it came to Stiles. Whatever it was that Stiles wanted to talk to her about would have to wait for at least another day.

Rena awoke to the silent sound of snow falling outside of her window. The weather was one of the things she always loved about Andover. Here it was, late fall, and it was already snowing. The first snow of the season. She stood at her bathroom window and peered out at the soft, but big flakes as they fell and draped the grounds and streets like a pure white blanket. She loved the way God showed His majesty in all things great and small. Following her routine, Rena took a bath, applied her skin lotion over her body, groomed her hair, and put on a dab of her favorite perfume and lipstick. She believed in the all natural look, so she didn't indulge in facial makeup, powders, and such. A touch of lipstick or gloss suited her hue just fine.

Since it was snowing and the temperature on her outside thermometer read thirty-eight degrees, Rena went to her walk-in closet to find the perfect outfit. She settled on a long sleeved, empire peri-dot jersey dress that stopped above the knees. Rena was a fashionista, so it was natural for her to expertly match the dress with leggings and a pair of flat heeled black suede boots. The cocoon cardigan was not too heavy, but just right for the weather outside.

It didn't take long for Rena to finish dressing. Before leaving, she went into the kitchen, smoothed a smidgen of butter on her blueberry bagel, and poured hot cider tea into her hot/cold tumbler. In weather like this, Rena was thankful for blessings like having a garage, which could go for a hefty price in Massachusetts. She took a small nibble from her bagel while she climbed inside her car and dashed off for a day of work at Andover Mass.

When she pulled into the staff parking lot, she spotted Robert's car right away. He was definitely an early bird. Knowing him, he'd probably been at school for at least half an hour, if not more. He loved his profession, and he was quite good at what he did. She stopped by his classroom to see if he were inside. He was.

With a broad smile, Rena positioned herself inside Robert's classroom. "Good morning, Dr. Becton. Tell me, did you pray for this beautiful snow?" she asked him, with her bundle of items in her hands, including her remaining tumbler of cider.

"Nope, I thought you were the one who called on the big man," Robert said and pointed up toward the sky. His smile was fresh. He walked to where Rena stood. He relieved her of some of her items which included books. Without saying anything, he closed his classroom door and proceeded walking alongside her to the library.

"How did you rest last night?" he asked.

"Fine, actually. Thanks for asking," was her reply.

"I prayed for you. You know I thought about that call from Stiles. Maybe the guy just wants to beg for your forgiveness. You know, start a clean slate. People do make mistakes, you know. And listening to what he has to say doesn't mean you're making a lifetime commitment to the guy. Who knows? It might relieve some of the weight from your beautiful, delicate, little shoulders," he said and used one hand to squeeze her shoulder gently.

Rena laughed. She was quite ticklish, and Robert knew it. "Will you stop it already," she said while laughing.

"Have you decided what you're going to do, or not do?"

"Not really. But I'm leaning toward calling him. I can't stand thinking all of these crazy thoughts about the reason he may be calling. I'm not ready to play head games with him, Robert." They approached the library, and Robert opened the door for Rena.

"Robert, I don't want to go backward. Things are opening up for me in Andover. I have a great job. I'm close to my family, and I'm closer to my older siblings." She walked over to her desk and plopped the rest of her things on top of the pile that she'd left there from the day before. She sat down and took a swig of her cider and a bite of her bagel while Robert placed the items he had of hers on the floor next to her chair.

"Okay, let's think this out. You have a great job, close to family and—"

"And I love my church family. Oh, oh, oh," she said and pointed one finger upward, "there's you and your kids. I've fallen madly in love with Isabelle and Robbie. And you're like the coolest guy in the world; my best friend, my confidante, my rock of Gibraltar, and need I continue to stroke your ego, sir?" Rena laughed and so did Robert.

"No, quite frankly, I thought you were just beginning. I have so many astounding and wonderful attributes you know," he said, but certainly not in a prideful manner. He stood up and then leaned slightly and kissed Rena's hair. "There's no guessing to it, Rena. You know how much I care about you, and how much I would like our relationship to be more than casual friends."

Rena stuttered. "I . . . I know, Robert. Please, let's keep things like they are for now. I don't know if I'm ready to jump into another serious relationship. And you, well you might be on the rebound. You've got a lot of healing to do yourself."

Robert nodded. "Still, Rena, I just want you to know that I'm here if you need me. I've got your back, and you tell that Stiles Graham, pastor or no pastor, I'll bust his chops if he tries to mess over my girl." Robert imitated several boxing jabs.

"You're so silly. Go on, Mr. Mad Scientist. I'll see you at lunch."

"Yeah, see ya, love. Duty calls." Robert swiftly turned around and walked out of the library.

Rena thought about her and Robert's relationship. He was everything a woman could want in a man, so why didn't she want things to go further than they had between them? The first time he tried to kiss her and become intimate, it frightened her. She didn't want to take the chance of loving any man again. Not after Stiles. Plus, Robert deserved so much more than she could ever give him. Once he found out she had herpes and had been involved in a lesbian affair for umpteen years, he would leave running like he was in an Olympic meter race. No, no matter if she liked him, loved him, or whatever she defined it, there was no way they could be anything but friends. No matter how badly she wanted to see how things could work out between them, she couldn't stand the thought of doing to him what had been done to her.

She looked at the time. It was far too early to call Memphis. Maybe this afternoon she'd give Stiles a call. Until then, she had plenty to do to keep her busy throughout the day.

The more she worked, the less time she had to focus on

Stiles. When lunchtime rolled around, she was so consumed in going through a brand new shipment of books that she failed to go to the Food Court. She heard the distinct ring of her phone indicating it was Robert. She dashed for it and reached it just before it went to voice mail.

"Hi, are you breaking up with me?" he teased.

"Breaking up with you? Is it that time already?" She looked at the clock on the wall of the library. "Oh my goodness. I didn't know it was past noon. I've been swamped. I had a temp that came in today, and I've been busy showing him some of the things I need to have done. I guess I'll eat at my desk. Are you in the Food Court?"

"Yep. You go on and do what you have to do. I'm sitting with some of the other staff, so I won't feel so lonely now that my best friend dumped me for a pile of books," he teased again.

"Oh, Robert, I'm sorry. I really am. The morning has zoomed by. I have been working my buns off. But hey, I have an idea."

"What's that pretty little head of yours thinking about?" flirted Robert.

"Why don't you and the kids come by after you pick them up this afternoon, and I'll treat you to my specialty," she said.

"I don't have to ask what that is - spaghetti with half dollar size juicy turkey balls." He sounded excited.

"You got it. So whaddaya say, five thirty?"

"Five thirty will be plenty of time. I'll bring the garlic bread and dessert."

Rena said, "Good. I'll see you this evening. Bye, Robert."

"Bye, Rena."

Chapter Fourteen

"Assumptions are the termites of relationships."
~Henry Winkler~

Stiles was on pins and needles, hoping and praying that Mrs. Jackson passed his number to Rena and that Rena would call him. It didn't register to him that it'd been barely twenty hours since he contacted Rena's parents. She had to give her the number, she just had to. Stiles taught his morning class and went back home to do some much needed paperwork. He was glad he was off work from the church today. It gave him time to do some real soul searching and praying about God's will.

He was surprised when he received a call from Detria. She wanted to know if he had talked to his father yet.

"Yes, I talked to him. And of course, he's fine with it. It's my mother who's going to give you the downright blues. She's a force to be reckoned with."

"I believe I understand. It's difficult for someone who was once so energetic and outgoing to suddenly become paralyzed and unable to basically do anything for themselves. Imagine your whole way of living being stopped, turned upside down and around. It's no wonder she's anxious and depressed."

"My, my, you do understand, don't you? So many of my mother's friends have stopped coming to see her, or even calling. I think they don't know what to say or do since Mother has practically turned her back on them. Mother seems to believe that if she can't share the same kind of friendship with them that she used to, she completely pushes them out of her life. It's hard to see my mother become more isolated and cut off from the world."

"I've worked around all kinds of people in my profession. You'd be surprised as to how important it is to continue to feed the body with nutritious foods that in turn can help boost the brain, the metabolism, the whole works."

"You really know your stuff, don't you?" Stiles sounded impressed.

"I'm just saying, if we paid more attention to what we ingest, we would be in much better shape, mentally, physically, and emotionally."

"You're in charge then. When do you want to start working with my parents?" asked Stiles.

"This afternoon, when I get off work, unless it's too soon," answered Detria.

"Okay, let me give you my parents' phone number. My father is expecting your call, but I'll call him now so he'll know that you'll be there this afternoon."

"Okay. Have a great rest of the day," said Detria.

"You too, talk to you later," replied Stiles and ended the call. He called his father and told him what Detria had said and that she would be coming to their home later this afternoon.

By the afternoon, Stiles had completed a full day's work. He was more on edge than ever after he didn't receive a call from Rena. He focused his attention on Detria and decided to drive to Emerald Estates to see how things were going with her and his parents.

Upon his arrival, Pastor greeted him with a pat on the back. "She's in the room talking to your mother," said Pastor before Stiles had a chance to say a word. Pastor smiled and stepped to the side.

Stiles hugged him, and then went to the bedroom. Before he went inside, he stood in the hallway and listened to his mother's laughter. It was something he hadn't heard in quite some time. "Whatever you can do to help me get out of this bed, then I'll be grateful. And if you can make my Stiles smile again too, girl you would have worked more than a miracle," Stiles heard Audrey telling Detria. That's when he decided it was time to interrupt the conversation. The last thing he wanted was for Detria to feel unduly pressured by his mother. He understood far too well how demanding Audrey could be when she wanted something her way. Seems like she was ready to play matchmaker, something Stiles didn't want to be in the middle of.

"Knock, knock," he said and opened the door wider while he peeked inside.

"There's my baby," Audrey said and reached her arms out toward him. He walked up to her and hugged and kissed her. Then he spoke to Detria.

"Hi, Sister Detria. Do you think you can convince this beautiful woman here to take better care of herself, as much as she can?" asked Stiles with a smile on his face.

"I think I can. Actually, your mother knows quite a bit already. All she needs from me is to teach her how to prepare some meals even though she's physically limited. Plus, like I explained to you and her," Detria smiled and looked at Audrey. Audrey appeared to glow with happiness. "I'll prepare some quick, easy meals that can easily be warmed in the oven by Pastor Graham or Mrs. Graham."

"Stiles, I tell you, Detria is going to work out fine. I'm praising God for her already. And do you know she's doing this from the goodness of her heart?" raved Audrey.

"Yes, mother. I know. Sister Detria is quite a woman. Well, don't let me stop the two of you from getting more acquainted with each other. Mother, I just came by to see my favorite girl," Stiles said lovingly. "I think I'm going back home and relax a little since I finished things early tonight. That way, I can get home in time, watch *CNN* and study the Word before I retire for the night."

"All right, baby. I'm glad you came by. I love you."

Stiles kissed his mother on the hand this time and repeated her words. He swirled in the direction of Detria and said, "Thanks for everything, Sister Detria. God bless your heart."

Detria's head nodded up and down, and she clasped her hands together.

Stiles did exactly as he said when he got home; he stretched out on his fabric sectional and watched *CNN*. After listening to what was going on around the world, he decided to put in the DVD of the taping he'd done for the *Loretta McNary Show*®. Watching it, he laughed at himself several times, and at other times gave himself a stamp of approval with a little slang, "Yeah, that's what I'm talking about." He nodded his head several times, and at the end of the DVD, Stiles presentation, his representation of Holy Rock, his members and the community was something he would be proud that he'd done for a long, long time. He made a note in his BlackBerry to send Ms. McNary an edible arrangement or flowers, when he got to the church office tomorrow. He removed the DVD and carefully placed it back in its holder.

Slowly, he walked back to his bedroom. The ring of his BlackBerry caused him to stop, turn around, and go get it from of the living room table where he'd left it. The number was restricted, and Stiles decided he would not answer it. It was probably some telemarketer trying to pitch a product. He held on to the BlackBerry so he could put it on charge in his bedroom. Then the phone rang again. The ID said PRIVATE CALLER this time. Stiles waited and then pushed the green button to answer the call. "Hello," he said. Not necessarily in an agitated tone, but one that showed that he wasn't in the mood to hear a sales pitch.

At first he stumbled, almost falling on the oak hardwood floor when he heard Rena's one of a kind voice on the other end.

"Stiles, it's Rena."

"Yes, I know," he said slowly. He made his way to his bedroom where he plopped down in his recliner.

"My mother told me you called looking for me. What is it that you want," she said in a bitter tone that was easy for Stiles to detect.

"It's good to hear your voice first of all, Rena. It's been awhile, you know," he said nervously.

"Yes, it has. Now tell me what's so important that you had to call my parents' looking for me?" she demanded.

"To be honest, I wanted to hear your voice, Rena. I know our relationship, well our marriage I should say, ended on a very sour note. And lately that's been bothering me," he told her.

"Is that right? What, you must want to badger me some more, or remind me of how much it was my fault that our marriage didn't last. Well, Stiles, I've accepted that. I've accepted a lot of things that I did. And I've gone before God. I don't feel the weight of my mistakes anymore, so if you're calling to drudge up something else that I did wrong, I suggest you go to God and not me." She spoke boldly and with force that surprised even Stiles.

Rena had always been a mild mannered, kind-hearted person, which is more than likely how Francesca was able to manipulate her so easily. But in his own way, as he listened to

Rena, he recognized that he'd done the same thing. No wonder she didn't want to talk to him.

"Rena, stop, please. Please, listen to me for a moment," he said in a modest manner. "I know I treated you badly. And I know that I didn't give you a fair chance or an opportunity to explain anything to me. But look at it from my angle too. I couldn't face it. I couldn't understand the reason you would not tell me about your affair with Francesca, or about the fact that you had an STD. Yes, I was angry; I was in a rage. I hated everything and everybody. I questioned God, something you and I both know I don't take lightly. But I'm telling you I did. But God, through prayer and studying His Word showed me that though I may not have done the things you did, that I am still just as much to blame as you." He stopped talking and swallowed.

Rena was silent on the other end of the phone. Stiles hoped she hadn't hung up on him. But then he heard her sweet voice. It softened as she spoke, maybe like she could have been crying. He really couldn't be sure.

"Stiles, I know I betrayed you to the fullest extent. But you hurt me too. You weren't exactly the kind of husband or person that I felt like I could come to. I loved you so much. You were the first and only man I've ever loved. When I got involved with Francesca, we were both young and naïve. Neither of us understood the repercussions of what we were doing. Then day after day passed; then month after month; and then before we knew it, we had been in a relationship for years. It wasn't until Francesca went overboard by losing jobs, doing drugs, and hanging with people that weren't really her friends, that my eyes were opened. It was like I discovered that both of us had been wrong all of these years. But she was still my best friend, and I couldn't turn my back on her. I had no idea she had been molested and raped. I would have reached out to her in a different way. I feel so much at blame for the way Francesca's life turned out."

It was like once Rena started talking, that she couldn't stop. "I didn't know how to help her by then, so I indulged her; I took care of her as best I could. I hid her drug addiction and her jail time from your parents. When you came home from college, the intimate part of me and Francesca's relationship had been over. But she was still my friend," Rena cried over the phone. Her voice raised a pitch. "Everyone seems to overlook that. She was my best friend. I couldn't leave her out in the world to fend for herself. I couldn't, and I won't apologize for that. But I didn't think about my own future, or my own needs. I wanted to have a man in my life. I wanted a family, kids, and the white picket fence type of life. I knew I couldn't have that with Francesca. I'm no dummy, Stiles."

"Rena, you don't have to go into all of this. I know it has to hurt you to talk about the past. All I want to tell you is that I acted hastily, too hastily," he said.

"What do you mean? Are you saying that you're sorry about our divorce?"

"I don't know what I'm saying. I'm sorry about a lot of things. I'm sorry about the way I reacted. I'm sorry about the way I treated you and my sister. When I went to see her, she welcomed me into her home, but she let me know that she didn't want to have anything more to do with our family. Can you imagine how much it hurt to hear her say that?"

"You, you've seen and talked to Francesca? How is she?" asked Rena.

"She's doing fine. A little on the thin side, and she's still having problems with that bum leg. She lives a couple hours outside of Memphis, has her own place. But you'll be elated to hear that she's surrendered her life to God; she's involved in several ministries to help others who have sexual identity crises and who're homeless; the whole nine yards. She has quite a testimony of the power of God to change lives."

"Oh, praise God," Rena screamed into the phone. "That's the best news I've heard in ages. I'm so happy, so happy for her," Rena continued to talk and cry.

Stiles remained silent for the next few seconds to allow Rena to rejoice. When she settled down he picked up the conversation.

"Rena, I was wondering if we could . . . talk again. I'm not asking you to feel sorry for me, and to be honest, I don't have a reason why you should want to talk to me. All I know is that I've been praying and asking God what to do. And it always comes back to making amends with you, Rena."

"Stiles, I'm trying hard to move on with my life. I want to leave the past behind me. I want to forget all the mistakes and the craziness of my life back then. Now you expect me to just jump on the bandwagon with you? I don't know. I really have to think about this."

Without thinking, Stiles blurted out, "Is there someone else? If so, I understand and I'm not calling to bring friction into your life. I'm glad you've moved on. Are you working?" he asked.

"Yes, I'm the librarian for a prominent school." She didn't say the name or where the school was located. "As for there being someone in my life, I don't think that it's fair for you to ask me that."

"I see. And I'm sorry."

"How are your parents?" she switched the subject.

"They're okay. I don't know if you heard, but my mother was in a serious car accident a few months ago. She's a paraplegic now, basically bedridden and depressed. As for Pastor, he's still Pastor. Still praising God and still encouraging others. He's doing well, praise God."

"Oh, Stiles. I had no idea. Do my parents know?"

"I doubt it, unless some of the long time members have kept in touch with your parents and maybe told them," answered Stiles.

"I guess they don't know because Mother didn't say anything when she gave me your message. And Pops, well, he would have told my mom if he had heard anything. But I'm sorry about your mother. I know that it must be hard on Audrey and the family. I'll be praying for her," she said. "Look, Stiles. I have a zillion and one things to do."

"Oh yeah, I'm sure you do. I do want to thank you for calling, Rena. And please, please think about what I said. I'd like to hear from you again soon," he urged her again.

"I'll see. Goodnight, Stiles," she said patronizingly, but with a mixture of softness.

"Goodnight, Rena." Stiles sat on the edge of the bed thinking about the last fifteen minutes. Rena had called and to him, that was a good sign. When he prayed, he thanked God for answering his prayer so quickly.

To hear Rena's voice caused an urgent rush, a melancholy smile that reminded him how much he truly missed her in his life. He was playing according to her rules now. There was no way for him to decipher from their conversation whether she would call him again or not. Stiles lay back on his bed and rested his hands on the down pillow and his head in his hands. Suddenly his face turned grim and his thoughts grew even dimmer. He needed love, the love of a woman; not just any woman but a woman sent by God. Stiles Graham needed a wife.

Chapter Fifteen

"Don't smother each other. No one can grow in the shade"
~ Leo Buscaglia ~

Rena's hands shook nervously as she placed her phone down on the kitchen table. She sat down in one of the kitchen chairs, rested her chin in her hands, and her mouth curved in an unconscious smile. Stiles's voice was the same. It caused Rena to yearn for what once was. She daydreamed about some of the happier times they had together.

A short lived relationship and marriage that held a lifetime of precious memories that lingered forever in a space in her heart.

Rena pulled her thoughts back to reality. She got up, exchanged her T-shirt and panties for a set of pale avocado pajamas, and prepared for a night of reading. She wanted to finish reading a novel that made her smile each time she picked it up. The title alone, *Girl, Naw*, was enough to give her a boost and the story the author weaved was one that made her feel a variety of emotions. She was three quarters of the way through the novel when the phone rang. Rena looked at her caller ID. It was one of her longtime friends who had always lived in Andover.

"Hey, girl," said Rena to Carolyn.

"Hey, what's going on? I haven't heard from you in a couple of weeks, so I thought I'd check in on you," was Carolyn's reply.

"Same ole, same ole. Working, that's all. How about you?" A smile played at the corner's of her mouth. "What's going on in your neck of the woods?"

"Same as you, work. Trying to keep my head above water. I call it recession proofing." Rena could hear Carolyn's signature giggling over the phone.

"You are too crazy for words. Any special plans for the weekend?"

"Me and my boyfriend are going to brave through the fierce snow and go winter hiking up at Harold Parker State Forest. You and Robert are welcome to come along if you don't have any plans made yet."

"Nope, don't think so. Robert's weekends are specifically set aside for his kids. I don't think taking them hiking will exactly be the kind of thing he'd want to do with small kids, if you know what I mean," replied Rena while she laughed.

"How are the two of you doing anyway?" asked Carolyn.

"There is no two of us, Carolyn. I've told you before that Robert and I are friends. That's it. We're really good friends, and nothing more." Rena pushed back the covers on her bed, raised her legs and hugged her arms around them.

"Sure. You can't tell me that Robert doesn't want more. He's just taking his time because he knows the two of you have had torrid pasts. But it's time to move on, girl. It's not like you're planning on ever going back to Memphis or that bum who mistreated you there."

Rena was quiet. She recalled her earlier conversation, but she wouldn't dare tell Carolyn that she'd talked to Stiles. Carolyn was a good friend, always had been, but not exactly the kind of friend to tell something that was not meant to be spread around in a gossip group. Carolyn had a good heart and great intentions, but Rena knew how far to entrust her.

"I'm not going to hold you on this phone. I just wanted to

say, hi. If you change your mind about this weekend, give me a holla," said Carolyn.

"I will, but I know we won't be joining you two this time. Maybe some other time, but thanks for the invitation. Talk to you later, Carolyn."

Rena unfolded her legs and crawled underneath the soothing warm, butter cream sheet and comforter. She turned over on her left side, picked up the copy of *Girl, Naw*, and resumed reading until her eyes began to droop. She bookmarked her page, prayed silently to God, then turned off her night lamp. Sleep met her and gave way to dreams of her and Stiles reuniting.

Early Wednesday morning, on her way to work, Rena stopped to get two dozen of fresh donuts from the bakery. Every so often, one of the staff brought donuts, pastries, or cakes and placed them in the teachers' lounge.

She parked in her usual space that was reserved for staff only, grabbed hold of her usual pile of what she called, *stuff*, along with the donuts. She trailed through the remains of snow that the snow plows missed, until she reached the entrance of the school, where a burst of warmth immediately welcomed her inside.

Rena went in the direction of the teachers' lounge, deposited the donuts and received thanks from some of the teachers already huddled inside and chatting. She didn't linger long, just long enough to fill her decanter with some fresh coffee, grab a donut, and then she was off to the library.

When she passed by Robert's class, Rena noticed that it was empty, and the lights hadn't been turned on in his classroom either. That was definitely unusual for Robert. Rena stopped momentarily, and then recalled that she hadn't seen his car outside. *Oh well, guess he's running late or maybe one of the kids made a last minute boo-boo.* She smiled at the thought and continued her trek until she made it to her world of books. She would check on Robert's whereabouts later.

Most of Rena's morning was spent checking in books, ushering classes in and out of the library, updating her computerized database, and delegating duties to the library assistant whom Rena determined was needed full time and not temporary. By twelve thirty, Rena stopped long enough to sit down at her desk and eat her packed tuna salad sandwich on sour dough bread, which is when her mind was quiet enough to notice that she hadn't heard from Robert. If he had been late, he still would have called or texted her by now. She searched through her oversize bag until she found her iPhone. No messages, except one from her mother. She listened to her telling her to be careful and to have a great day. Rena smiled. No other calls.

Rena dialed Robert's cell phone. His phone went directly to voice mail. She found her assistant and told her that she would be back shortly. Rena went downstairs until she reached Robert's classroom. No Robert. There was a woman teaching his class. She turned around and went back to the library and called Robert again. Still no answer. She didn't know why she was becoming so jittery. It wasn't like Robert had never missed a day of work before. Maybe Isabelle or Robbie had come down with something and he had to stay home with one or both of them. She finished off her sandwich with a bottle of water, then went back to work. The rest of the afternoon passed by like a breeze. She was out the door and heading for home by three o'clock. Her iPhone rang. She talked through her Bluetooth.

"Robert, am I glad to hear from you. What happened to you today?" asked Rena. Her eyebrows raised, and she waited on his response.

"I had an issue starting last night after I talked to you." He sounded tired and agitated.

"What happened? Are the kids all right?" Rena was concerned when she heard Robert's tone.

"Yeah, they're fine. It just so happens that their long lost mother decided to show up on my doorstep at ten o'clock last night, demanding to see her children. Can you believe that? I am so freaking mad I don't know what to do." The anger was certain in Robert's voice, and it worried Rena because Robert was a mellow, even tempered man. It took a lot to make him go off, and even then, he would do it in such a manner that sounded more like a boring lecture than anything.

"My goodness, Robert, what did you do?"

"First, when she came banging on the door and ringing the doorbell like her finger was glued to it, I didn't know who in the world it could be. And at that time of night too. It woke up both Robbie and Isabelle, and I had just gotten Robbie settled down for the night. You know how much of a fuss he makes about bedtime," Robert explained.

"Yeah, I know. Look, before you go any further, I'm on my way over there. She isn't there, is she?" questioned Rena.

"No, that's another story in and of itself. She didn't leave until two o'clock this afternoon, and I had to practically threaten to call law enforcement on her to get her to leave then." The frustration mounted in his voice. "Just come over here. I could use a friend right about now," he told Rena.

"I'll be there as soon as I can. Do you want me to bring you or the kids something to eat, drink, anything?"

"Yes, that sounds great. Just pick up something for them; Mickey D's will be fine. I'll reimburse you when you get here. I just haven't regrouped yet from all that's happened, Rena."

"I'll stop, get the kids something, and you just try to relax as best you can until I get there," she told him.

Rena changed driving directions and sped to the closest McDonald's to get the kids some food, and then off to Robert's she drove. She already felt sorry for what Robert and the kids must have gone through last night and most of the day. Karen hadn't been seen or heard from for about as long as she and Stiles had been divorced, and Robert's kids barely knew her. It was only through pictures and the positive things Robert told them about their mother that the children knew of her existence. Last night must have been an ordeal for all three of them. Robert was such a good father, a wonderful man that any woman would be proud to call husband.

Why don't you see him like that? Rena looked over her shoulder quickly. The voice sounded like someone was inside the car with her, which she knew was impossible, but she had to be sure. She didn't know the answer to the question her spirit had posed. Why didn't she want more out of their relationship? Why did Stiles's voice last night give her a slight glimmer of lost hope, but hope nonetheless. Was she mad, crazy, or what?

Then there was Robert. A decent, loving, handsome, and perfect man who loved God and did the best by every one whose path he crossed. And even though Karen had popped up at his house unannounced, Rena knew that there was no way that Robert mistreated her or was harsh to her. He was just that kind of man.

Rena arrived at Robert's house. In a flash of a second, Robert opened the door. He kissed Rena on the cheek, then took the bags and sodas out of her hand. "Thanks for coming over, Rena. You know your way around here."

"Hello, Auntie Rena," both Isabelle and Robbie said.

"Hello, you guys. Something tells me that you two didn't go to school today," Rena said in a teasing tone and reached out to tickle Robbie's tummy. Both of the children were still in their pajamas.

"Mommy came over last night," said Isabelle. "Robbie was scared of her."

"Nooo, no Mommy," Robbie began to whine.

"Okay, come on you two. Auntie Rena brought you happy meals. How does that sound?" he said and tried to put on a face of laughter, but Rena detected that it was hard for Robert to do.

"Yay," said Isabelle as Robbie tried to copy her every word. He was at the age of doing whatever he saw the next child do, especially his older sister. The kids ran to the kitchen and Rena followed behind them. She helped Robert with getting them seated and quiet long enough to say grace and begin to eat.

"There's a sandwich and fries in there for you and me," she told him.

"I saw them, and thanks, but I don't want anything to eat," Robert told her.

"You are going to eat," she insisted. "Come on, we can go in the family room where we can still see the kids in the kitch-en. We can talk there," she told him. She walked over to the fridge and grabbed two ginger ales. Robert always kept at least a case of in the house. She put in some ice cubes and poured the fizzling ale in cups, and then went into the family room with Robert in tow.

Robert didn't fight against her instructions. He did as he was told and the two of them sat Indian style on the floor of the family room.

"Now, tell me what happened, and are the children all right? I mean, from the sounds of things, they don't appear traumatized or anything like that," remarked Rena, and then she took a bite of the regular size cheeseburger.

"No, they've calmed down now. But when she first came last night, it was simply awful. I didn't know how to react, what to say. I had no idea if she planned on trying to stay here; I didn't know anything. The children woke up, and

Robbie began to cry frantically. Karen reached for him, and he went totally out of control, which made Isabelle cry. She didn't know this woman from some stranger on the street. At that time of night, she didn't remember that Karen was the woman I talked about on the pictures I showed them. "

"What did she say she wanted, Robert?"

"She looked totally spaced out, first of all. She kept babbling incoherently about her children. She needed her children. She wanted her children. She kept saying that over and over again. She pulled at her hair, her clothes were smelly, and she was, she was, I don't know what to call it, Rena. Between trying to get the kids settled down enough to explain to them who she was, and with her becoming more and more impatient because they didn't want to go near her, it was well past one in the morning before things settled down a bit. I offered Karen something to eat, some leftovers I had in the fridge; thank God for that. She wolfed that food down like she hadn't eaten in ages. I talked to her as calmly as possible so she could get a little more relaxed, and then once she finished eating, I suggested that she take a shower and comb her hair, that way the children would calm down. I explained that they were frightened to see her in the condition she was in. She listened to me and so I was able to convince her to take a bath. I found one of her old pair of pants in some of the things I had boxed up to take to Goodwill, and I gave her one of my shirts to put on.

"Oh, Robert, this all sounds so terrible." Rena rubbed his hand gingerly.

"While she was bathing, Robbie couldn't fight sleep any longer. He fell asleep in my arms while Isabelle cuddled underneath my other arm, like a frightened kitten. I put Robbie to bed, and then I talked to Isabelle. I told her that Karen was her mother, the lady I showed her and Robbie in the pictures.

But Isabelle kept saying that she didn't look anything like the lady in the pictures and that Karen wasn't her mother. Isabelle cried so hard, Rena, and I didn't know what to say or do."

Robert began to shed tears and Rena reached over and hugged him. She could feel him relaxing in her arms, and she rocked him back and forth.

"Daddy, I'm finished with my Happy Meal." Isabelle came bursting into the family room, interrupting Robert's meltdown. Isabelle's smile was big and showed off several gaps where she had shed her teeth. Like clockwork, Robbie came toddling into the family room with ketchup all over his face and hands.

Robert began to stand up.

Rena stopped him. "No, you stay parked right where you are and finish eating. I've got this. I'll take care of the kids." Rena led Isabelle and Robbie to the bathroom and helped them wash their hands and faces.

"Mommy," Robbie said and reached up for Rena to hold him.

"She's not Mommy," Isabelle tried to explain to him, but Robbie insisted.

"Mommy," he said again until Rena picked him up.

"Don't worry, Isabelle. It's okay. He's just confused. It's been a long night and day for both of you." Rena pushed the locks of fallen hair out of Isabelle's face, and Isabelle held on to Rena's leg. Rena refused to let the tears spring forth from her misty eyes. Robbie laid his head on her shoulders and held on to her like he was afraid she would let him go.

"Isabelle, come on, sweetie. Why don't I read you a story? Won't that be fun?" asked Rena.

"Yes," said Isabelle. Robbie still lay quietly on her shoulder. She led Isabelle into her room, and Isabelle picked out a book she wanted Rena to read to her. Rena carefully pulled Robbie away from her, but each time she tried to lay him down, Robbie clung to her that much harder until Rena gave in to his hold on her. She read the story to Isabelle until the little girl's eyes could no longer remain open. Robbie was in deep slumber so that Rena could at last lay him down in his twin bed without him pulling against her. She sat on his bed for several minutes and watched both children as they slept. She started to think of how much she longed to be a mother one day, with little ones like Isabelle and Robbie vying for her love and affection. Herpes wouldn't make it impossible for her to have children, but it sure would make it almost impossible to get a mate who would accept her once she had to tell him about her STD. Rena bowed her head and stifled her tears. She thought of Stiles's phone call, and his voice; his words still attracted her like a magnet to him.

"God, I thought he was the one," Rena spoke softly. "I wanted to be a good wife to him, to have his babies, and to love him for the rest of my life, Lord." Rena stopped her conversation with God and stood up. She smiled somberly and gazed at the children a final time before she walked out of their bedroom and closed the door.

When she went back to where Robert was, she found him lying on his side asleep on the sofa. She noticed a coral blue blanket lying on the back of the chair. She picked it up and spread it over him up to his neck. He twitched slightly, but didn't wake up. Rena moved around the room and started picking up some of the children's toys and clothes from the floor. From the family room, she went into the kitchen. There were only a few items in the kitchen sink, and Rena washed the dishes and put them away. A quiet peace overcame her as she performed light chores. She was comfortable in the space where she was — at Robert's house.

Robert woke up an hour or so after falling asleep. He rubbed his eyes, and allowed his brain several seconds to diffuse what had transpired over the past twenty-four hours. He looked around. Everything was quiet. The family room was clean. He yawned, pushed back the blanket, stood up, and stretched. He quickly deciphered what had happened. He went into the kitchen and saw that it was clean as a whistle. The clock displayed 9:45. For a moment or two, Robert had to stop and gather his thoughts to determine if it were 9:45 A.M. or P.M. When he determined that it was nighttime, he went directly to the kids' room and saw them asleep.

"Rena," he called out lightly and walked through the remainder of the house, peeping inside each room when he fully recalled the events earlier. "Rena," he called once more with no answer. He looked outside in his driveway and saw that her car was gone.

Robert turned and walked back into the family room and picked up his cell phone that was lying on one of the tables. He pushed speed dial and called Rena.

"Rena, how long have you been gone?" he asked and yawned again. "Excuse me," he said quickly.

Rena giggled through the phone. "I've been gone for quite a while. Do you remember me telling you that I would take care of the kids?" she asked Robert.

He hesitated like he was baffled by her question. "Yeah, and that's about all I remember," he answered.

"I didn't have the heart to wake you. You and the children were exhausted from the surprise visit, huh?" she commented.

"Yeah, Karen's unexpected visit threw me for a real loop. I don't know how it's going to affect the children."

"You never told me how you got her to leave. You had fallen asleep by the time I got them settled down."

"I'm sorry about that, Rena." Robert's voice took on a sorrowful tone. "I didn't mean to doze off and leave you to see about my kids."

"Man, puhleeze. Those kids are like family to me. I love them, Robert. And you . . ." Rena's voice trailed. "Well, you're my best friend, Robert. There's practically nothing I wouldn't do to help you. It must have shaken you to the core to have Karen knocking on your door. And the children, I'm sure they didn't know what to do."

"None of us did. I tried to be as nice as I possibly could toward her. After all, she is the mother of my children and there was a time when I truly was in love with her. But seeing her in the state that she was in, made me feel nothing but pity for her. One minute, she was rambling on and on about things that didn't really make much sense, if any. The next moment, she was extremely irritable. When she tried to talk to the kids, they ran away from her. That sent Karen into a tangent. She started accusing me of turning the children against her. She picked up whatever she could put her hands on and started throwing it at me. That's why you saw some of the kids' things spread all through the family room. It was a horrible scene that lasted all night and most of the day.

"I couldn't allow her to continue to upset the kids. I mean, none of us could sleep once she came. She was basically uncontrollable. I kept talking to her in a low key voice, assuring her that things were fine and that she was safe. For a while she seemed to understand what I was saying. I told her that the kids were tired and needed to sleep. I asked her how she got here. She said she couldn't remember, but she thinks she took the bus. I asked her about her meds, and she couldn't remember how long it had been since the last time she took them. That was when I called 911. I explained to them what was going on and they sent a police car to pick her up and take her to be mentally evaluated." Robert's voice rang with sadness.

"Robert," remarked Rena, "I am so sorry this happened."

"I didn't want the kids to see her being dragged out of the house by the police. They were quite good with her, which was truly a blessing. There was a female police who came inside of the house. At first, the kids looked frightened. Their mother was hollering and talking and swearing out loud. But the police lady talked calmly to her and treated Karen with dignity and respect. She talked to Karen and explained that they were going to take her to get her meds. After almost an hour, Karen was calm enough to be transported to the hospital.

The female police officer came back inside of the house after they placed Karen in the squad car. She talked to the kids and explained everything she was about to do, which I thought was exceptional on her part. It's still heart wrenching that they had to witness their mother in such an uncontrolled state of mind, Rena."

"I know, I know. But they're children, Robert. Children bounce back quickly. And you're such a good father. They know they're safe with you. They know you would never let anything bad happen to them. As they become older, they'll understand their mother's illness more. You did everything right, Robert. Don't allow Satan to place any guilt on your shoulders about what happened and about the measures you were forced to take to remove her from your home," Rena told him in an endearing voice.

"Thank you, Rena. I don't know what I would have done without you today." His voice sounded tired and worn.

"That's what friends are for, Robert. Now you go and get some more rest. I expect you to be at your official duty station, the science lab, first thing tomorrow morning, bright eyed and bushy tailed." Rena laughed into the phone and Robert did too.

When Robert ended the call, he held the phone in his hand and regarded it slowly. "I love you, Rena. I love you so much," he said, and then he retreated to his bedroom.

Chapter Sixteen

"Having someone wonder where you are when you don't come home at night is a very old human need."
~Margaret Mead~

Stiles approached Detria in the church kitchen shortly after noon Bible Study. "Detria, I don't know what it is you've been doing the past two weeks, but all I can say is, keep doing it," he said with a mixture of happiness and a rather cool tone.

Detria replied with her own mixture of laughter. "What on earth are you talking about?"

"Oh, you know very well that you are responsible for the positive attitude my mother has had since you've been going to Emerald Estates. She adores you. I think, if I know my mother," he spoke assuredly, "and I do, she thinks she's going to match the two of us up with one another."

"For real? I had no idea. I mean, when you happen to pop up nearly every time I'm over there, I just took it as you being the kind of son who visits his parents two or three times a day is all." This time Detria laughed loudly.

"So, you do detect the same thing?" Stiles responded.

"Yeah, I do, Pastor Stiles. But I don't pay Mrs. Graham any mind. I love doing what I can to help your parents. They are such a lovely couple. When I get married, I would love to have a loving relationship like your parents have with each other.

They remind me of my mom and dad's marriage. They even finish one another's sentences at times. I mean, it's amazing the kind of relationship they have. And your father, Stiles, I have to admit, he is a man of God if I've ever seen one. He showers Mrs. Graham with affection, and he rarely leaves her side."

"Yep, that's my dad all right. I can't say that they haven't had their troubles, but through everything they've been through, they've remained together. And that is a testimony, Sister Detria." Suddenly Stiles's voice and expression took on a different tone. A slight frown came upon his face and his voice sounded sad. "I wish I could stand here today and say the same thing about me, but I failed at marriage. I don't know if God will allow me to go down that path again."

Sister Detria washed her hands at the industrial sized sink, and then tore a paper towel off the rack and dried them. She focused her full attention on her pastor. "Pastor Stiles, I don't know, and I don't care to know what happened that caused your marriage to fail. I've heard gossiping around the church, that much I can't lie about. But as for me, all I can tell you is that we all make mistakes. You're a true man of God, just like your father; at least that's what I see, and that's what I feel in my spirit about you." Her voice became more reserved and softer as she spoke. Stiles's eyes were glued to hers.

"I do know one thing, and that is that the God I serve, and the God you preach about is a loving, kind, and forgiving God. He's a God who looks beyond our many faults and He sees our needs. He's a God that doesn't hold a grudge, and He doesn't keep a list of all the wrong we've done. All I can say to you is, if you've repented for your wrongdoing, whatever it was that you say was your fault and caused your marriage to fail, God has forgiven you. Isn't it what you teach us all of the time, Pastor Stiles? Don't you tell us that God is a God of non-condemnation? Don't you tell us that we can go to God and we can ask Him for the desires of our hearts? If you truly want another chance at loving someone again, or trying to reconcile with your wife, or whatever it is you're wrestling with as a man, then go to God with that thing, Pastor. Give it to God. Turn it all over to Him. That's all I can say about that." Detria ended boldly and with conviction.

"My, my, my," Stiles said with a rasp of excitement bouncing in his voice. "Sister Detria, thank you for that word from God. I bless you, and I thank God for you, my sister." Stiles's face had turned a shade lighter; he was pale. He opened his arms and without saying a word, Detria stepped into them. He held on to her and she held him. There was nothing tainted or immoral about their embrace. It was the Spirit of the living God that comforted them.

Stiles stepped aside and looked at Detria. "You are a true, woman of God, Sister."

"To God be the glory, Pastor. Now come on over here and get the food for your parents. Be sure to tell Mrs. Graham I'll see her tomorrow."

"I'll be sure to do that. Have a blessed afternoon," he told Detria and strolled out of the kitchen.

Stiles placed the food on the floor of his car. He drove to Emerald Estates like he did every Wednesday following noon Bible Study. He hadn't heard anything else from Rena, and he was about to lose hope of her ever calling him again. Maybe it was time to give up on the desire to rekindle anything with Rena. He transferred his thoughts to Detria. By the time he arrived at Emerald Estates, he had made up his mind that he was going to ask Detria to go out with him the next time that he saw her.

Detria was a single woman from a good Christian family. She'd never been married, and the best thing about Detria,

Stiles reasoned, was that the two of them easily communicated. It was one of the things that he and Rena seemed not to have done very well. Their communication had been way off base; that's probably why Rena didn't feel like she could come to him with the truth.

Stiles, like always, placed the food in the kitchen after Pastor opened the front door and let him inside.

"How's Mom doing today?" Stiles asked his father.

"She hasn't been feeling too well, son. Her sugar level is up, and those bedsores are getting worse."

"I don't recall you telling me she had bedsores. Doesn't that mean she's not being moved enough?"

"Not necessarily. She's being moved as much as possible, but being immobilized like she is makes it difficult. The nurse has a call in to the doctor. She thinks that they're going to have to hospitalize Audrey. You know your mother is upset about that," said Pastor.

"I'll go in and talk to her." Before he walked up the hallway and into his mother's bedroom, Stiles stopped. "Pastor, you know that it's not a good sign; I mean her having the bedsores. She's already paralyzed, for goodness sakes, and bedsores and diabetes can be a deadly match."

"God is able," was Pastor's reply and he turned and walked away from Stiles.

"Mother," Stiles called as the nurse opened the door for Stiles to enter. Audrey barely turned her head to look at her beloved son.

"She's not feeling too well today," the nurse told him.

"I know, my father told me." Stiles walked over to Audrey's bedside. "Mother," he called again. Tears were rolling down Audrey's face when she turned to look at Stiles.

"I hate living like this. I wish God would call me home." Audrey voice sounded fragile and shaky. Stiles saw the weakness in her eyes.

"Mother." He caressed her right arm tenderly. "I think you need to go back into the hospital. You'll do better there. The doctor can get your sugar level regulated, and they can tend to the bedsores before they get any worse. I know you don't like the sound of all of this, but it's for your good, Mother. You have to remain strong and courageous." There was gentleness in Stiles's voice that denoted how much he loved his mother. "You have to fight and you have to live, Mother."

"Baby." Audrey's voice changed from one of impending death to a gleeful tone. Stiles looked over at the nurse, who shrugged her shoulders, and then back to his mother.

"What is it, Mother?"

"I want you to have a good life. You need a good woman by your side. Detria is a good woman, Stiles. And before you say anything, let me finish what I have to say."

"Yes, ma'am," was all Stiles said in return. He was not about to tell her that he didn't want to hear her match making schemes. Audrey was too weak for him to upset her any more than she already was.

"I've been watching her every time she comes here. That girl is a good girl, Stiles. She treats me and your daddy real good. She not only helps with our meals, but she spends time talking to me, like I'm a real person and not some patient." Audrey glared past Stiles and looked at the nurse who was sitting in the chair reading a magazine. "She's nothing like that Rena; deceiving, backstabbing, and downright evil, her and your sister," Audrey emphasized even though she sounded weak.

"Mother, I wish you wouldn't say things like that about Rena or Francesca. Neither of them is totally to blame for my divorce."

"Oh, yes, they are. Don't you go blaming yourself and nobody else, but her and that sister of yours. And speaking of your sister," Audrey's voice grew stronger with every word she spoke, "if she loved me so much, why hasn't she called here one time or come to see me. Pastor told me that he talked to her and that you went to see her. You thought I didn't know, didn't you?" she said in a nasty tone that reflected her bitterness toward Francesca and Rena.

"Mother, you're lying here sick. You shouldn't be focusing on negative thoughts. You should be focusing on getting better, not on the past. Dear God, Mother, let the past stay in the past." Stiles's spoke with light bitterness. He didn't want to make his mother angry, but she was doing a good job of making him angry.

Audrey managed to point a finger at Stiles. "You better listen to me, son. I won't be around here always. I'm telling you that God is about to call me home. I can feel it. I know Pastor doesn't want to hear it, and you don't want to hear it, but it's the truth. And so you better listen to what I have to say," she said. "That Detria girl is your wife. God is giving you the woman you deserve, not some woman like Rena who you can't trust as far as you can throw her. I'm telling you, you better hear what I'm saying."

"I'm listening," Stiles said in order to appease his mother.

"That's my boy. I knew you would listen to your mother. Now, here's what I want you to do. I want you to call her up and ask her to go out with you. Take her to a fine place to eat or something. Not some rinky dink place. Do it the old fashioned way."

"What's the old fashioned way, Mother?" Stiles managed to smile.

"Court her. That's what you do. She still lives with Brother and Sister Mackey."

"How do you know that?" asked Stiles.

"I know because I asked her, that's how. She said she's been dating some man that goes to Brown Baptist, but never mind that. She likes you. I know it," said Audrey in a choked voice. She started coughing and Stiles looked at the nurse.

The nurse rushed to Audrey's bedside. "Come on, sit up a little," the nurse told Audrey and started pumping the side of the bed with her foot to raise the bed up. Audrey's coughing slowly subsided. "Hon, it's time for me to give you your insulin."

"Stop calling me, hon. I told you my name is Mrs. Graham. My momma, God rest her soul, didn't name me, hon," barked Audrey between several more coughs.

"I'm sorry, Mrs. Graham. It's just a habit."

"One you need to get rid of," Audrey rebuffed.

"Mother, settle down." Stiles patted her arm.

The nurse gave her the insulin injection, and Stiles resumed his place by Audrey's bedside.

"Mother, get some rest. We'll talk about Sister Detria another time. I have to be at church for evening worship, you know."

"Don't try to change the subject. You have plenty of time before you have to be back at church. I may be in this bed, but I ain't no fool. I can still read and tell time. And I'm telling you that it's time for you to get married again. It's not good for a young, handsome man like you to be preaching two or three times a week and not have a helpmeet. It's too many women out there trying to get hold of you, wanting to be the first lady. It's like the Bible says, the harvest is plentiful but the laborers are few."

"Mother, I don't think that finding a wife has anything to do with that passage of scripture.

"Oh, yes, it does. It means that there are plenty of women out there who would love to become the next Mrs. Stiles Graham, but they aren't worthy. Their motives aren't right. This

Detria girl is the right one. I like her, Pastor likes her, and I can tell that you like her too."

Stiles let out an exasperating, audible breath. There was no getting through to Audrey once she'd made up her mind about something. The best thing for him to do was to let her have her say. He wouldn't even tell her that he'd already thought about asking Detria to have dinner with him. But it would be in his time and no one else's.

The nurse's cell phone rang in the middle of Audrey talking to Stiles. She answered it and placed her hand lightly over the phone. "It's her doctor," the nurse whispered.

The room became quiet as Stiles and Audrey deciphered what the doctor was saying on the other end by the nurse's movements. When the nurse hung up the phone, she told them what they already knew. "Mrs. Graham, the doctor wants you to be admitted to the hospital this afternoon."

"I'm not going to do it," Audrey said.

Stiles tried persuasive tactics hoping that he could encourage his mother to do as the doctor had ordered. "Mother, this is the best thing for you. You need more care than Pastor and the nurse can give you. Plus, this terrible cough that you're having isn't good either. I'm sure it'll only be for a few days and then you'll be back at home."

"Stiles, I've had enough of this." Audrey started coughing again. This time she coughed so loudly and so badly that Pastor heard it and came into the room.

"What's going on in here?" He looked nervous and walked over to Audrey's bedside. She continued to cough. The nurse explained to Pastor what the doctor had suggested and that Mrs. Graham had refused to follow his advice.

"Audrey, this is one time when you can't have your own way. You are going to the hospital, and that's that." Pastor swished around like he would in his younger days when he was full of zest and zeal. "Nurse, please call, or do whatever you have to do to make sure the hospital and doctor know we're on our way. Stiles, you help get your mother in her chair, unless you think we should call an ambulance." Pastor looked at Stiles for an answer.

"I think it would be easier and less uncomfortable for mother if we did," replied Stiles.

"Stop discussing my well being like I'm not here," she scolded both of them. "I'm fully capable of making a sound decision about my health. If you call an ambulance, I'll just tell them that I refuse to go, and that's that," Audrey said between hard, guttural coughs.

"I tell you, I won't have it. If Stiles has to pick you up and carry you to the car, then so be it. But one way or the other, you're going to the hospital, and that's not up for further discussion," Pastor bit back.

Stiles had never seen this side of his father. He was always soft spoken, even in his anger, but this afternoon, he was commanding, and he was not about to give Audrey the winning hand.

Pastor turned to the nurse again. "Will you get her cleaned up and ready for us to take her to the hospital?"

"Yes, sir," the nurse quickly remarked and began gathering some clean clothes for Audrey to put on.

"Honey, I don't want to hear another word out of you. Stiles and I are going to step out of the room while Nurse Pettigrew gets you cleaned and dressed. Then when she finishes, we are going to take you to the hospital. Son, am I right?" he looked at Stiles, not for an answer, but for confirmation that Stiles understood Pastor's orders.

"Yes, sir," Stiles replied.

Audrey's coughing spell simmered down, but she had broken out in a heavy sweat. She could hardly speak, so she certainly couldn't fight against what her husband ordered. She exhaled after another cough before she resigned herself to doing what Pastor said.

On the other side of Audrey's bedroom, the two men walked down the hallway and into the study. "You put on quite a show of authority in there," remarked Stiles and patted his father on the back.

"I can count the times on one hand that I've had to use that tone with her during our marriage. Other than that, I usually don't balk against your mother. I'm a peacemaker. I don't like arguing. I don't like confrontation, and I sure don't like dissension in a marriage or any type of relationship if I can help it. What you heard back there was a decision that was best for your mother. It hurts me to see her going through this. But it would hurt me even more if I sat back and let her dictate about her health when it could be a matter of life or death. That cough is the worst I've heard since she started doing it a couple of days ago. She has bedsores forming on her buttocks and legs. She can't feel them, nor see them, so she thinks that she's fine. She's becoming weaker, and despite the insulin injections, her sugar level teeters on the high end. Enough is enough." Pastor paced back and forth across the carpeted floor in the study. His hands were tucked behind his back, and there was an edge in his voice that Stiles had never heard before either.

When Nurse Pettigrew knocked on the door to the study and said she had finished grooming Mrs. Graham, even though she had continued to fuss, Stiles and Pastor went back to her bedroom.

"Honey," Pastor said in a voice that forbade any questions or discussions. "Do you want me to call for an ambulance to transport you, or do you prefer Stiles to drive us to the hospital?" He looked at her sternly and waited on her answer.

Stiles couldn't believe what he heard. His mother's voice wasn't high pitched and forceful like it was when they left the room before. Audrey spoke in a calm, almost childlike tone. "I'd like an ambulance to take me, but I want you to ride in the back with me," she said.

"That's my girl," Pastor remarked and kissed her on the lips. Everyone in the room released a welcoming sigh of relief. The nurse called 911 and Stiles went to the front of the house to wait on the ambulance. The nurse rode with Stiles in his vehicle, while Pastor and Audrey rode in the ambulance. They sped to Methodist University Healthcare in midtown. The admissions department of the hospital had performed it's job well. They already had a room ready and waiting for Audrey's arrival.

"Baby, I'll be on up to your room as soon as I complete the rest of this intake paperwork," Pastor said in a consoling voice.

Audrey nodded her head.

"Pastor, I'll stay down here with you, and we'll go to Mother's room together," Stiles stated.

"Son, you don't have to wait for me. I can make it by myself."

"Stiles, don't listen to Pastor. You stay down here with him," Audrey instructed as a patient orderly began wheeling her away. "Wait just a minute." Audrey crooked her neck upward until her eyes landed on the young face of the orderly. "Don't you hear me talking? Where are your manners?" she scolded the young man.

"Sorry, ma'am," he said. He stopped and gave Audrey the time to say what it was she wanted to say.

Audrey focused her attention back on Pastor. "If I have to come to this God awful place, then the least you're going to do is let your son stay with you. You need a wheelchair yourself to get to my room. This hospital is too big for you to think you can just walk along one or two corridors and that's it. You know for yourself this hospital is like a giant maze. So Stiles," Audrey pointed her fingers flippantly at him, like she was shooing him away from her, "stay with Pastor."

"Yes, ma'am," answered Stiles respectfully.

Pastor huffed but gave in without a fuss. Whatever pleased Audrey and would help her remain settled is what Pastor wanted to do.

After completing some additional intake paperwork, Stiles located a wheelchair and coerced Pastor into sitting in it. Audrey was right. It took two elevator changes and countless long, winding corridors before they made it to her hospital room. When they opened the door, Audrey had been placed in a hospital bed and was hooked to an IV. She held the television remote in her free hand and surfed the channels.

"We made it," said Pastor. "They sure work fast around here. They already have you in the bed, and you got yourself an IV too?" remarked Pastor.

"You would have thought I was some famous celebrity or something, the way they moved to get me in here." Audrey laughed slightly.

"You're my celebrity," Pastor flirted. Stiles stood back and watched his parents' love interaction.

Stiles's cell phone chimed a gospel tune. He reached on the side of his hip and pulled it out of its slender black case.

"Hello," he said.

"Pastor Stiles, this is Detria. I was calling to check on Mr. and Mrs. Graham. I called the house and no one answered, so I took the liberty to stop by Emerald Estates. There was no one home. Is everything all right?"

"Let me call you right back."

"Oh, okay," Detria said.

Stiles went back inside of his mother's hospital room. He called Detria on the patient room phone.

"Detria, I'm sorry about that. I'm at the hospital with mother. The doctor told us to bring her here. Her sugar level is high, she's developed some serious bedsores, and she has a terrible cough. Thank you for being concerned about my parents."

"It's no big deal. I've known Pastor and Mrs. Graham since I was a teenager. Now that I've been interacting with them almost on a daily basis, I've grown rather close to them. You have great parents, Pastor Stiles."

"Thank you, Sister Detria."

"I'm not going to keep you on the phone. Please tell Mrs. Graham that I'm praying for her. And if there's anything I can do, don't hesitate to call me."

"Sure, God bless you."

"Pastor Stiles," Detria blurted. "I mean it; if Mrs. Graham needs or simply wants someone to sit with her to keep her company so you and Pastor Graham can go home, rest, and you can attend the services you need to attend, just call me. I usually make it home from work around three o'clock."

"Again, God bless you and thank you so much, Sister Detria. I'll pass that on to Mother. I know she'll be glad to know that you're praying for her."

"Okay, I'll talk to you later, Pastor," Detria said softly, and then she ended the call.

Stiles heard the dial tone, stood still for a moment, then smiled and refocused his attention on his mother.

"That was Sister Detria. You don't have to tell me," Audrey said with a wide smile on her face. "I'd know that angelic voice anywhere, and then when you left the room, I knew for sure it was her. Did you do what I told you to do?" asked Audrey in a raspy tone of voice.

"No, Mother. I didn't. That's the last thing on my mind right now. I'm concerned with making sure you get better." Stiles looked in the direction of his father who was sitting in the hospital recliner and nodding. "Pastor?" His dad's eyes sparked open when he heard Stiles call him. "Sister Detria asked me to tell you and Mother that she is praying for you. Mother, she said if you need her to come sit with you, or do anything for you, then tell me and she will be here. I hope that makes you feel better."

"It does. You see what I mean about her? She's so thoughtful and caring. And she sure likes you," insisted Audrey.

"Mother, please. What's ticking in that head of yours now?" asked Stiles.

"She could easily have gotten my hospital room and phone number from you, but she didn't. She told you," Audrey pointed at Stiles, "to call her if I needed her. She didn't say she would call me, now be honest. I can read between the lines. I know how other women think."

Pastor shook his head, grinned, and continued to nod. Stiles folded his arms together. "Mother, you're a true piece of work." He started grinning like he'd been caught with his hand in the cookie jar.

Stiles remained at the hospital with Audrey for another hour. Pastor insisted on spending the night with his wife.

On his way home, Stiles called Francesca to tell her about Audrey. Francesca didn't sound overly concerned or caring. She told Stiles to call her if something serious happened. Stiles and Francesca engaged in an argument because of Francesca's lack of concern for their mother.

"Look, don't try to call me like I'm supposed to get up and run down there every time Mother or Pastor sneezes. You're there. You're her golden boy, so you handle the situation. I have faith in you," taunted Francesca.

"Francesca, what happened to you? You're all up in the church pretending like you've got it all together and—"

"Don't even try it, Stiles. Nothing you say is going to make me feel guilty. So let me tell you how it's not going to be," yelled Francesca. "You know what; I think I'll show you instead."

Stiles heard her end the call. He was furious. "I can't believe she hung up on me." He hit the lower palm of his hand on the console of his car. "Stupid," he mouthed.

Twenty minutes after leaving the hospital, Stiles was at home. He called to check on his parents again, and Pastor answered the hospital phone. He told Stiles that Audrey had just been taken to have some x-rays done. Father and son chatted for a minute or two. At first Stiles was going to tell Pastor about his tiff with Francesca, but then decided that it would only upset his father more than he already was. After he finished talking to Pastor, he did his usual end of the day duties, and then sat back in his recliner and turned on the television. He flipped through channels until he settled on *ESPN* Sports channel. He didn't know he had dozed off until the ringing cell phone woke him. He popped open his eyes and reached on his side for the phone.

PRIVATE CALLER, the ID read.

"Hello," Stiles answered.

"Pastor?"

Stiles's breath deflated when he heard the throaty voice on the phone. It was not who he wanted it to be. *Why would it be Rena*, he thought. *She isn't going to call me again.* "Yes, Brother Jones. What can I do for you?" asked Stiles.

Stiles listened to Brother Jones who played many roles in Stiles's life: friend, church deacon, and confidante; of which, by choice, Stiles didn't have many. Brother Jones confided in him about a relationship matter that he'd gotten himself entangled in. The two of them talked until Stiles convinced his friend of the right thing to do.

I don't know how I just gave him advice when I don't know what direction I'm headed in myself. I just wish she would call, one more time. Rena, I wish I hadn't messed up what we had. If I had the chance, I'd say things differently. I would have acted differently. I woulda, woulda, woulda. Just shut up. You woulda, but you didn't. He turned off his cell phone and the television and slowly walked to his bedroom. The day had been one that had really tested his faith and his strength to hold up under taxing situations. On top of all that had transpired today, he didn't feel the need to stay up any longer with thoughts of Rena bobbing around in his head. He needed an escape. He needed sleep.

Chapter Seventeen

"Nothing is more sad than the death of an illusion."
~Arthur Koestler~

For the next few days, Audrey's hospital care intensified. Her cough continued to worsen, and it was difficult to treat her bedsores. Audrey's immune system weakened, and her blood sugar level and blood pressure remained elevated.

Stiles sat beside her hospital bed. He had finally convinced Pastor to go home and get some rest. Pastor had never left her side since the day she was admitted, but his energy had waned, and Stiles pushed him to leave for a few hours.

"Pastor," Audrey called out and looked around the hospital room. Her eyes were droopy and her voice sounded weak. Stiles jumped up when he heard her call for his father.

"Mother, Pastor has gone home to clean himself up. Get some sleep. It won't be long before he comes back."

"Stiles, I don't feel so well." Stiles noticed the tiny beads of sweat forming on her forehead. He touched her head slightly and she felt unusually warm. He poured her a cup of ice water. She took only a few sips from a straw before she turned her head aside.

"Mother, maybe I should get the nurse in here to check your temp. She can give you something to help you to feel better."

"Wait," Audrey said in a weak voice. "I want you to know

how much I love you, son. I want to tell you that I'm sorry for all of the trouble I caused."

Stiles looked at Audrey and tears started forming. "Mother, please, get some rest. There's no need to apologize about anything."

"Ye . . . Yes there is," she began struggling to talk. "I did wrong by Francesca. I was so wrong. God forgive me. Please, Lord, forgive me." Stiles saw tears run down his mother's smooth cheeks.

"Mother, I'm calling for the nurse." Stiles pushed the call button and asked the nurse to come in to check on Audrey. Audrey didn't put up a fuss. This heightened Stiles's concern for his mother even more. The nurse came in straight away and took Audrey's temperature. It was elevated: 103 degrees.

"I'm going to call her doctor. I'll return shortly with something to help decrease her fever," she said to Stiles. She patted Audrey on the arm, and then turned around and exited the room.

Before the nurse returned to the room, Audrey screamed loudly. Stiles pounced up from the chair beside her bed.

"Mother, what is it? What's wrong?" he asked in a terrified voice.

Audrey's eyes rolled upward and her body jerked like she was being electrocuted. She took the hand with the IV embedded in it, and flopped it across her heart. Stiles ran toward the hospital room door and yanked it open. He collided with the nurse who had returned to administer medication to reduce Audrey's fever.

The nurse dropped the medicine cup when she saw Audrey convulsing. She buzzed for assistance. "Code Blue, room 402, Code Blue, room 402," she announced when Audrey went unconscious.

Suddenly a team of nurses, doctors, and a medical cart

rolled through the door. One of the nurses pushed Stiles outside and instructed him to go to the patient waiting area, where someone would let him know what was going on. Stiles rubbed his hand nervously through his hair. It took him a minute to get himself together enough so he could go to the waiting area. Once there, he continued his pace, back and forth, back and forth. He reached on his side and pulled out his BlackBerry and called Brother Jones.

"Look, I need you to go and get my father right away. Bring him to the hospital." Stiles almost screamed into the phone. He was terrified.

"What is it, man?" Brother Jones talked to him like the best friend that he was to Stiles instead of Pastor and church member.

"It's my mother, man! She just, she just went unconscious. They called a Code Blue. I'm in the waiting room." He spoke nervously and his voice trembled. "Get Pastor here as quickly as you can. I'll call him and tell him you're on the way, but don't tell him that Mother is unconscious. I don't want him speculating anything. Just get him here," Stiles said in a pleading voice.

"Will do, man. And you hold on. I'll be praying." Stiles called Sister Detria next. Her voice mail came on and he left her a quick message.

"Lord, please. Help my mother; do it, Lord. Please." He begged God with tears pouring from his eyes.

"Mr. Graham?" he heard the throaty sound of someone calling his name. Stiles did an abrupt turn and wiped his tears with the back of his hand.

"Yes, that's me. I mean, I'm Stiles Graham," he said in a confused state. He looked at the doctor's ashened colored face, and Stiles suspected what he didn't want to face. "How is she? Can I go see my mother now?" Stiles asked.

"I . . . Mr. Graham, we did..."

Stiles fell down to his knees and onto the tile floor. "Noooo," he screamed. The doctor knelt down and another person in the waiting room rushed over and they helped Stiles to his feet.

"We did all we could. But your mother went into sudden cardiac arrest. We couldn't revive her. I'm sorry."

"No no no. Not my mother. Not my mother." His cries turned into sobs of pain. The doctor held his hand on Stiles's back.

"Is there anyone you'd like me to have our staff call? Are you here alone?" The doctor asked with true concern.

"My father is on his way up here," Stiles managed to tell the doctor. "I'm a pastor. I'm going to call my church. Some others will be here shortly."

"Good. You don't need to be alone at a time like this," the doctor told him.

"Can I see her?" asked Stiles and looked up at the doctor with eyes bloodshot from crying so hard.

"Yes, but it'll be a few minutes. I'll have one of the nurses come get you when it's okay for you to see her."

"Thank you, Doctor," said Stiles. He looked at the stranger who sat beside him; the person that had helped him up when he collapsed. "And thank you too."

The stranger nodded his head once before he returned to his original seat.

For Stiles, it seemed like time had stood still. A wave of thoughts about Audrey rushed through his mind. The nurse came shortly after the doctor left. He led Stiles to his mother's room. She was lying in the bed and looked like she was asleep. Stiles saw the crooked expression on her face, one that looked like she had been in pain when she died. It hurt so bad to see her lying so still. He heard the cries of his father, as he came down the hallway and joined Stiles in the hospital room. The doctor or one of the nurses must have told him that Audrey had gone into cardiac arrest and died.

Pastor's cries filtered through the vents and along the corridors. Father and son were in agony. Brother Jones embraced each of them as he fought back tears of his own. Audrey Graham was dead. Pastor's first lady was gone forever. It was a sad day; a sad day indeed.

Chapter Eighteen

"You come to love not by finding the perfect person, but by seeing an imperfect person perfectly."
~Sam Keen~

The day of Audrey's death was extremely hard for Pastor, so Stiles made the decision to stay at Emerald Estates as long as needed to keep an eye on his father. Something as devastating as this could easily send Pastor's health reeling, and Stiles wanted to do everything he could to make certain that Pastor was going to be all right.

Francesca's display when he called and told her about what happened caused Stiles to build an invisible wall between him and his sister. He couldn't believe Francesca said she wasn't going to come to Memphis. All of the years that she'd done wrong to herself and to others; all of the scary nights and days Pastor and Audrey spent praying for her safety when they hadn't heard from her; all of the trouble she'd caused in their family, and now she couldn't or wouldn't try to support the family in some small way.

Stiles's grief turned ugly. He got up from where he was sitting in Pastor's study, and with one fell swoop of his hand, he cleared Pastor's desk of all that was on it. Everything found a new destination on the floor. Giant tears poured from his eyes. Stiles slammed his fist down on top of the oak office desk again and again, until the side of his hand turned beet red and was bruised from the pounding. Stiles's cries echoed through the empty house. It was good that Brother Jones had taken Pastor to the church where Pastor said he wanted to go and pray before God.

Stiles's body trembled. The woman who had given birth to him, loved him, and looked after him was no more. Stiles's heart pounded like it was trying to escape from prison. He fell down on his knees and bowed his head. He placed his face in his hands, but it wasn't enough to hold back the flood of tears that pressed through his fingers.

"Mother, oh God." Stiles cried out. "Not my dear, sweet mother."

Mrs. Jackson's phone rang while she held it in her hand, still stunned at what she'd just heard. She pushed the talk button.

"Hello, Rena. I'm glad you called. I was just about to call you. I'm afraid I have some bad news," Mrs. Jackson told her daughter.

"What is it, Momma? Is Daddy all right?" Rena was anxious, nervous, and frightened all rolled into one huge ball.

"No, everyone in the family is fine. But I just received a phone call from Stiles."

"About what? I returned his call weeks ago."

"Oh, you never told me you talked to him," replied Mrs. Jackson.

"I'm sorry. I thought I did. It wasn't about anything. He wanted to put on this sad story like he missed me so much, and that he was sorry about how things ended between us. But Momma, I'm not buying it. I can't trust Stiles ever again." Rena's eyes narrowed. "Momma, I know that I did a lot of wrong. I'm not denying that, and neither am I trying to make an excuse for my past actions. But I will not be condemned over and over again. I believe God has forgiven me."

"God has, Rena. But this time, he didn't call about you."

"What did he want then?" A cold edge of cynicism rang in Rena's voice.

Mrs. Jackson spoke slowly. "It was about Audrey, honey."

"What about Audrey?" Rena's hand shook and an unexplainable feeling of alarm consumed her. "What has she managed to screw up now?"

"She was in the hospital. I don't know the details; don't know how long she was in there. But she died. She went into cardiac arrest."

Rena gasped and placed her hand over her mouth. "When?"

"Earlier today," Mrs. Jackson answered.

"That is so sad. I know Stiles is about to have a fit. And Pastor; I know he's taking it hard."

"I'm sure he is," added Mrs. Jackson.

"What else did he say?" asked Rena.

"Nothing, just that he was notifying people."

"Did he say when the funeral is going to be held?"

"No, but it's probably going to be sometime next week, I suppose. He said he would call back and let us know. He sounded like he was crying."

"He probably was, Momma. He was Audrey's only son, and they were extremely close. And Francesca; did he say how she was doing?" Rena asked in a melancholy tone.

With a sound of ridicule ringing in her voice, Mrs. Jackson replied, "He didn't say, but who knows what that child is up to anyway? May be one of the reasons poor Audrey died. From all the stress Francesca brought on her."

"Momma, don't say that. Francesca has her ways, that's for sure. But she doesn't deserve to be blamed for Audrey's death. That's a low blow."

"I'm just saying, that's all. And whether you want to admit it or not, it's the truth. I'm not going to lie on her."

"Momma, I don't want to talk about Francesca or any of the Grahams anymore. I need to get back to work. I have a ton of paperwork to enter into the computer." She ended the call and stifled her overwhelming desire to break down and cry.

Rena tried to use work to help conceal the sense of hurt she felt about the news of Audrey's death. *The woman was a tyrant at times, but it was only because she wanted the best for her children.* She went to the nonfiction aisle and started shelving new and returned books. It would be more than enough to keep her busy for the remainder of the day. Usually the library assistant and some of the upper school kids kept the shelves stocked, but Rena needed the extra duties to keep at bay while she tried to soak in the reality of Audrey's death.

Rena managed to giggle softly when she felt welcoming arms encircling her from behind. She looked over her shoulder and smiled affectionately at Robert.

"Robert, stop it," she whispered, and then giggled again. "We don't want the kids to see Dr. Becton making out with the librarian now, do we?" She looked at him and noticed the intensity of his gaze.

"I can't help it when the librarian is so cute," he joked and continued by turning her body toward his and kissing her tenderly on the tip of her nose.

Rena pushed him back slightly. "You are so bad," she said. "How many times do I have to tell you that we're friends?"

"You can stop feeding yourself that line because you and I both know that what we have is far deeper than friendship. I'm crazy about you. All you have to do is admit that you're crazy about me too." He affectionately nuzzled her on the neck before he walked away and out into the open.

Rena followed Robert, leaving the cart of books behind. "Robert," she called. A flood of grief rushed over her body.

Robert stopped, turned around and saw the color leave from her gorgeous face. "Baby, what is it?"

She tried to swallow the lump that had formed in her throat. Her mouth felt dry and her tear ducts went into overload.

"Rena, tell me. What's wrong?" Robert's mounting concern for her wellbeing intensified.

"My mother called me today. A little earlier as a matter of fact. She . . . she told me that my ex-mother-in-law passed away. She went into cardiac arrest, and they were unable to revive her." Rena burst into tears. Robert quickly scanned the large library.

He tenderly grabbed Rena by the elbow and led her to one of the private meeting rooms to keep students from seeing her cry. He closed the door behind them, and then pulled her into his arms lovingly. Robert rubbed her hair and Rena lay against his chest.

Rena couldn't fight the overwhelming need to be close to him. He gave her a sense of security, more than a shoulder to lean on. For the first time, she felt that she could easily fall in love with Robert. He was so genuine and so kind. But now was not the time to get all mushy. She allowed Robert to ease her troubled thoughts with his caress.

"Rena, I'm sorry to hear about your ex-mother-in-law. You never told me that the two of you were so close."

Rena looked at Robert. He still held her by her shoulders. She could feel his passion and see the fire of desire that appeared in his chestnut eyes. She refused to be captured by them or Robert himself.

"We weren't close. Well, let me take that back. We used to be very close, but things changed. I don't want to go into the details with you right now, Robert."

"I'm not asking you to. I just want you to know that I'm here for you—all the way, Rena. Do you know when they're going to have her funeral?"

His gaze was like a gentle caress as she talked to Robert. "No, but Momma said Stiles was going to call her back and let her know."

"Whenever it is, I'm going with you," he told her.

"You're going to do what?" Her eyes bucked.

"I said, I'm going to Memphis with you. And I'm not going to accept no for an answer. I know Mr. and Mrs. Jackson are going, but I want to be there to support you. There's no way I can let you face your ex-husband alone. Not after the way you two split up. It was nasty, and I don't want anyone, especially him, disrespecting you. I care about you too much to allow that." He hugged her again and Rena relaxed inside of his arms without putting up a fuss. She didn't have the strength even if she wanted to.

"Look, let me think about it, Robert. Anyway, what would you do about the children?" Rena massaged her forehead with her hand.

"Let me worry about that," was Robert's reply. "I don't want the kids to go through any unnecessary trauma by attending a funeral, especially for someone they don't know. So we'll see how things work out. I might check with my sister. Maybe she can watch them for a couple of days. But like I said, you let me be the one to figure that out."

"Thanks." Rena smoothed down her hair and rubbed the tears from her face. She opened the door and stepped back into the openness of the library. She had to pull herself together if she planned on making it through the last few hours of her workday.

Chapter Nineteen

"What the caterpillar calls the end of the world, the master calls a butterfly."
~*Richard Bach*~

"Momma, I don't know if I'm going to Mrs. Graham's funeral. It might drudge up too much of the past for me," Rena told her mother over the phone.

"Honey, that's a personal decision you have to make. But your father and I are going. The Grahams were good to us when we lived in Memphis, and you know as well as I do, that the Grahams deserve our respect and our sympathy. I know how you felt about Audrey, but we both know that God wants us to forgive one another. The woman is dead now, Rena; time to let bygones be bygones."

"I know," Rena said sluggishly, "but it's still going to be hard to do. I'll have to see Stiles, Francesca, Pastor, and all of those people from Holy Rock. I don't think I can deal with it. I just don't." Rena's voice broke.

"You can do all things through Christ who strengthens you. How many times have I told you that, child?"

Rena listened at her mother's words. She bit her bottom lip before she responded. "You're right, Momma. This isn't about me anyway. I guess I'll go. Robert said if I decided to attend the funeral that he wanted to be there with me. He thinks it'll do me good to have a friend by my side."

"Now, that's my girl. And Robert is a sweetheart. If you ask me, and you haven't," she said and waved and shook her head simultaneously, "I'd say the man is in love with you. But you didn't ask me," she reiterated and smiled. "Your father and I are checking on flights, so we'll include you and Robert. I'll let you know what we come up with."

"That's fine. And I'll pull up some flights online too; we can compare what we find."

"Good," her mother answered. "You have a good night, dear."

"You too, Momma. G'night."

Rena thought about Stiles and Francesca. What must they be going through? Rena surmised that Stiles was totally devastated and in despair, while Francesca — well who could tell how Francesca reacted to her mother's death? Rena settled back in her favorite position. She stared at the phone. Should she call Stiles? Without much further thought, and before she could change her mind, she picked up her phone, scrolled through her contacts until she found his number, and hit the call button.

Rena exhaled with relief when Stiles's phone went directly to his voice mail. She waited a second or two to decide if she should leave a message, and then proceeded to do so.

"Hello, Stiles. This is Rena. Momma told me the news about Audrey's death. I wanted to call and let you know that you and your family have my sympathy. I know how close you and Audrey were. I'll be praying for y'all. Buh-bye." Rena paused, and then pressed the red END button on her phone.

Detria insisted on accompanying Stiles and Pastor to the funeral home to finalize the arrangements. There were still a few details like who would style Audrey's hair, what outfit Pastor wanted her to wear, and a list of minor things that neither Stiles nor Pastor wanted to do.

By the time they left the funeral home, the three of them were exhausted, probably just as much emotionally as they were physically.

"Pastor, let's stop somewhere and get a bite to eat," suggested Stiles.

Without much energy, Pastor answered, "Sure, son. Whatever you or Detria want will be fine with me."

Stiles looked over his shoulder at Detria. "Sister Detria, do you have a preference about where we can get a quick bite to eat?"

"There's Interstate Barbeque on Third Street. That's about the closest place I can think of. We can dine in or they have a drive-thru. It depends on what you all want to do."

"Barbeque sounds good," Pastor said. "I haven't had their rib tips in a long time. But I'm drained, so if y'all don't mind I'd rather we get it to go."

"Okay, next stop, Interstate Barbeque," said Stiles. He made the proper turns and arrived at the popular restaurant located at the intersection of Third Street and Mallory Avenue. Stiles drove around to the side of the restaurant and pulled up at the drive-thru window. After he ordered and they received their bag of food, he headed home. Stiles didn't want to keep Pastor out much longer, knowing his father was drained. Tomorrow was going to be another full day, with more relatives and guests stopping by.

Stiles tilted his head and peered back at Detria. "Detria, if you don't mind, I'm going to drop Pastor off first. We have some relatives there who can look out for him until I take you home."

"That's fine," answered Detria. Twenty minutes after leaving the restaurant, Stiles pulled into the driveway of Emerald Estates.

"You sure you don't want to come inside?" added Pastor in

a groggy voice as he opened the heavy passenger door to get out of the car.

"No, but thank you, Pastor Graham. Stiles, take your time and get your father settled in. I'll wait," she told him.

"Thanks, Sister Detria. I won't be long." Stiles picked up the bag of food from the floor and walked alongside Pastor. He stopped and turned to look at Detria. "Sister Detria, you can move to the front seat. I don't want anyone thinking I've been hired as your chauffeur," he said and then laughed.

Something in Stiles's manner of speech soothed Detria. He was such an honorable man and Detria was drawn to his gentlemanly ways. She opened the back door of his car and did as he suggested; moved to the front passenger's seat. True to his words, Stiles returned only a few minutes after leading Pastor inside.

"Did you get him settled?" Detria asked Stiles.

"Yeah, he's in the family room eating his food. Some of our relatives are in there to help him, so he'll be fine until I get back. They'll make sure of that. He's having a hard time, and I can't say I blame him. He and my mother have been together since I was four years old. Now, he's without his helpmeet. He looks lost and confused." Stiles turned on the car and backed out of the driveway.

Detria listened and whenever his eyes locked on hers, it sent her heart into flips. Detria had never admitted that she was attracted to Pastor Stiles. Initially, she offered her help innocently. But a handsome man like Pastor Stiles, who had such buoyancy about himself, drew her closer to him.

"Pastor Stiles, the kind of marriage your mother and father had is becoming a rarity these days. So many people don't give their marriage a chance to survive. It takes good and bad in a relationship for it to grow strong."

Stiles cleared his throat. "I agree. Without discussing the

break-up of my marriage, I will have to say that I should have been more willing to fight for our relationship and for our love. I should have been the one to do whatever I needed to do to make my marriage work, but I didn't, and so I failed at any chance of reconciliation."

"I'm sorry to hear that." Her eyebrows flickered a little. "I wasn't saying anything about you or your marriage. I was talking about marriages in general."

"I didn't take it personally. But the truth is the truth. I still could have done more to save my marriage. I didn't. Now I have to move on. As for Pastor, it's different. They were literally together until death. And that's the way a marriage should be. Nothing but death should be able to separate a husband and wife. I long for that kind of love, and I thought I was going to have it when I fell in love with Rena."

Stiles turned on Detria's street and rode past several houses until he arrived at her parents' home. He turned off the ignition and sighed. "I want to express how much I appreciate everything you've done to help my family, Sister..."

Detria shushed him by placing one finger over his lips. "Detria," she said.

Stiles's face turned a shade darker when he felt her finger purse his lips.

"Detria," he said slowly. "Thank you for your help and your kindness. I don't know how I, well me or my father, could have made it these past few days without you."

"I'm glad to help," Detria answered. "Mrs. Graham was a lovely person; a woman to be admired; a strong personality is what she had. She could chew you up and spit you out with one of her stares." Detria and Stiles burst into laughter.

Stiles leaned toward Detria. Still laughing, he transfixed his eyes upon hers. His thick brows drew together in an agonized expression.

Detria stared back. Her lips tremored when Stiles's hand rested on the side of her face. Her pulse raced, and Stiles's lips moved closer to hers. His warm breath ignited passion in Detria that she didn't want to reveal, but she was at Stiles's mercy now.

Stiles's lips were soft, tender and arousing. Gusts of desire for him could not be hidden. Their kiss grew more intense. Slowly, Stiles's hands moved downward while Detria, fully aroused now, drew in closer to him. His fingers caressed her thighs and seemed to burn her tingling skin. She suddenly cried out for release.

"Stiles, Pastor, Stiles . . ." she didn't know what to call him . . . lost for words at what to say. Stiles's mouth covered hers hungrily. She forced herself away from him.

"I'm sorry, Detria," he told her, but his body said differently. "You're just so beautiful."

"Stiles, we shouldn't," she said and bowed her head in shame.

"Don't say that. We're two adults, Detria. I like you. I like you a lot," Stiles admitted. "I didn't realize how much until this week. I know I probably sound stupid, but it's the truth. Mother told me you were the girl for me. She told me two days before she was taken to the hospital. I promised her that I would ask you out on a real date." Stiles smiled at the pleasant thought he had of his mother. His face remained flushed. His voice hoarse and thick.

"Really?" Detria said. "I'm glad she liked me. That means a lot to me, Pastor Stiles."

"Uh, I think after what just happened, you can drop the Pastor in front of my name, of course unless we're at church or at a formal setting," he said and giggled. He hugged Detria again and kissed her on the lips.

"I better go inside, so you can get back to your father. Plus, I want to eat this delicious smelling food you bought me," she told him.

"Wait, I'll get the door for you." Stiles jumped out of his car and ran to the other side to open Detria's door. He picked up her bag of food, and used his other hand to hold hers. He walked her to the door and leaned down to kiss her again. "Detria, I want to see you again. Not on business either. Will you consider going out with me maybe to dinner, lunch, whatever? I mean, it'll have to be after mother's funeral. But I'd like to spend more time with you. You make everything so much easier," he said softly and kissed her again.

"Stiles, I'm here for you. Don't ever forget that," she said. She pulled her key out of her clutch bag and opened the front door and went inside.

Stiles stood at the door for a second or two before he walked slowly back to his car and drove back to Emerald Estates.

Once at Emerald Estates, Stiles checked on Pastor who had picked over his food and was preparing for bed. On the contrary, Stiles ate most of his food, chatted with some of his relatives, and then he enjoyed a hot shower. Afterward, he read several scriptures from his favorite Bible. He checked on Pastor again and found him already in his bed, asleep. The house was eerily quiet even though it was far from empty. Stiles took advantage of the silence. It gave him time to reflect on everything that had happened in the span of a few days. He shed more tears when he thought about his mother. A flood of tears poured down his face when he thought of Francesca's coldness. When he couldn't cry anymore, he walked back to the family room and located his BlackBerry so he could put it on charge for the night. The red message light was blinking. He dialed his voice mail and heard several messages from friends and family sharing their condolences over Audrey's demise. The message that caused a lump to form in his throat was the one from Rena. She had called. He listened to her voice on the voice mail more than once. She sounded sweet, sincere, and loving.

Like changing a channel, he switched to the scene of him and Detria in his car moments earlier. Detria was a good girl. Her spirit was one of giving, and she would be easy to fall in love with. But he couldn't shake his feelings for Rena; she was still in his heart and in his thoughts. But it was over between them, so why couldn't he get over her? He could have a life with Detria. Like Audrey said before she died, he needed to give Detria a chance. Stiles hit the button on his BlackBerry one more time and listened to Rena's message. This time after he listened to it, he deleted it. He went to the last empty bedroom, where he further prepared for bed. He got down on his knees, clasped his hands and prayed.

It was early afternoon, on the next day, before Stiles stopped and settled down. The day had been exhausting, which was good for him in a way; it kept his mind from the obvious, the death of his mother. Stiles pulled out his BlackBerry and called Francesca.

"I'm on my way to Newbern," he said without asking for her permission. "We need to talk."

"Knock yourself out. I'll see you when I see you." Francesca sounded cold and void of emotion when she hung up the phone in Stiles's ear.

Stiles didn't know whether he was furious because of Francesca's selfishness, or if he were furious because of the pain Francesca had endured in her youth.

He told Pastor that he was going to talk to Francesca about coming back with him to Memphis, at least until after the funeral.

Pastor looked relieved that Stiles was going to hopefully bring his baby, Francesca, home.

"Do you want me to go with you?" Pastor offered.

"No, that won't be necessary," one of the out-of-town relatives stated. "Pastor, we're here to help out too," she told him.

Pastor nodded.

"Pastor," Stiles said before he left, "remember, there's plenty of food and drink."

"Yeah, I know. Be careful, son."

"I will."

Stiles made the usual two-hour drive to Newbern in an hour and a half. His mind was consumed with wave after wave of thoughts. Thoughts flourished about him and Francesca growing up in the Graham household. He thought about the good times they used to have as kids; before life took a drastic turn. For Stiles, it seemed like all of it had been a dream and that somehow he'd missed out on it.

When he arrived at Francesca's apartment complex, he piggy backed off the car ahead of him and rushed through the wrought iron security gate.

Stiles parked, got out of his car, and walked up to Francesca's apartment. He knocked on her door, but there was no answer. He continued to knock several times until he realized that either Francesca wasn't home or she was inside and ignoring his knock. His face turned an off color. He was mad. "I can't believe this girl let me drive all the way up here when she knew she wasn't going to be home." Stiles seethed as he returned to sit in the car. His exhaustion apparently caught up with him because he drifted off to sleep. A banging noise woke him up. He jumped, cocked his head up and balled his fists. On the outside of his car stood Francesca. She had her hand over her mouth, and she was enjoying a good laugh, or so it seemed.

"You should see yourself?" she told Stiles. "Looking like that, you can scare anybody off," she continued with her teasing.

Stiles fumbled with the electric button on his car until he located the unlock button. He was furious and it showed. He unlocked the car and jumped out.

"Woooo," said Francesca. "I sho' is scared now, sir," she said, pretending like she was uneducated and about to take off running.

"I fail to see the humor," Stiles bit back. He looked at the time on his phone. "I've been sitting out here for an hour wondering where you were. And you can't say that you didn't know I was coming because I called and told you. Why would you leave?" he asked her as the rapid pace of his heart began to calm down.

"Oh, I was at my friend, Cheryl's apartment." Francesca pointed to her right and waved. Stiles saw an older lady standing on her porch waving back at Francesca.

"Everything's all right," Francesca yelled at her friend. "It's my brother," she told Cheryl and refocused on Stiles. "Come on in. Unless what you have to say, you can say right here."

"Why are you so bitter?" he asked and trailed Francesca as she walked the few steps to her apartment.

Francesca blew him off with the wave of her hand. She opened her front door and barely left it ajar for Stiles to follow her inside. Stiles sat down on the couch and watched Francesca go to her refrigerator. She opened the fridge door, pulled out a diet soda, a package of cheese, and a package of bologna. She opened the package of wheat bread that was sitting on the counter, and proceeded to make herself a sandwich without offering him a bite. She didn't say a word until she was finished preparing her meal.

"You can fix yourself something to eat if you want to," she said between bites, and after taking a swallow from her bottle of diet soda.

Stiles watched her. Blood pounded in his temples. "Some things never change," he told her.

"Look, you're the one who called me," Francesca emphasized, as she reacted angrily to his challenging voice. "You didn't bother to ask me if it was a good time for me, or if there was something else I had to do. So don't come in here like you run things because you don't." She took another bite of her sandwich and a gulp of her soda.

Stiles tried to keep his emotions in check. He didn't want to argue with Francesca. He wanted to persuade her to come back with him to Emerald Estates, at least until after their mother's funeral and burial.

He waved up a hand in surrender. "You're right, sis. And I'm sorry." He swallowed before he continued talking. "I should have asked you if today was a good time for me to come up here. But I didn't think. I've been too distraught, Francesca." Tears pushed to the front of Stiles's eyes. "I feel like I, like I have this heavy boulder resting on my shoulders." A tear leaked out. "Francesca, I need you. Pastor needs you," said Stiles.

Francesca's tone of voice softened. "Pastor will be just fine. You just wait and see. He's a strong man. Stronger than you or I could ever imagine." She sat down in a nearby chair and took the last bite of her sandwich. She chewed slowly until she finished, and then pushed the last bit of food down with another swallow of her soda.

Stiles looked at her. His eyes were red and his cheeks crimson. "I don't know what to do," Stiles told her.

"Who's with him? Some of Audrey's folks, or what?" she spoke nonchalantly.

"There's a mixture of some of Pastor's and Mother's relatives, which equates to *our* relatives. I know you'll be glad to see some of our cousins. I have people camping out at Emerald Estates, my place, and some of the members from Holy Rock and in the neighborhood set aside a room in their houses just in case we need more space."

"Good for you. You've always been good at faking in front

of folk; just like Audrey." Francesca nodded. "Audrey had a lot of friends. That much I can say about her."

"Is that all you can say about our mother? Don't you understand?" Stiles stood up and spread out his hands. "Mother is dead, Francesca. D-e-a-d," he spelled. "Like she's never coming back? Are you in some kind of denial, or what?"

"Denial?" Francesca repeated and remained seated. "What's there to deny. Audrey is gone. Ding, dong, the wi—"

"Stop, it! Don't you dare make fun of our mother." He pounded one fist against his chest.

Francesca's voice rose and her chest puffed outward. "Why shouldn't I? You can't stand the truth; that's what it is. All while you were away having fun at some school activity, or hanging out with one of your cute little chicks, I was being molested." She pointed an excusing finger at Stiles. "You were so into what you had going on. You're no better than Audrey or Pastor. All of y'all were busy, wrapped up in doing everything for the Lord," she started to say in a mocking voice. "Now you come prancing up here like I'm supposed to be all torn apart. Well, here's the truth big brother—I ain't," she said and sat down.

Stiles sat back down on the couch, like he'd been knocked down. "How many times do I have to tell you that I didn't know, Francesca. You're right. I was busy. Busy having fun in and after school. I was a teenager, for Christ's sake! Then I was off to college, doing my own thing. I had no idea that anything bad, especially like what happened to you, was going on," Stiles lashed out. "I am not the one you should be mad at. Why do I have to keep telling you that?"

"Well, tell me, who should I be mad at? Audrey? Pastor? Or maybe we shouldn't stop there. Let's put it all out on the table, shall we? Maybe I should be mad at God. Is that what you're trying to say?" Francesca's words dripped like venom from a poisonous snake.

"You are so selfish," he replied with contempt. "There's no getting through to you. And you say you've changed? You're supposed to be all brand new on the inside, but you're the same. The same, selfish, whining, wannabe the center of attention person you always were." This time Stiles refused to hold back his furor. He stood up and turned toward the front door.

"Are you going to need a funeral car to pick you up for the funeral?" Stiles asked.

"Nope. If I decide to come, I'll get my own way," she remarked. "Don't think I'll be riding in the family car or nothing like that." Francesca swished her hands back and forth.

"If you decide . . ." Stiles repeated, then stopped in midsentence and opened the door.

"Until then, try to be strong, Stiles." Francesca's words bordered on mockery when she quoted a scripture from the Bible. "Precious in the sight of the Lord is the death of His saints. God must have truly loved Audrey to let her get away with all the dirt she's done."

Stiles whirled around and pointed his finger directly at Francesca. Francesca waved her fingers back at him and started laughing. "Oooh, I guess I'm supposed to be scared of my big, bad brother. Well, I'm not, so whatever else you have to say, say it and get out of my apartment," she screamed.

"You haven't changed a bit, Francesca. You always did have a way with words. What is it about you two? Or should I say, what *was* it about you two?"

Francesca gathered her eyebrows like she was wondering what on earth Stiles was talking about.

"I mean, your mother, our mother, is dead," he went back and forth. "She's gone forever, Francesca, and all you can do is make snide remarks about her." Stiles was infuriated by Francesca's lack of caring.

"What, you want me to put on a sad, fake face for everybody? You want me to act like I lost my mother, when in fact the truth of the matter is I lost my mother a long time ago. I lost her when I was an innocent, little girl. I lost her and she was replaced with nothing but evil and bad things in my life. She's the one who made me this way, and now you expect me to shed tears over her, or go to her funeral and sit next to you and Pastor and pretend like I'm so heartbroken when I don't feel one darn thing?" Francesca's face was beet red. "Well, I won't do it. I'm through pretending. I'm me, Stiles. I'm just me," she yelled, and hit her chest with the open palm of her hand. "Doesn't anybody see that? Am I invisible or something?"

Stiles yelled back and stood on his tip toes, a sign of his mounting anger. "I do see you, Francesca. I've always seen you, but you're just like Mother. All you ever see is yourself. It's always been about poor Francesca or Frankie or whatever you're calling yourself these days."

His words were stopped as Francesca landed an open handed slap across Stiles's face that sent him spiraling backward, and holding on to the blood red hand imprint she left on his face.

Stiles rubbed the side of his stinging face. "You know what; I've had enough of you, Francesca. Live your life exactly the way you want," Stiles bellowed. "I'm just the messenger. Don't take your hurt out on me. But I will tell you this. I'm so sorry for all the bad things that happened to you. I wish I had been there to know what was going on but I wasn't."

Her words sounded harsh when she replied. "No time to talk about what should have been or could have been. No matter how bad, evil, or wrong I've been in the past," Francesca said sternly, "I know God loves me. There was a time, not long ago, that I didn't believe that. But now I feel the exact opposite. So when my number is called, I don't need y'all worrying about me, just like you shouldn't be worrying about Audrey. I'm sure she's either at peace or stirring up trouble. She's probably having the time of her life, putting on a real show for all of heaven . . . oops, or hell." Francesca laughed lightly.

Stiles stepped outside and onto Francesca's small porch. The sun suddenly felt blazing hot. Sweat formed on his brow the moment he stepped outside.

"One thing is for sure, bruh."

"What's that?"

"I know that God has forgiven me for everything, and it makes no difference what you, Mother, Pastor, or anyone else thinks of me. God knows my heart, and I'm so glad He does."

Stiles was quiet. "Sis, it's still good to see you. I hope you're at the funeral."

Francesca responded by closing her front door.

Stiles pounded off of the porch and got back in his car. He drove back to Emerald Estates with his foot heavily on the accelerator. The longer he drove, the more resentment mounted against his sister.

While driving, Stiles changed direction and ventured in the direction of his house. He needed to check on his house-guests. They were three ladies who had grown up with his mother. Stiles had basically given them free reign of his home while they were in town to pay their last respects. When they assured him that they were fine, Stiles told them he was going back to Emerald Estates to be with Pastor.

When he approached Emerald Estates, cars filled the drive-way and lined the street. Stiles had to park a few houses down. He walked the short distance, and once inside, he was met by a room full of friends and family. He sat down and mixed and mingled with them although he was still fuming over Francesca's insensitivity. Pastor was in his bedroom taking a nap, one of the church members informed Stiles.

A knock on the front door pulled him from their conversation. He went and opened the door and was presently surprised when he saw Detria standing there. Out of sight from the guests, he affectionately pulled her into his arms and squeezed her.

When he released her, he stepped back and looked in her eyes and grinned widely.

"Wow, what was that all about?" Detria said and placed one hand on her hip and returned his smile with an uplifted brow.

"God sent me a much needed deterrent from what I'm doing, and I must say you are a welcome deterrent. Come on in." He stepped aside to open the door wider and ushered her inside.

"I've never been called a deterrent," she said as she strolled inside. Her hair lightly bounced. "But I'll accept being a deterrent, since I am welcome." She stopped in the kitchen and smoothly turned around. She saw trays of covered food almost on every space.

Stiles rubbed his head with his hand. "I guess that's not exactly the word I was looking for," he said and looked rather embarrassed. "What I should have said is that I'm relieved that the knock on the door came and there you were, standing on the other side looking gorgeous and my heart goes, yes." Stiles used his body to evoke a round of positive emotion.

Detria pointed a finger. "Now that worked," she said and laughed. "I thought I'd stop by since I was on my way home. I wanted to know if there's anything I can do to help you get some things done," Detria said seriously.

"You are truly a godsend, Detria. I've spent the past couple of hours talking with a house full of guests. Those from out of town who said they were coming are here, so that's not the problem."

Detria walked into the family room, and with a fresh smile, she introduced herself to those who didn't know her and chatted lightly with church members who did know her.

She excused herself and told Stiles. "I'm going to go in the kitchen and make sure all of that food is stored properly. I'll take some of it to your house for the people over there," she told Stiles who followed behind her. When she looked at him, she saw the frustrated look on his face. She stood in her tracks. "Is there anything I can do to help?"

"No," he rubbed his hair back with his hand. "I guess I'm just frustrated. You know I went to see if Francesca was going to come to Memphis. Pastor was looking forward to her being her."

"And what happened?" asked Detria.

"You see she isn't here." He stretched out his hands. "I don't know if she's even going to come. Pastor will be devastated. Detria, I don't know what to do." Tears crested in his eyes.

Detria's heart swelled with hurt when she saw the discouraged look on his face. "Stiles, pray. Trust in God. That's all you can do. It's Francesca's decision whether she's coming or not. As for Pastor, keep doing what you're doing; loving him and sticking by him."

"But you don't understand, Detria. Mother's viewing is tomorrow, and her funeral is the day after tomorrow. I haven't had a free moment to look over her eulogy. Instead, I feel like I'm having an out of body experience or something."

"Why don't you go to your church office? I'll stay here with Pastor and your relatives. Plus, there are some church members in there who I know are just waiting to help out in any way that they can." Detria patted Stiles's shoulder. "Now go. You don't have to worry about a thing. We'll make sure everything is fine. Where is Pastor anyway? I didn't see him in there." Detria asked.

"He's in his room taking a nap."

"See, it's the perfect time for you to get out of here." She shoved him playfully. "Go. Stay away as long as you need to."

Stiles leaned down and kissed Detria on the cheek. "God bless you, sister." He felt inside of his pants pocket for his keys. Finding them, he exited through the side door and left.

Chapter Twenty

"If we claim we have not sinned, we make him out to be a liar and his word has no place in our lives."
1 John 1:10

Rena folded the last few items and placed them neatly in the small suitcase. She was planning on being gone for one, maybe two days at the most. At first she turned down Robert's offer to accompany her to Audrey's funeral, but after more thought, she agreed with him when he told her that she needed someone to lean on. Her parents would have each other, but facing Stiles and Francesca was going to be a chore for Rena. Folding her dark navy fitting dress, Rena thought about something Francesca had told her. *"Wantin' folks to think you so much. You deceived my brotha. You tricked him into believing that you were so pure, so holy, when all the time you just as nasty as me."*

"Rena, are you in there?" she heard the voice of her mother calling her out of her daydream.

"Yes," she hollered back. "I'm back here in my bedroom," she answered.

Her mother came into Rena's bedroom and saw the clothes and suitcase lying on the bed.

"I saw your car in the drive. I rang the doorbell and I knocked, then I just used my key to let myself in when you didn't answer. I wanted to make sure you were all right. I guess you were in one of your trances, huh?" Her mother knew Rena like the back of her hand.

"Yeah, I was just thinking." Rena sat down on her bed. "Momma," she said solemnly, "I've messed my life up so bad."

"Now, Rena, don't go doing this to yourself," she told her daughter and sat down next to her. She wrapped her arm around Rena's shoulder. "What have I told you about self-condemnation? Whatever you've done wrong, you've asked God to forgive you . . . right?"

"Yes."

"And He has. Your sins are scattered now as far as the east is from the west. God has thrown them into the sea of forgiveness, never to be remembered again. Are you bothered about the fact you'll see Stiles and Francesca?" her mother asked, already knowing the answer that her daughter was going to give.

"Yes. And I don't want to cause a scene. I guess I'm having second thoughts. Maybe you and Daddy should go. I know how ugly Francesca can get, and Stiles, well, when we talked he sounded nice enough, but I still can't understand his motive for calling me, and that was before Audrey died. I did call and extend my condolences to him after you told me about her death. His phone went straight to voice mail."

"Did you leave a message for him?"

"Yes, ma'am, but I didn't leave my telephone number. I don't want him to have free access to call me whenever he chooses."

Mrs. Jackson continued to embrace her daughter. "Rena, I think Robert's offer to go with you is great. He's a nice man, you know."

Rena raised her head from off her mother's shoulder and gazed at her.

"Don't say a thing." Mrs. Jackson stopped Rena before she could say one word. "All I said is that Robert is a nice man. And he is. One day you'll open your heart again and allow love to come in. It might be Robert that you let come into your life and share the wonderful love the two of you can give to each other. Then again, it might be someone you've yet to cross paths with. Whoever it is, God is going to restore all that the enemy has taken from you, my child. We've all messed up and that means me and your poppa too. You're not the only one in this world that feels ashamed about something they've done in life, Rena, and you won't be the last. But give whatever it is you're trying to carry on your own shoulders, over to God. He's the only one whose shoulders are large enough to carry our burdens."

Rena laid her head against her mother's shoulder again and the two of them sat silently.

Robert called Rena's cell phone early and woke Rena from her troubled sleep. She had spent the night at her parents' house to make it easier for Robert since he was going to drive his car to Boston Logan Airport. He would only have to make the one stop to pick everyone up for the thirty-minute drive. Rena turned to her side and sleepily looked at the clock.

"Good mornin'," she said groggily.

"Time to get your pretty self up. Our flight leaves at nine thirty. We need to get our bags checked through security at least an hour before the flight departure."

"Yeah, I know. I hear Momma and Daddy in their room shuffling around. Sounds like they've been up for a while," she said as she sat up fully in the bed and the sleep began to leave. It felt awkward sleeping at her parents' house in her old room. But it worked out fine so Robert could pick them up all at one place.

"I'll be there to pick y'all up by seven," he told her.

"Are you still going to park your car in short-term parking?" Rena asked and flopped both legs out and on to the side of the bed. She yawned again and stood. The sun was barely up. "What about Isabelle and Robbie?" Rena asked with concern. "You never told me who's going to watch them."

"Didn't I tell you not to worry about them? If you just have to know, my sister is here right now. She's going to sleep over here with the kids until I get back. She'll get them off to school and daycare. So that's settled. Now get your fanny moving, and tell Mr. and Mrs. Jackson that I'm on my way."

"Believe me; they remember what time you told them to be ready. I'm surprised they hadn't pounded on my door before you called to wake me up." Rena placed her hand over her mouth to stifle another yawn. "Let me get dressed. I already have everything packed and sitting by the door, so see, I've been a good girl." Rena laughed into the phone.

"You might just get a special treat for that," Robert joked. "See ya," he said and ended the call.

Rena stretched on her way to open the door to her bedroom. "Morning, Mom. Morning, Dad," she yelled out into the hallway.

"Good morning, baby," they replied in unison.

"Robert said he's on his way," Rena yelled again. "He should be here by seven o'clock."

"We know. We're ready. Do you want some breakfast?" Rena's mother asked when she walked out of the bedroom fully dressed with Rena's father right behind her.

"I'll have something light. Like a slice of sour dough toast and a cup of grape juice," Rena answered.

"Okay, you finish getting ready, and we'll see you downstairs."

"Yes, ma'am."

Rena closed her bedroom door and went into the small connecting bathroom to take a bath.

She refused to let more negative thoughts control her mind. She finished her bath, and after drying off, she lotioned her body, squirted a dab of perfume on her wrists, and then put on the clothes she had laid out the night before to wear to the airport. Summers in Memphis could be hot and being that it was the end of June, Rena had prepared to dress cool and comfortable. She slipped on a bold Caribbean green tieback sundress and a pair of open toed sandals. She was ready in a jiffy. She grabbed her one carry-on bag, and then went downstairs to join her parents for a light breakfast before Robert arrived.

The twenty-four mile ride to Boston Logan airport was a mixture of quiet, chattering between mother and daughter, and Robert and Mr. Jackson talking politics. Robert and Mr. Jackson sat in the front, and Rena and her mother in the back, which was orchestrated by her father.

The foursome arrived at Boston Logan, parked, and completed check-in and security check effortlessly. It wasn't until they were boarded safely on the Air Tran flight that Rena felt like she could finally relax a bit. She sat next to Robert and looked across him and saw her parents involved in conversation as the plane took off. Rena leaned her head against the semi-soft head cushion and closed her eyes.

Robert laid his hand on top of hers as the plane's altitude heightened. Rena fell to sleep quickly, while Robert pulled out a science magazine and started reading. Rena slept until the pilot announced that they were about to land in Atlanta. They had a one hour layover which went by rapidly once they waited their turns to exit the plane, helped Rena's parents get their carry-ons, and then caught one of the airport carts so they could make it in time to get on the flight that would take them into Memphis.

"Robert, thank you for coming with me." Rena sat next to a window in the plane but her eyes were on Robert. "You know you didn't have to do this," Rena told him and squeezed his hand lightly.

"That's where you're wrong," he answered. "I did have to do this. You mean a lot to me, Rena. You're near and dear to my heart." His voice was sensuous and his stare was certain.

Rena relaxed her head against his shoulder, then she popped it up again.

"What is it?" Robert asked.

"The kids." She looked at her watch. "I wonder how they're doing. They're not used to you leaving them, except when you're at work, of course. This is going to be a huge adjustment for them, Robert," Rena sounded worried.

"Stop it, will you? The kids love their aunt. I've not only told you that, but you've witnessed it for yourself. You've met her, and you know she's great with the kids. As far as the kids are concerned, it's like I'm at work anyway. She's already taken Isabelle to school and Robbie to daycare. She was leaving to take them at the same time I was leaving to come and pick you and your parents up this morning. So they're fine." He kissed her on the cheek and grinned. "I'm glad she's staying at my house too."

"Okay, I give." Rena sighed. "You're right. That way, maybe they won't miss you as much."

"Good, finally that's settled." Robert chuckled and leaned his head back against the headrest.

"Robert, on second thought," Rena blurted suddenly, "we should have brought Robbie like we said we were going to do originally."

"I think *we*," he said, "made the right decision. If I had taken Robbie, then Isabelle would be that much lonelier. By both of them being together, Isabelle gets to practice on her big sister skills, and they both can keep one another company."

Rena patted the side of Robert's arm like she was puffing up a pillow. Content with the answers Robert had given her, she laid her head on it.

Rena's tummy bubbled with nervousness. Audrey's viewing was in five hours. In between that time, Robert had to pick up the rental car and then they had to check into their hotel. It was going to be a long day, but one that Rena was prepared to endure for the sake of the Graham family.

They arrived in Memphis safely. They checked in at the Radisson Hotel. Robert and Mr. Jackson shared one room, and Rena and Mrs. Jackson shared another. The men placed the luggage in the adjoining rooms, and the four of them had a quick bite in the hotel restaurant before they returned to their rooms to get ready for the viewing.

The viewing was just as Rena had imagined. Flowers were everywhere. She walked farther into Holy Rock. The sanctuary was packed with people. They had to stand in line to sign Audrey's guest registry. Robert must have noticed Rena's nervousness because she felt his hand go gently around her waist. She looked over her shoulder and smiled at him.

Mr. and Mrs. Jackson stood in front of Robert and Rena. The line moved slowly, but the Jacksons didn't seem to be bothered as they greeted familiar faces from their years of having once lived in Memphis.

Rena found herself consumed in saying hello to people too; some whose names she'd forgotten, but whose faces she remembered well. When it was her turn to sign, she perused the long list of names that had already signed the guest registry and then proceeded to add her name. She stepped to the side and allowed Robert to sign in before they weaved through the crowd and into the church.

When they finished chattering and greeting people, they soon arrived in front of Audrey's casket. Rena placed her hand against her mouth, and Robert planted his strong hands on each side of her shoulders.

Mr. and Mrs. Jackson stood and looked down on Audrey's lifeless body. Mrs. Jackson saw the tears streaming down her daughter's face and she hugged her lightly.

"I've got her," Robert softly whispered. Mrs. Jackson nodded, and Mr. Jackson led her away to find a seat. Rena was motionless. She was face to face with the woman who once loved her like a daughter, but in the end despised her like her worst enemy. She didn't know why her tears were so heavy, but they were. Strong arms surrounded her and she was glad because she felt like she would collapse if they had not.

The woman lying in the casket looks so peaceful, so at rest. Could this be Audrey? Rena thought as she stared intensely. Audrey would be proud of the way Pastor, Stiles, and Francesca had her fixed up. She always had to be the center of everyone's attention. Rena wanted to touch her. She wanted to touch the platinum white couture fabric. The front neck and waist panels were encrusted with beads and rhinestones. The matching camisole and skirt completed the fashion statement that only First Lady Audrey Graham could pull off. Even in death, she looked like a million bucks. Rena half smiled, and then reached for Robert's shoulder. She was ready to be seated.

Mr. and Mrs. Jackson had saved a space for Rena and Robert. Rena heard people talking all around her, but she was oblivious to what they were saying. She couldn't draw her eyes away from the woman lying in the casket. They were several rows away, but Rena felt like she was sitting right next to Audrey. She replayed Audrey's wicked words over in her mind.

'You deceitful little tramp' Audrey had called Rena just after she'd hit her so hard that it sent blood pouring from Rena's mouth. Rena reached inside of her purse for tissue. But Robert offered her his handkerchief, which she accepted.

Rena heard bellowing and sobs emanating from behind. She looked back over her shoulder and saw Pastor, Stiles, and Francesca being escorted into the sanctuary. Francesca's voice was loud and her limp was more pronounced. Someone was holding her on each side. She looked better than Rena remembered. Was that a good thing or a bad thing? Rena didn't know whether to be glad or sad. To hear Francesca's screaming seemed to scare some of the small children that were there. Rena was grateful for Robert's decision to leave the kids with their aunt.

"Ohhh, Lord. Ohhh, why, Lord? Why my mother?" Francesca screamed.

Rena became almost physically ill; confused at Francesca's response over Audrey's death. *Is this one of Francesca's acts? She despised Audrey.* Rena's mind was spinning with bewilderment, confusion, and swirling emotions. Her nails dug deep into Robert's jacket when she saw Stiles and Pastor. Stiles was handsome as ever. A lump formed in Rena's throat, and her tears poured as the family came nearer. Pastor looked like a broken man. His shoulders slumped and his head hung low. His sobs were deep and penetrating.

They reached the row where Rena and her family sat. For a quick moment she met Stiles's gaze. His eyes were hollow. Holding his hand and walking next to him was a woman who was exquisitely dressed. Underneath the woman's hat, Rena saw that she was as beautiful as the outfit she wore.

The family passed by her as if in slow motion. One by one they were led to Audrey's casket. In unison, they cried, sobbed, screamed, and begged for God's mercy.

Francesca collapsed. Ooohs and ahhs of pity could be heard throughout the sanctuary. Two men who were walking by her side, helped to carry her out of the sanctuary. Pastor was consoled by Stiles, and Detria consoled them both. They lingered at Audrey's casket until other relatives and friends gathered around them and ushered them out.

Rena eased up, and then leaned over to her parents. "I'm going to go speak to Pastor," she whispered.

"Honey, do you think you have the strength to do that?" asked her father.

"I have to."

"We're coming with you, then," said Mr. Jackson and proceeded to stand, followed by his wife and Robert.

Robert held on to Rena's hand and led her out into the vestibule. She looked back once more at Audrey's body lying peacefully in the casket.

It took Mr. Jackson to find where they had taken Pastor, Stiles, and Francesca. Holy Rock had been remodeled since the Jacksons and Rena left Memphis. There were several additional rooms and corridors.

"I'll check with one of the armor bearers," Mr. Jackson told his wife with Rena and Robert in earshot. Mr. Jackson approached a gray-haired, short, stocky gentleman. After talking with him for a few minutes, Mr. Jackson returned to his family.

"What did he say?" Mrs. Jackson asked her husband.

"He said they're in one of the rooms reserved for the family and some of their closest friends. He said it would be too much for the Graham family to remain in the sanctuary for the viewing. I explained that we were longtime friends of the Grahams. I asked him if he could allow us to see the family for just a few minutes to let them know that we were here and that our prayers go out to them," Mr. Jackson explained.

"And?" Rena asked.

"He said we could, but only for a few minutes. The family is taking Sister Graham's death really, really hard."

Rena and her mother followed Mr. Jackson and Robert. The armor bearer led them down a corridor, turned to the left, and opened a door marked PRIVATE. He ushered them inside where the Graham family members were gathered. Rena spotted Francesca right away. She was seated in a chair next to several other people who Rena did not recognize. It was at this time that she wished she'd told Robert everything about her past. There was no way to tell what kind of mood Francesca was in, or what she would say.

Robert took hold of Rena's hand and caressed it without saying anything. Rena exhaled. It felt good to have someone standing next to her that cared about her wellbeing.

Stiles was engaged in conversation with some people, one or two of whom Rena recognized. Pastor was in the same huddle. Rena took her parents' lead and she and Robert followed them to where Pastor and Stiles stood.

"Pastor," Mr. Jackson said. Pastor turned around. His eyes immediately glistened with tears. He hugged Mr. Jackson and then Mrs. Jackson.

"God bless you. God bless you for coming." He cried heavily until Stiles turned and patted him on the back. Stiles's eyes were glued to Rena's. "I'm glad you came," he told her while he eyed Robert up and down. "You don't know how much this means to me, I mean our family," he corrected himself.

Rena's tears started. "I am so sorry," she said. "So very sorry about Audrey," Rena repeated. Detria remained close by Stiles. Neither Detria nor Robert said anything. At the moment, it seemed that maybe the two of them felt like outsiders. This moment belonged to Stiles and Rena, Pastor and the Jacksons. There would be time to include others, but not now.

"Are you all going to be here for mother's funeral tomorrow?" Stiles asked and looked from Rena to the Jacksons. He hugged Mr. and Mrs. Jackson while he waited on their response.

"Of course," Mr. Jackson assured Stiles and Pastor.

Stiles half-turned slightly and rather quickly. He placed his arm around Detria's shoulder. "This is Sister Detria Mackey. I don't know if you remember Rena or not?" he looked at Detria and then at Rena.

"I'm sorry, I don't," Detria responded softly.

"Well, Detria, this is, well no other way to say it but to say it—this is my ex-wife, Rena Graham and her parents, Mr. and Mrs. Jackson. I'm sorry, I don't know you," he said and looked at Robert.

"Nice to meet you," said Detria and nodded at each of them as she shook each of their hands.

"Hello, Sister Detria." Rena extended her hand and Detria accepted the handshake. "I don't remember you either, but it's nice meeting you, even if it is under these circumstances." Rena looked at Robert and took hold of his hand. "This is Dr. Robert Becton. Robert's a very dear friend of mine," Rena seemed to emphasize as she introduced him. "When I told him about my Audrey, he insisted on coming with me for support, and I'm so glad he did. She looked at Robert with gratefulness sparkling from her tear drenched eyes. He kissed her on the cheek.

Stiles looked somewhat taken aback when Robert kissed Rena, but he reached out his hand and the two of them shook hands.

"Well, well, well, look who's popped up. My best friend. You mean it took Audrey's death to bring you back to Memphis," Francesca remarked as she walked up and planted herself in the middle of the huddle.

Rena's face immediately changed shades. *God, please don't let her make a scene. Please, God.*

"Francesca, it's good to see you. Certainly not under these circumstances, but it's good to see you still. You look well," Rena said nervously. She leaned over and hugged Francesca. Surprisingly, Francesca reciprocated. "Francesca." Rena called her name.

Francesca slowly looked up at Rena with enlarged eyes. Like a person with a split personality, Frankie's tone of voice and sharp look changed. "Oh, Rena. Thank God you're here. Thank God the only person who ever really loved me and understood me is here." She kissed Rena one on each cheek.

Robert and the rest of the brood stepped to the side slightly and allowed Francesca to release her grief.

Rena was finally able to break their embrace. "Frankie, I'm so sorry about Audrey. I don't know what to say."

Francesca glanced at the man who stood close to Rena. 'Who is this?" Frankie asked.

"This is Dr. Robert Becton; he's a dear friend of mine. He was gracious enough to come with me for support."

"Oh, I see," Frankie responded. She stretched forth her hand. "I'm Francesca Graham, a long time friend of Rena's." The two of them shook hands. "It's nice to meet you, Robert," Francesca said first. "Did Rena tell you how close we used to be?" she asked him.

Rena wanted to crawl in a hole and die when she heard what Francesca asked him.

"She's mentioned that the two of you were close friends when she lived in Memphis," Robert responded casually and placed his arm around Rena's waist.

Rena started talking. "I hate to see Pastor so heartbroken; and that goes for all of you," Rena told her.

"We all have to go some time or other," Francesca said.

Stiles interrupted the conversation. "Francesca, I don't think this is the time to talk about whose friend was who's or a lot of other unnecessary banter."

"And who died and made you king?" Francesca said with a look of bitterness. "Oops, I forgot. Audrey did. Well, excuse me. Next time I'll make sure I get permission from my dear old big brother here," she mocked.

Rena closed her eyes and thanked God that Stiles interrupted.

"No problem," Robert said. "I do want to say that I'm sorry to hear about the loss of your mother. I can imagine how you feel. My mother died when I was nine years old."

Rena stared at him. Robert had told her he was young when his mother died, but he didn't tell her how young. It made her think about all the things they still had to learn about one another.

Stiles and Francesca both said, almost at the same time, "I'm sorry to hear that."

Next, Mr. Jackson walked up and butted in. "Francesca, darling it's good to see you. I'm sorry, honey, about your mother. I really am."

"Thank you, Mr. Jackson."

"Francesca, child you look wonderful." Mrs. Jackson stepped up next and hugged her. "But are you all right? I mean you fainted; are you sure you're going to be okay?" Mrs. Jackson's voice radiated genuineness.

"Thank you, Mrs. Jackson for asking. But I'm fine. It's a lot to take in, and I hadn't had much to eat. And seeing Audrey like that, well it was just too much to take." Francesca said and held her stomach.

"Mrs. Jackson touched Francesca's shoulder. "You take care of yourself, Francesca."

It was Mr. Jackson's turn to interject. "That's why, we're

not going to keep lingering. I know all of you are probably tired and tomorrow is going to be an even longer day," Mr. Jackson told them.

"Yes, it is," added Pastor. He started crying again. "My poor Audrey. We have to put my sweet angel to rest," he said.

"We're sending up prayers for you, Pastor," Mr. Jackson said before he embraced Pastor.

Rena caught Francesca's eyes rolling up in her head, but ignored her. Instead, when her father stepped aside, Rena hugged Pastor and tried to console him the best way she could. She then hugged Stiles, Detria, and Francesca again.

"Good-bye. We're here for you," Mrs. Jackson said while they walked away.

Back at their hotel, Rena and Robert met up and had a bite to eat in the hotel restaurant, while Mr. and Mrs. Jackson ordered room service.

"Are you feeling all right?" Robert asked. He touched her hand; it was reassuring the manner in which he lightly caressed it.

"I don't know, Robert. It's so much you don't know about my past. I shouldn't have invited you to come to Memphis."

"First of all, you didn't invite me. I offered. And what else do I need to know about your past? If that's the case, there's a ton of stuff you don't know about my past. Like the fact that my mother died when I was nine. You didn't know that because I never told you. You didn't know that my older brother raised me because my father died two years later from lung cancer. You didn't know I worked three jobs to put myself through school, and I even flunked out of school one of those times."

Rena's eyes widened though she was tired and sleepy. "No, I didn't know any of those things. But it doesn't matter. You're a great man, Robert, and an even dearer friend."

"See," he pointed one finger up, "that's the problem I have with you, Rena Graham." Robert half smiled.

"What on earth are you talking about?"

"What I'm talking about is that I don't want to be classified as a dear friend. I've told you that. Don't get me wrong, we do have an awesome friendship, but I want more. And I believe you do too. Maybe being in Memphis for your ex mother-in-law's funeral isn't the perfect setting, but the truth is the truth. Then again, maybe it is because it reminds me that tomorrow is promised to no man." Robert toyed with her slender fingers. "Don't you know that I'm in love with you, Rena? I love you so much," he said.

Rena didn't move. She didn't say a word. Stiles kept flashing through her mind. Stiles had been the only man she ever loved. Stiles was the only man that she'd given herself to completely. She didn't know how to respond to Robert.

"Robert. I . . . I . . ."

"Let me save you from embarrassing yourself and me. You don't feel the same way," he blurted out. A muscle flexed in his jaw. "You like me as a friend. You love my children. But . . ." He paused and his face split into a wide, fake grin. "You don't love me. You're still in love with the man who treated you like crap."

"Robert," Rena reached out for him, but he moved back out of her reach.

"Are you done eating?" he asked coldly. "You have a long day ahead of you tomorrow. Better try to get some rest," he said as he placed the money in the check holder and stood up.

"Robert, please try to understand." She ran at his heels as he walked out of the restaurant. "This is the first time I've seen or heard from Stiles. It's sort of, well, it's all so screwed up."

"What's so screwed up, Rena? The fact that he was with another woman? The fact that it's over for the two of you? What don't you get, Rena? When are you going to wake up and smell the roses?" He stormed off in the direction of the elevator. Upon reaching it, he continuously pushed the UP button.

"Where do you get off assuming anything about my feelings or what I'm thinking? How was I to know that the only reason you came with me is to add brownie points to your list so you'd have a better chance of getting with me." She stood frozen waiting on his response. None came.

Robert pushed the elevator button again. A cold expression filled his reddened face.

The door opened and he stepped in. His heavy heel clicked the tiled elevator floor. Rena scooted in before the door closed.

"Robert, are you listening to what I said?" she screamed on the elevator that, thank God, held only the two of them.

"Loud and clear," he said. The door opened much too quickly for Rena.

Robert stormed off in the direction of his hotel room. He pulled out his card and unlocked the door. He hoped that Mr. and Mrs. Jackson were done with their dinner. When he walked inside, the sitting area of the suite was empty and he saw Mr. Jackson lying asleep on the double bed.

Rena stomped her feet and then pulled her door key out and ran into the adjoining room. She didn't want to wake her mother, who she heard snoring lightly when she walked inside. She eased out of her clothes and took a warm shower. Upon finishing, she placed the towel on lid of the closed commode, and then sat down. Seeing Stiles tonight had stirred up so many mixed emotions. And then Francesca. Thank God Stiles interrupted Francesca. There was no telling what she was about to say. Something had to be done. And Rena had to figure out what that something was; maybe before she left Memphis.

Rena tossed and turned in the bed. After sleep continued to avoid her, she eased up, so as not to wake her mother and went and sat on the sofa in the living room suite of their hotel room. She couldn't escape thoughts of Stiles. Of all times, why did Robert decide to tell her he was in love with her? No matter how hard it would be, she had to be truthful to Robert, totally truthful about her past. She would see how much he loved her then. But confession would have to wait until after Audrey had been laid to rest. It also would have to wait until she found out if there was any hope of reconciliation for her and Stiles. There was no way she could move forward in her life unless she knew for sure, one way or the other, if there was chance for a future with her ex-husband. The woman he was with gave Rena cause to think that Stiles had moved on with his life. Detria stuck by him like glue to paper. It was obvious that something was going on; at least it was to Rena. Somehow she had to be sure.

Chapter Twenty-one

"The spaces between your fingers were created so that another's could fill them in."
~Unknown~

When the Jackson family and Robert arrived at the funeral, it was close to standing room only. Rena scanned the aisles until she found a large enough gap that the four of them could squeeze in. The usher passed out the obituary that read like a short story. A gorgeous, graceful looking picture was on the front of the obituary, which was covered in a linen paper. Audrey looked like the queen she always demanded that she was. Past the picture, there was a poem that Rena read silently before the funeral started. It fit Audrey to a T. It also gave Rena cause to think about her own future.

The funeral service began promptly at noon. The choir sang at full force, and from what she could see of Pastor, he looked like he was well pleased with the way Audrey was being honored. The program moved along nicely until Francesca started up. She flailed her arms when the choir sang, "I Shall Wear a Crown."

"Mother, oooh, Mother," she screamed continuously. Ushers on duty from Holy Rock rushed to her side to calm her down. Rena noticed some of the people in the large sanctuary were shaking their heads from side to side, and she heard someone behind her whisper to someone else, 'She know she ain't doing nothing but clowning. She's the one that drove her poor momma to the grave."

The ushers took Francesca out of the sanctuary; a replay of last night's viewing. Only this time, minutes later, Francesca returned holding a huge wad of white tissue up to her face. She was seated again and the attention she'd brought on herself subsided.

One by one, people walked up to the front, next to Audrey's closed coffin. They paid glorious tributes to her, spoke eloquent words, talked of her service to Holy Rock and her love for her family, especially Pastor Graham.

The icing on the cake came when a young woman with blond dreads came forward. She identified herself as 'Siren,' one of the members of Holy Rock. Rena recalled exactly who she was and smiled when she saw her stand on the side of Audrey's casket. Siren was a wonderful speaker, and anyone who listened to her was touched by her majestic words.

"I've been a member of Holy Rock church since I was a little girl," Siren said. I grew up under the leadership of Pastor Graham, Sr. Now I'm privileged to continue my growth under his son, Pastor Stiles," she said and looked tearfully in the direction of the family. "God has truly blessed my life, and I'm thankful for the Graham family. First Lady Audrey was always the epitome of grace and eloquence. She stood out among the crowd."

The young woman wiped tears from her eyes, but continued to speak. "When it comes to death and dying, I know what the Word of God says. I believe that First Lady Audrey is with the Lord. But yet, when I thought about her and her death, it caused my spirit to shutter. I have to admit, that dying, not death, is a little scary to me, even though I believe with all of my heart that when I do die, I will go to be with God. I wrote a poem some time ago about death that I asked to have placed in First Lady Audrey's obituary. As a spoken word artist, I've frequented various venues in Memphis, determined to make a name for myself in the literary world. When I talked to Pastor Stiles and recited the piece to him, he was emotionally touched by it. And so here I stand today before each of you to recite, "Fear of Death."

Lord, Please don't let me die in Winter
A season of loss and regret
Amends not made yet
Memories of love lost
Combined with snow, sleet, frost
Moaning winds blow bitter and bold
The earth like my heart, still and cold
I will surely die a sinner
If you should let me die in Winter.

Lord, Please don't let me die in Spring
When eternal hope shines in my eyes
And my future is as clear as the morning skies
When all is yellow, blue, and green
Like dew my soul is new and clean
When my spirit is full of faith and light
And like an eagle my soul takes flight
The voice in my heart will cease to sing
If you should let me die in Spring.

Lord, Please don't let me die in Summer
When I am unruly and careless like a sunny day
Like heat, steamrolling and trampling all in my way
My will is strong and seemingly invincible
And rejects logic and all things sensible
Brash, brilliant, and bright as a sun ray

Treating life and love like child's play
Everyone will gasp in awe and wonder
If you should let me die in Summer.

Lord, Please don't let me die in Fall
When what once was new begins to fade
And resolve diminishes from too much shade
As promises like leaves drift in the wind
Briefly stand still then take off again
When from death creeping things start to crawl
And I'm reminded of the fleetingness of it all
Before my soul flies it will surely stall
If you should let me die in Fall

Winter, Summer, Spring, or Fall
Lord, Please don't let me die at all
For until I draw my last breath
I will not escape my fear of death
Siren~ ©

When the talented, young word artist was finished, there was barely a dry eye in the church, including Rena's. For Rena, the poem perfectly explained how many people view death. No one wants to die, even though we all have to. No one wants to see what's on the other side, but Christians, Rena thought, should long to be at eternal rest where death, sorrow, and no worries about tomorrow exist. Yet, much like the young poet, Rena sometimes felt the fear of the unknown.

Robert pulled Rena's shoulders lovingly toward him. Last night's argument hadn't stopped him from being by her side. Rena glanced over at him as he tightened his grip around her shoulders. He felt strong, and he felt perfect. She looked at Stiles on the front seat, and next to him, Sister Detria, planted between Pastor and Stiles. Rena watched her too. Something about her was refreshing and real. Rena thought that perhaps Stiles had found a woman he could trust for real. Why would she want to even entertain grand illusions of Stiles and her getting back together and living happily ever after? *It was not an illusion; it was delusional*, Rena thought.

Stiles approached the pulpit and stood bravely before the crowd of mourners. "That was truly a touching poem. Thank you for that, Siren," he said and looked over to the right of the sanctuary where the young woman was seated. "That's how many of us view death. I know some of you may be asking yourself why I asked Miss Siren to recite her poem at my mother's home going. But you see, that's exactly what many people fear. They fear dying, and by fearing death, they sometimes miss out on living. Because you see, for us, death never comes at the right time. And when it does come, we're never quite ready to go. That doesn't necessarily mean that we don't have things in order with God, but what it does mean," he said, "is that we're so fixated on this world that we're fearful of what's on the other side. We fear death because it comes so quickly. It doesn't give us a warning. It doesn't ask our permission. It just shows up." Stiles's voice was strong. It was evident that God was speaking through him. "I won't be long winded today. It's a hard task to perform—eulogizing my mother." He choked back tears. "But the truth remains that whether it's spring, summer, winter or fall, death is surely coming. Nothing can stop it. No amount of pleading with God. No amount of doctor visits or living right. No amount of anything can stop what is inevitable. And my friends and family, death is inevitable. I'm going to miss my mother. In fact, I miss her already. She was a remarkable woman. A woman who didn't hesitate to speak what was on her mind." Silent, but respectful giggles could be heard in the sanctuary when Stiles made that statement.

Rena listened and thought about how harsh Audrey could be one minute and sweet as cherry pie the next.

"My mother was a loving wife for well over thirty years to my father, Pastor Chauncey Graham. Pastor Chauncey Graham built Holy Rock. He built it on strong Christian principles and moral values taken directly from the Word of God. And my mother, First Lady, as she loved to be called, was forever by his side."

Several people could be heard saying, "Amen, Yes, sir." Some nodded their heads in agreement. "First Lady Audrey Graham loved her husband. Pastor Chauncey Graham loved his wife. They were a living example of what it means to be equally yoked and joined together by God 'til death did them part. I'm not going to keep you much longer. But I do want to tell you that my mother is not gone. Pastor," Stiles looked over at his father, "your wife is not gone. Francesca, Momma is not gone. Friends and family, Audrey is not gone." Stiles's voice began to rise. "For the Bible states clearly that to be absent from the body is to be present with the Lord. And I'm here to tell you that I'm not worrying about where my mother is. I'm not wondering where she went. I know that nothing is lost when you know where it's found. So I'm telling you that if you don't have your house in order, now is the time to get your life straight with God. It doesn't matter if your sins be as scarlet because the God I know, the God my mother knew, the God Pastor knows and many of you all out there know," Stiles pointed out to the crowd, "will make you whiter than snow. He stands ready to welcome you into His loving, forgiving arms. The God First Lady Audrey Graham knew for herself, stands ready to accept you into His kingdom. He will forgive and forget your sins and separate them as far as the east is from the west. I'm thankful that I had a godly mother because that means that one day," Stiles pointed his finger upward, "I said, one day, Pastor, one day, we'll see her again."

Stiles said a moving prayer after his eulogy. The church seemed to be on fire with praises and thanksgiving.

During the remainder of the funeral, Francesca barely made another sound, that is, until the casket was opened for final viewing. People filed along past the casket in tears, sobs, and others were quiet and sullen. When it was time for the family's last viewing, Pastor could no longer hold back his grief. He bent over and kissed Audrey and touched her cold skin and sobbed heavily. He seemed barely able to stand. Stiles stood next to him and supported him; Detria stood next to Stiles and held on to his arm with one hand while she wiped tears from her face with the other. Rena saw the tears Stiles shed too. Her heart fluttered. He was handsome as ever. He stood erect, wearing a black suit with his signature white starched shirt and shining black shoes. Pastor and Stiles were dressed alike, both with purple ties adorning their white shirts. Purple had always been Audrey's favorite color. Francesca was surrounded by ushers and funeral directors. She leaned over the casket like she was about to climb in it with Audrey. Stiles looked at her with a stern face. He removed his hand from Detria. Detria automatically stood aside and Stiles latched hold to Francesca and tugged her along with him and Pastor.

The procession to the burial was long, probably sixty cars or more. Afterward, people returned to Holy Rock Banquet Hall for the repast. Rena hoped at the repast that she would get to talk to Stiles. She wanted to tell him what a beautiful eulogy he'd done over his mother.

The kitchen ministry had done an outstanding job. Rena saw Detria rushing about in and out of the church's kitchen. Long tables had been strewn together, and there was more food and beverage than anyone could imagine.

"They put Audrey away nicely," Rena's mother said. She took several bites of food from a hefty sized plate.

"Yes, they did. When some of the people start thinning out, I'm going to see if I can go talk to Pastor Graham before we leave," Mr. Jackson commented.

Robert was quiet; he looked around the large banquet hall while he ate his food.

"I agree with you, Momma. Everything was nice. If Audrey could give a review, she'd definitely give it an A for excellent," Rena said.

"Yes, she would," the familiar voice said from behind Rena. She looked up and into the eyes of Stiles. "Mother was a stickler for professionalism mixed with a little flamboyancy," Stiles said and twisted his hand from side to side.

"Stiles," Mrs. Jackson said and wiped her mouth. "Everything was put together extremely nice. Come, sit with us," she said politely. The ill feelings she had toward him were pushed aside. Now was not the time to hold on to grudges.

Stiles sat down. "How long are you all going to be in town?" he asked and looked around the table. His eyes appeared to linger a little longer on Robert.

"We'll be leaving early tomorrow morning," Rena spoke up.

Stiles eyes shifted to Robert. "I'm sorry, but I don't recall your name," Stiles said to Robert.

"Robert . . . Robert Becton." Stiles excused himself and reached across Mrs. Jackson as he extended his hand toward Robert. The two men shook hands. Afterward, Robert rested his arm around Rena's shoulder, like he was staking his claim.

Stiles leaned back in his chair. "So, you're a librarian as well?" he asked.

Rena cleared her throat. "No, he's a science teacher and an assistant basketball coach," she spoke on behalf of Robert.

"I see. That's interesting," said Stiles and then he stood up. "If you all will excuse me, I want to make my rounds; speak to some of the others who came out to celebrate Mother's home going." His eyes focused on Rena one last time. "Rena, have you spoken to Francesca again?" he asked.

Rena stopped chewing the piece of food she had in her mouth. She picked up the glass of iced tea and swallowed a bit of it. "Uh, no I haven't. I'm sure I'll talk to her before we leave the repast. She seemed to take Audrey's death pretty hard."

"Yeah, she did, didn't she? Well, again, thank you all for coming. I hope I get a chance to say good-bye before you all leave. And Robert, it was nice meeting you." Stiles turned and walked away. Rena's eyes remained glued on him until he stopped at another table.

Rena wiped her mouth with her napkin. "Excuse me; I see someone I know. I'll be back shortly," she said.

Robert stood up and helped to pull out her chair from the table. "Do you want me to go with you?" he offered.

"No, that won't be necessary. I shouldn't be long. I'm going to meander around the banquet hall."

Robert sat back down and entered into conversation with the Jacksons.

Rena stopped at various tables of people she'd known when she lived in Memphis. It felt good to talk with old friends and acquaintances.

She caught up on what was going on in people's lives and exchanged her glad news about her life changes since her move back to Andover. The table she ventured to next was where Francesca sat. Rena didn't know how to react when they met each other's gaze. Was Francesca going to make a scene or what? Rena forced herself to put on a fraction of a smile.

"Hello, Francesca."

"Hello, Rena. I'm glad you're here." Francesca stood up and with the aid of her cane, she took several steps, and then slightly tilted her head for Rena to follow her. Rena looked back for a second, and then presumed to trail Francesca to a portion of the room where no one was standing or sitting.

"It's good to see you again." Rena told her and licked her lips nervously.

"Sure it is," Francesca answered rather calmly. "How are you doing?"

"I'm fine," was Rena's response. "But the real question is, how are you? The past couple of days have been exceptionally tough for you."

Frankie didn't acknowledge Rena's concerns. She immediately voiced concerns of her own. "What made you come here? It's not like you or I was a big fan of Audrey's," scoffed Francesca.

Rena's lips parted in total surprise when she heard Francesca's spiteful remark about, of all people, her mother. "Francesca, Audrey was your mother. How could you say something so mean?"

Francesca leaned against the wall of the building for added support. "The truth is the truth. You know it and I know it." Francesca looked over Rena's shoulder. "Is that your new man?" she asked Rena and lifted her head in a forward nod in Robert's direction.

Rena pressed her lips together, upset that Francesca was being so callous. "Let's just say that he's a special friend of mine." Rena's facial expression became serious. She sucked in a deep breath before she started talking again. "How has your health been?"

"What you mean to ask is, do I have full blown AIDS or am I still HIV positive?" Rena's face reddened. "I'm doing okay," answered Francesca.

Like a person with a split personality, Francesca's demeanor and voice changed. Rena saw her shoulders relax and the frown that was etched on Francesca's face slowly disappeared. "Rena, I've done a lot of wrong in my life. I've made a lot of mistakes. Because of some of those bad choices, I have herpes and I'm HIV positive."

Rena saw the familiar frightened look on Francesca's face. It was the same endearing, pleading look that Francesca had often used in the past to suck Rena in and have her doing any and everything to help her. Somehow, things were different this time because Rena didn't feel that same tug or pull on her heart strings.

Rena raised her hand up in an effort to halt Francesca's words.

"No, let me finish. I've needed to say this for a long time. It's one of the reasons I made a last minute decision to come to all of this fancy get up," Francesca said and looked around the packed banquet hall. "I figured you and your family would be here. Did you know that Fonda is here?"

"No, no I didn't see her," Rena said awkwardly.

Francesca pointed in the direction to the left of Rena, and told her where Fonda was sitting with her husband and kids. "You see how happy she looks? People like her need to be rotting away in hell. She needs to be the one feeling the pain I feel," Francesca said harshly.

Rena reached out to take hold of Francesca's hands, but Francesca pulled back. "I don't need your pity anymore, Rena. I've settled everything with God. I'm trying to right some of the wrongs I've done in my life. I'm not all prissy like you; I never have been. I'm not ashamed of who I am, but I am ashamed of some of the things I've done. I can't help it if I don't feel sad like most of you all do over Audrey's death. I've been praying about that too. But I just don't feel it," Francesca said.

"Then why all of the balling and the charades at the viewing last night and at the funeral today?" Rena's expression was strained; it was hard looking at the woman Francesca had turned into.

"It wasn't a charade. To tell you the truth, I cried for of all of the years when I wasn't allowed to cry. I cried for all of the years the woman in that casket held back her love from me. I cried because for the first time in my life, I think I can go on now. I can live my life. Now maybe that sounds cruel to you; and if it does, then I can't apologize; I won't apologize. I have only one person to answer to and that's the man up above. I'm sad for Pastor because he loved Audrey. I'm sad for my brother because he's just like Audrey. And I'm sad for you because you were an innocent bystander, found guilty because you loved me and you loved Stiles."

Rena teared up. "Stop it, Frankie . . . Francesca. I never meant to hurt you. I never meant to be deceitful to Stiles. And I'm sorry. I'm so sorry." Rena's tears fell freely.

"Come on, let's step outside. You don't want everyone having something else to talk about," Francesca said and walked in the direction of the back door.

They stood on the porch behind the banquet hall, out of sight from everyone. "Look, Rena, you were always my best friend. I can never deny that; although there have been times when I did. But you were there for me when no one else cared enough to see about me. I'll always be grateful to you for that. I was wrong in so many ways and on so many levels. I've repented; I've asked God to forgive me. But I have a long way to go. I still have anger in my heart toward Stiles and toward my dead mother. I have anger in my heart toward a lot of people, including Fonda and Pastor Travis. I have anger for Kansas, God rest her soul, for placing this death sentence on my life. So you see, I still have a whole lot to work on. I want to forgive like God has forgiven me, Rena. It's just so hard." This time Francesca's voice trembled and her eyes grew misty.

"Francesca, you're not totally responsible for what happened between us. We were young, we were best friends. Yet, I had no idea how badly you had been hurt mentally, physically, and spiritually. I allowed myself to be a crutch for you to lean on. I'm just as much to blame for my actions as you are. When God looks at us, He doesn't look at us and judge us together, he looks at us and he loves us equally."

Francesca reached out and hugged Rena. "I love you, Rena. I'm sorry for everything. I was mixed up back then. If anyone is responsible for the breakup of your marriage, it's me. I know I can never make that right, but I can ask you to forgive me." Francesca released Rena just as the door opened. It was Stiles. The expression on his face looked hard and tight with strain.

"Sorry. I didn't mean to interrupt." His voice dripped with sarcasm as he held the door ajar.

Francesca listened and Rena turned her head away from him, hoping he wouldn't see that she had shed fresh tears.

"You always have had a knack for walking up where you don't belong," Francesca bit back sternly. "Rena, I meant what I said. I hope I see you before you leave." Francesca opened the door and left Rena and Stiles standing outside.

"So what was that all about? The two of you making up, or what?" he asked with a bitter edge to his voice.

Rena faced him head on. "Look, I don't owe you an explanation about anything I do or who I talk to; nothing," she said angrily. "I'm not your wife anymore—remember?" she snapped.

"No, you aren't. And seeing you sneak out of the repast with my sister reminded me of the reason why you aren't."

Rena tried to push past him so she could go back inside, but Stiles blocked her way. "I'm not going to stand here and listen to your insults and badgering, Stiles, so get out of my way," Rena demanded.

"Not until we talk," he said.

"We have nothing to talk about."

"Oh, I think we do. I don't know what that was all about with you and Francesca, and frankly that's no concern of mine anymore. Because my heart tells me that there's nothing between the two of you. In the past, when you were young and naive, yes. But what you and I had was real. I know that now. We were in love." Stiles spoke gently and carefully. "I just got bent out of shape. I snapped when I was told that the woman of my dreams was also the woman of my sister's dreams. But I still had no right to be unkind to you and treat you harshly. I know now that I reacted hastily when we broke up, and I pushed you completely out of my life. I should have listened and weighed the situation out more carefully, but I allowed my heart to rule my emotions instead of going before God."

Rena's head popped up at the sound of his voice. Her eyes bore into his. She felt herself weakening and hated the fact that Stiles had this effect on her. Why couldn't she dislike him? Why did he still have the power to tug on the love strings of her heart?

"Stiles," she fidgeted nervously. "What's done is done. We can't look back on yesterday. I've moved on with my life, and it seems that you have too. I'm standing out here face to face with you with my heart fluttering and my cheeks probably crimson, and you know what, Stiles? I can honestly say that I don't love you." Rena seemed surprised by her own words.

"If you're saying this because of the relationship you think I have with Detria then you're seeing something that isn't there. I do like Detria. Could I fall in love with her? Yes. She's been a godsend to me. She runs the kitchen ministry at church, plus she stops by almost every day to help prepare nutritious meals for Pastor and Moth..." Stiles stopped. His face turned a shade darker. "She's a wonderful, smart woman. One day she's going to make some blessed man a good wife."

"I'm sorry. I didn't mean to come off so strong." Rena reached over and took hold of his hand. "I know it hurts, Stiles. You and Audrey were close. But she's with God now. And she doesn't have to suffer anymore. As for Detria, maybe you need to open your eyes and see the love that woman has for you."

Stiles held his head down. He stepped closer to Rena and embraced her like he was holding on for dear life.

The door swung open. Rena and Stiles stared. Both of them speechless.

"I didn't mean to interrupt," Robert said, turned, and walked quickly back into the banquet hall. As the door closed Rena saw Francesca positioned behind Robert with a smile of sick pleasure on her face like she'd accomplished her purpose—she had.

"Oh my, I didn't want this to happen. Look, I have to go back inside." Rena brushed hastily past Stiles. She had one hand on the door as she turned to him and kept talking. "Keep moving forward with your life, Stiles. I hope you can forgive me for all the problems I caused. I loved you once. And I loved you with all of my heart," she said tearfully. "I'll be the first one to take responsibility for our failed marriage. I was deceitful, I lied, I subjected you to an STD; the list of wrongs I've done is endless. I didn't know if I wanted to come to Audrey's funeral or not. I had mixed emotions about her too. But then I realized that Audrey has to answer for her own wrongs, and so does Francesca, me and even you, Stiles," she said in a choked voice. "I can't keep running away from my past, but I won't allow my past to keep running after me either."

Stiles reached out and removed her hand from the door. Rena didn't resist. "Wait," Stiles said." We need to get this out in the open, once and for all. Tell me, Rena. Is it because of the man you brought with you? Did you bring him here to show me that you've moved on, or to flaunt him in my face? Is it another one of your game plans?" Stiles said coolly.

Rena's brows frowned. "He's here for the same reason Detria is here with you. I don't know if you've told Detria about me and Francesca; I frankly don't care. But when I see Detria, I see a part of me; the part of me that once loved you like crazy. I watched Detria standing next to you last night, and being there for you and your family today. Now she's inside the banquet hall serving people on behalf of your family. She loves you, Stiles. Can't you see that? She's a woman that I believe is willing to do anything for you," cried Rena. "Stiles, I'm telling you, if you have the chance at love with Detria, I suggest you take it. It's like God has suddenly opened my eyes. I know for sure now, more than ever, that what we had is over. Robert is a good man. He loves me. But I wouldn't allow myself to love him in return because I was weighed down with feelings of guilt over my past. I thought I was still in love with you."

"So you're saying that you don't love me anymore? You're saying that we can't right the wrongs and make a new start?"

"That's exactly what I'm saying. You always have wanted what you can't have, Stiles. You have a beautiful young woman inside that banquet hall who loves you. My advice to you is you better open your eyes and your heart and accept the blessing God desperately wants to give you."

A powerful feeling of relief consumed Rena. "I hope I haven't lost Robert. I hope I can explain to him that what he witnessed was simply two ex-lovers saying their final good-bye. Now, if you'll excuse me, I have to go inside and find the man I love and make things right with him. And this time around, I'm willing to lose him because I won't live a lie anymore. I'm going to tell him everything about my past, and pray that if

Robert truly is the man for me, and I believe that he is, that God will open up his heart and allow me to love him as much as he loves me." Rena reached for the handle again, opened the door, and swiftly went inside. This time Stiles didn't try to stop her.

Rena hurried to the table where her parents were seated. "Where's Robert?" she asked when she didn't see him as she scanned the room with red eyes.

"He said he was going back to the hotel," Mr. Jackson told Rena. "We told him we would get the church shuttle they provided to carry us back. I thought you went with him," her father added.

"No, I was outside talking to . . . to Francesca and Stiles."

Mrs. Jackson's eyebrows lifted and she dabbled the sides of her mouth with her cloth napkin. "What's going on, Rena?" she asked. "You look like you've been crying."

"I don't know. I think Robert must have gotten the wrong idea about me and Stiles."

"Why would he get the wrong idea when there's nothing going on between the two of you?" her father asked.

"Honey," Mrs. Jackson said, "why don't you go back and mingle with some of the people and talk to Pastor before we leave? I need to talk to our daughter alone."

"Um, huh," he said and moved his seat from the table.

"Tell me, Rena," her mother said. "What exactly did Robert see or hear?"

"Nothing, really." Rena swallowed hard. "Except he saw me and Stiles hugging."

"Oh, Rena, what were you thinking about? Please don't tell me you're letting Stiles fill your head with a bunch of empty hopes and dreams. Not after the way he reacted when he discovered the truth about you, Francesca, your health," Mrs. Jackson leaned over and whispered.

"Mother, it wasn't anything like that. Yeah, I admit Stiles was trying to come on to me, but I told him there was no way I was going to enter into a relationship with him again. I told him that Detria Mackey loves him." Rena used her head to point in the direction of where Stiles and Detria stood. Stiles had his arm comfortably placed around Detria's waist. They truly looked like a couple in love. "That woman loves Stiles, and I told him he would be foolish not to pursue her," Rena explained. "I talked to Francesca too. After all of her, 'I'm sorries,' she still was the cause of Robert coming outside and seeing me with Stiles."

"How do you know that?" asked Mrs. Jackson.

"Because when Robert opened the door and saw us hugging, I saw Francesca standing behind him with a big smile of satisfaction on her face just as the door closed. Momma, I don't want to hurt anyone else. Robert means so much to me. He's been by my side since I met him. He loves me, Momma, and I realize that I love him too. But I may have lost him forever, all because of my lack of thinking." Rena softly cried and kept her head down.

"Shhh, don't do this to yourself." Mrs. Jackson took hold of Rena's hand and stood up. She led her outside to the front of the banquet hall. "You get on the next shuttle that comes and take your butt to the hotel room, and tell Robert everything."

Rena's eyes popped wide and she gasped. "Tell him everything! I hope I can, Momma."

"Do you love him, Rena?" Mrs. Jackson asked.

Rena didn't hesitate to answer, "Yes, I do love him. I really do love him, but I'm afraid, Momma. What makes you think Robert will want me after he learns everything about my past?"

"Love and acceptance," answered Mrs. Jackson. "Look,"

Mrs. Jackson pointed outside. "Talk about perfect timing; there's the shuttle. If you want to start anew, start by telling the truth, Rena. Now get out there and get on that bus. Me and your father will catch the next one," her mother said. Rena ran outside to the spot where others were gathered to get on the shuttle bus.

Rena stepped up on the shuttle bus, looked over her shoulder one last time at her mother, who had followed her outside. "Thank you, Momma."

"I'm praying for you, angel," Mrs. Jackson said.

Rena arrived at the hotel and rushed to Robert and her father's room. She knocked on the door, but there was no answer. Rena knocked again, harder this time. Robert opened the door.

"May I come in?" she asked him.

Robert hesitated. He gave her a narrowed, glinting glance before he stepped aside so she could come in the room. He closed the door behind her.

Rena saw his packed bag sitting on the floor next to the entrance of the room. "Robert, where are you going?" she asked like she didn't already know.

"Where do you think I'm going? I have kids to see about, Rena." He refused to make eye contact with her. "Seems like you have everything worked out here; no need for me to hang around." He started talking fast. "Oh, I'm going to catch the shuttle to the airport; so will you make sure Mr. Jackson turns in the rental car since you all aren't leaving until tomorrow morning?" He sounded like he was trying to mask his hurt.

Rena walked up to him and planted her lithe body in front of his. "Robert, I don't know what you're thinking, but please don't leave like this."

Robert stepped away from her. "Leave like what, Rena? It's obvious that you're still in love with your ex-husband. What's wrong with that?" He looked at her questioningly. "It is what it is." He stood for a minute and gazed at her.

"Robert, I do not love Stiles. What you saw was the two of us saying good-bye," she waved her hands outward. "That's all, Robert."

"Why are you wasting your time trying to convince me? We're just friends, remember? You already made that perfectly clear. You've told me that you don't love me and that's fine. As a man, I can only respect you for being honest."

Rena moved in front of him again, trying to keep him from walking out of the door. "I do love you," she blurted.

Robert stopped and focused his eyes on hers. "What did you say?"

"You heard me; I said, I do love you, but there's so much about my past that you don't know. I wouldn't admit to you that I loved you; I've been so confused, so mixed up, Robert. I've messed up the lives of so many people, and I don't want to destroy yours." Rena cried and then walked toward the bed and sat down on the edge.

"There's nothing you can tell me that I can't forgive you for. There's nothing you can say that will stop my heart from loving you. Nothing. No past relationship; no immoral affair."

Rena's tears poured down her face and she looked at Robert; the color drained from her face at what he was saying. She tried to speak but nothing came out of her mouth. She sat still as a statue and listened. A heaviness centered in her chest as her heart pounded like never before.

Robert knelt down on one knee in front of Rena and took both of her hands inside of his. "Not even an STD you contracted from a same sex lover." Robert's eyes were tear-filled this time. He looked at her sitting on the bed. "I love you, Rena Jackson Graham. I don't know what else I can say to convince you of that. I don't know what else to do."

A look of love mixed with embarrassment filled her face. "How? How did you know?" she asked. She cocked her head slightly from side to side in wonderment. "Fran—"

"Yes," answered Robert. "While you were outside talking to Stiles, Francesca had me cornered inside. She told me everything. Don't think that I wasn't hurt. And shocked is not the word I can use," he said but without condemnation. "All that I can tell you is that after she finished trying to convince me that you were not at all who you pretended to be, I realized that she was right."

Rena sighed and gently pulled her hands away from his. "She was right?" Rena was confused.

"Yes, you are not who you pretended to be. You're the woman I love. You're a woman who's made mistakes in life, and I'm a man who's made just as many, if not more. But there's something I know about life and love, Rena." Robert sat next to her on the bed and placed his arm around her shoulders.

"What is it that you know?" she asked.

"I know that we are human. We do things, we say things; we are imperfect people. That's why I've chosen to believe God, Rena. I'd rather believe in a God who was willing to die for me so that I might live life eternally, than for me to die and not believe that He is who He says that He is. I'd rather believe that God forgives, and then He casts out sins as far as the east is from the west, than to walk around full of pinned up anger, rage, and unforgiveness. I'm not saying our relationship will be easy. But what I am saying is that I knew from the moment I laid eyes on you, that God had sent you my way. I knew God had smiled on me and given me another chance to love; that in you, my children would be loved unconditionally."

"But what about the STD, and what about my affair with Francesca?"

Robert tilted her head to face him. "Shhh. Haven't you heard a word I've said? It does . . . not . . . matter," Robert said slowly. "It truly does not matter. What we have is now, not yesterday, Rena. This is our tomorrow. All I ask of you is that you love me as much as I love you. I'm willing to spend the rest of my life giving my all to you so that you will one day give your all to me."

"Oh, Robert," Rena said. A shudder passed through her. His mouth hungrily covered hers and her hands explored his body. A quiver fluttered through her as their kiss deepened. Rena Jackson Graham had been given another chance. This time she wasn't going to let it go.

"Everything turned out well. I believe your mother is up in heaven smiling down on you and Pastor with pleasure," Detria said to Stiles as they pulled up into her parents' driveway. Stiles turned off the ignition and got out to open the door for Detria.

"I believe Mother is extremely happy." Stiles managed a light smile and glanced toward heaven. "Detria?" Stiles called her name and then paused.

"What is it, Stiles." She reached out and took one of his hands inside of hers and gingerly rubbed it.

"I want to spend as much time with you as I possibly can; I want to get to know all about you. I don't want to live my life without someone to love, without someone to share it with," Stiles told her. "I'm not just talking. I mean every word I'm saying. I learned a lot these past few days. It's amazing how God used the death of my mother to orchestrate closure of my past. I don't want to hurt anymore, Detria."

Detria smiled back at him as they stood at the entrance of her front door. "I'd like to do be there to help you, Pastor—"

"Ah, ah, ah," he said

Detria giggled and corrected herself, "Stiles."

Stiles encircled his arms around Detria's upper body and kissed her lips lightly. "Thank you for all you've done, Detria. I'll talk to you tomorrow?" he asked rather than assumed.

"Yes, tomorrow," she answered, and then unlocked the door and went inside.

Stiles turned, placed both hands in each one of his pant pockets and walked toward his car. He replayed the scene between him and Rena. Everything she said had been true. He was so busy passing judgment on her and Francesca that he didn't see his own imperfections. He needed to repent and ask for forgiveness so he could let go of the past, his hurt, and his shame. Shame because he didn't fully comprehend until now that God's love is so vast and so deep that it hides a multitude of sins. He had been blessed with a woman who loved him, a woman he could and would easily love. His mother was right. He needed a wife, and hopefully, one day that wife would be Detria— His First Lady.

Stiles looked up toward heaven, "Mother, I know you're watching. I'm going to do right by Detria," he said out loud. "I miss you already," he said and then finished the walk to his car, got in, and drove off.

Chapter Twenty -two

"Forgiveness is giving up the possibility of a better past."
~Author Unknown~

Francesca was glad to be back in her apartment. The past two days had been long and she was glad everything was over. Francesca undressed, and Jabez jumped up on her lap when she sat down. "Hey there, pretty boy," she said soothingly to the cat and stroked him around his neck. She started to open-ly talk to God. "God," she said out loud. "I know I messed up again. I don't know what it is, but every time I try to do right, I do wrong, and every time I want to speak the right words, the wrong words come out. I know over the past few days that I haven't exactly radiated the love that you have placed in my heart, and for that I ask your forgiveness. I have a long way to go, Father. I want to forgive Fonda; I want to forgive Audrey. I didn't mean to say and do the things that I did toward Rena, someone who has been nothing but good to me, but I did. Lord, forgive me. Keep working on me."

Francesca leaned her head back against the neck of the chair and continued to stroke Jabez. Tears cascaded from her eyes. She had gone to Stiles and confessed what she'd done and how she tried to set him and Rena up to fail again. But she felt convicted for trying to do to someone else what had been done to her so many times in her life. She didn't want to hurt people; she wanted to learn how to truly forgive. She wanted to make her life worthy.

Stiles listened to his sister with an open and forgiving spirit. Pastor stood next to him. Afterward, she and Stiles were in each other's arms hugging and crying. It was an answered prayer for Pastor. In the midst of sorrow, God had brought renewal, repentance, and restoration.

Francesca was glad she listened to the conviction of the Holy Spirit almost as soon as she'd done the terrible thing to Robert, Rena, and Stiles. She caught them just before the next shuttle bus was scheduled to come. Rena told Mr. and Mrs. Jackson what she'd done earlier toward Rena, and pleaded for their forgiveness. After she finished confessing, the Jacksons prayed with Francesca and forgave her.

Mrs. Jackson felt the spirit leading her to give Rena's cell phone number to Francesca. "Do what God tells you, my child," she said to Francesca and hugged her tightly before they left the repast.

Francesca arrived home that night hours after everything was over. She was totally wiped out, but she was determined to be obedient to what God had placed in her spirit. She sat in her favorite chair and picked up her cordless phone sitting on the charge next to her. She then searched in her pocket for Rena's phone number and without hesitation, dialed it.

The phone went straight to voice mail. Francesca didn't hang up. She had to do what God told her to do, so she began to speak. "Rena, it's Frank . . . Francesca," she corrected herself. "I know you probably won't ever speak to me again, and that's because of my own doing. But it's time to stop the hurt. And the only way I can stop hurting is if I stop hurting other people. I'm sorry for telling Robert about your past; I'm sorry for trying to destroy your relationship; I'm sorry for all I've ever done to hurt you. I love you, Rena. You're my best friend. And I'm asking you one more time, to forgive me. Have a wonderful life. Good-bye," Francesca said and hung up the phone.

On the way back to Andover, Rena felt like a totally new person. She finally felt free from the weight of her past. God had revitalized her life. She had a man who loved her and whom she loved, and he had children who loved her and that she loved. God had stripped away the stench of her past.

Once in Andover, Robert and Rena stopped by his house first. He was glad that Rena wanted to see the kids just as much as he did. The kids rushed out of the front door and into Robert's waiting arms.

He picked them up one at a time, twirled them around, and hugged and kissed them. Rena watched the love shared between Robert and his kids. Isabelle ran over to Rena next and hugged her around the neck while Robbie toddled right behind his sister. Rena picked him up and kissed his chubby cheeks.

"Come on, you guys. Let's go take Rena home." They jumped for joy and waved good-bye to their aunt who was standing in Robert's doorway.

Finally home, Rena saw her BlackBerry message light blinking as they walked up the steps to her house. "Robert, here's the key. Let me listen to this message. I can't imagine who it's from, unless Mom and Dad forgot something," she told Robert as he removed her luggage from his car.

"They probably did leave something. Go on and listen to it. Come on, kids," Robert told them, still chuckling and happy to be with them.

Rena tapped the key to her voice mail as she slowly made her way toward her house. When she heard Francesca's voice, her first inclination was to hang up and delete it, but the Holy Spirit outweighed her own fleshly decision. She listened to Francesca's message. Just as she finished listening to it a second time, Robert came back outside with Isabelle and Robbie happily trailing behind him.

He walked around Rena and grabbed her from behind in a loving hug. "Is everything all right?" he asked.

"Everything is perfect. Absolutely perfect," she said and turned around to kiss him.

Words from the Author

Rena was ruled by the mistakes of her past. She couldn't move forward because she was far too busy looking backward. Have you ever been ashamed of mistakes you've made in your past? Have you ever been afraid that your past mistakes will reveal themselves and destroy your future? Have you done something to someone; wronged someone; acted in an ungodly way, or intentionally done something wrong in your past? I can speak for no one but myself when I say that I, too, am guilty. I have been guilty because I've done wrong; I've been guilty by association; I've been guilty because of my thoughts; I've been guilty of intentionally inflicting hurt on someone else for my own revenge. But those things are in the past. I am so grateful that we have the kind of God that forgives the mistakes of the past, the mistakes we make right now, and the mistakes of tomorrow. I am a new creation because of Jesus, my Lord and Savior. I still fall short, and I still make mistakes, but God never leaves me or forsakes me. He stands ready to forgive me and because He is no respecter of persons, He will do the same thing for you. All you have to do is repent, turn away from that which you have done that was wrong, and ask God to forgive you. I know from experience that He will. He's proven over and over again in my life, that though my sins be as scarlet, He will make them as white as snow because He loves Himself some Shelia!

Discussion Questions

My Son's Ex-Wife: The Aftermath

1. Do you think Audrey learned a lesson about forgiveness in *My Son's ex Wife*? What does she learn or fail to learn?

2. Did Stiles truly still love Rena?

3. Did Rena still love Stiles?

4. What are your thoughts about Pastor's role in this story?

5. Do you think Robert and Detria will get a fair chance in the relationships they have formed with Stiles and Rena? Why or why not?

6. Do you believe Rena was prepared to tell Robert everything about her past?

7. Why did Francesca tell Robert about Rena's past?

8. Did Francesca truly change in this story?

9. What is the most important positive thing you got from this story?

Reader Discussion Questions

10. Was the relationship between Rena and her mother realistic?

11. Why or why not?

A Personal Invitation from the Author

If you have not made a decision to accept Jesus Christ as your personal Lord and Savior, God Himself extends this invitation to you.

If you have not trusted Him and believed Him to be the giver of eternal life, you can do so right now. We do not know the second, the minute, the hour, the moment, or day that God will come to claim us. Will you be ready?

The Word of God says,

"If you confess with your mouth, Jesus is Lord, and believe in your heart that God raised Jesus from the dead, you will be saved. For it is with your heart that you believe and are justified, and it is with your mouth that you confess and are SAVED." (Romans 10:9-10 NIV)

Author Contact Information

To send your comments, feedback, remarks, and questions to the author please contact the following:

Website: www.shelialipsey.com
E-mail: shelialipsey@yahoo.com
E-mail: shelialipsey@gmail.com
Blog: http://www.shelialipsey.blogspot.com
Follow Me on Twitter: http://twitter.com/shelialipsey
Join Me on MySpace: www.myspace.com/shelialipsey
Bookclub Website: www.UCHisglorybookclub.net
Join my FB Fan page: www.facebook.com Shelia E. Lipsey Readers

Author Contact Information

To arrange signings, book events, speaking engagements
with Author, Shelia E. Lipsey
E-mail: quikhandyasst@gmail.com
Or contact the author directly: shelialipsey@gmail.com

Shelia E. Lipsey Books
Are Available At Bookstores Nationwide!
and Including the Major Online E-tailers listed below

Amazon.com
www.bn.com
www.borders.com
www.booksamillion.com
Indiebound.org
www.shelialipsey.com
"Search these sites under <u>Books - Shelia E. Lipsey</u>
http://www.shelialipsey.blogspot.com
www.uchisglorybookclub.net

ORDER FORM
URBAN BOOKS, LLC
78 E. Industry Ct
Deer Park, NY 11729

Name: (please print): _____

Address: _____

City/State: _____

Zip: _____

QTY	TITLES	PRICE
	A Man's Worth	$14.95
	Abundant Rain	$14.95
	Battle Of Jericho	$14.95
	By The Grace Of God	$14.95
	Dance Into Destiny	$14.95
	Divorcing The Devil	$14.95
	Forsaken	$14.95
	Grace And Mercy	$14.95
	Guilty & Not Guilty Of Love	$14.95
	His Woman, His Wife His Widow	$14.95
	Illusion	$14.95
	The LoveChild	$14.95

Shipping and Handling - add $3.50 for 1st book then $1.75 for each additional book.

Please send a check payable to:

Urban Books, LLC

Please allow 4 - 6 weeks for delivery

ORDER FORM
URBAN BOOKS, LLC
78 E. Industry Ct
Deer Park, NY 11729

Name: (please print): _____

Address: _____

City/State: _____

Zip: _____

QTY	TITLES	PRICE
	16 ½ On The Block	$14.95
	16 On The Block	$14.95
	Betrayal	$14.95
	Both Sides Of The Fence	$14.95
	Cheesecake And Teardrops	$14.95
	Denim Diaries	$14.95
	Happily Ever Now	$14.95
	Hell Has No Fury	$14.95
	If It Isn't love	$14.95
	Last Breath	$14.95
	Loving Dasia	$14.95
	Say It Ain't So	$14.95

Shipping and Handling - add $3.50 for 1st book then $1.75 for each additional book.
Please send a check payable to:
    Urban Books, LLC
Please allow 4 - 6 weeks for delivery

ORDER FORM
URBAN BOOKS, LLC
78 E. Industry Ct
Deer Park, NY 11729

Name: (please print):_____

Address: _____

City/State: _____

Zip: _____

QTY	TITLES	PRICE
	The Cartel	$14.95
	The Cartel#2	$14.95
	The Dopeman's Wife	$14.95
	The Prada Plan	$14.95
	Gunz And Roses	$14.95
	Snow White	$14.95
	A Pimp's Life	$14.95
	Hush	$14.95
	Little Black Girl Lost 1	$14.95
	Little Black Girl Lost 2	$14.95
	Little Black Girl Lost 3	$14.95
	Little Black Girl Lost 4	$14.95

Shipping and Handling - add $3.50 for 1st book then $1.75 for each additional book.

Please send a check payable to:

Urban Books, LLC

Please allow 4 - 6 weeks for delivery

ORDER FORM
URBAN BOOKS, LLC
78 E. Industry Ct
Deer Park, NY 11729

Name: (please print): _____

Address: _____

City/State: _____

Zip: _____

QTY	TITLES	PRICE

Shipping and Handling - add $3.50 for 1st book then $1.75 for each additional book.
Please send a check payable to:
Urban Books, LLC
Please allow 4 - 6 weeks for delivery